Outcasts

A novel of Mary Shelley

Mary Wollstonecraft Godwin Shelley
(1797-1851)

Posthumous miniature (c. 1857)
by Reginald Easton.
National Portrait Gallery, London.

Outcasts

A novel of Mary Shelley

Sarah Stegall

Increase of knowledge only discovered to me
more clearly what a wretched outcast I was.

—*Frankenstein, or, The Modern Prometheus,*
Volume II, Chapter VII

WingsPress

San Antonio, Texas
2016

Outcasts: A Novel of Mary Shelley © 2016 by Sarah Stegall

A note on the edition cited throughout: Except where noted, all quotations are from the first edition of *Frankenstein, or, The Modern Prometheus*, published in 1818. Though the 1831 edition, heavily revised by Mary, is more commonly known, the concern in this novel is with the story Mary began in 1816.

Cover image: "The Creature," line drawing by William Blake, 1791.

All images used in *Outcasts* are in the public domain in the United States: 1. All were first published outside the United States. 2. All were first published before 1978 without complying with U.S. copyright formalities. 3. All were in the public domain in their home country on the URAA date.

ISBN: 978-1-60940-516-8 (paperback original)

E-books:
ePub: 978-1-60940-517-5
Mobipocket/Kindle: 978-1-60940-518-2
Library PDF: 978-1-60940-519-9

Wings Press
627 E. Guenther
San Antonio, Texas 78210
Phone/fax: (210) 271-7805
On-line catalogue and ordering:
www.wingspress.com

Wings Press books are distributed to the trade by
Independent Publishers Group • www.ipgbook.com

Library of Congress Cataloging-in-Publication Data

Stegall, Sarah.
    Outcasts: A Novel of Mary Shelley / Sarah Stegall. Historical fiction.
    pages cm
    ISBN 978-1-60940-516-8 (trade pbk. : alk. paper) -- ISBN 978-1-60940-
517-5 (epub ebook) -- ISBN 978-1-60940-518-2 (Mobipocket ebook) --
ISBN 978-1-60940-519-9 (pdf ebook)
    1.   Shelley, Mary Wollstonecraft, 1797-1851--Fiction. 2. Shelley, Mary
Wollstonecraft, 1797-1851. Frankenstein. 3. Romanticism--England--History-
-19th century--Fiction. 4. England--Social life and customs--19th century-
-Fiction. | BISAC: FICTION / Biographical. | FICTION / Historical. |
GSAFD: Biographical fiction.
    PS3619.T4478 O94 2016
    813/.6--dc23   2016004202

Contents

Part One: June 14, 1816

Part Two: June 15, 1816

Part Three: June 16, 1816

Preface

The Emotional Roots of *Frankenstein*

The publishers of the Standard Novels, in selecting *Frankenstein* for one of their series, expressed a wish that I should furnish them with some account of the origin of the story. I am the more willing to comply, because I shall thus give a general answer to the question so very frequently asked me: "How I, then a young girl, came to think of and to dilate upon so very hideous an idea?"

—Introduction to *Frankenstein, or,*
The Modern Prometheus, 1831 Edition

Context is everything. Countless works have explored the scientific and historical roots of one of the most enduring and influential novels ever written, but few of them have explored the psychological or emotional roots of *Frankenstein*. We know about the science of the time, the advances in chemistry and biology, the raging debates on mesmerism, vitalism, magnetism, the fascination with electricity. We know about the social revolutions that accompanied the political revolutions in America and France, movements that fired Mary Wollstonecraft Godwin and her cohorts with ideas about perfectibility. But it is not 18th century science that has kept the book in print for 200 years, but rather the profound insight into human nature that the Creature, and even Victor, present us with.

Victor Frankenstein has been depicted as a rogue, a mad scientist, or a colossal fool. I think Mary Shelley saw him as a deadbeat dad, a man who usurped unto himself not the prerogative of God, but the role of woman, and attempted to create life. But having done so, he rejects his Creature, abandoning it and trying to run away. One need not look far to discover the well of frustration, longing and alienation from which a high-spirited eighteen-year-old author drew what she later called her "horrid progeny." There was the cold and distant father who rejected her, the society which spurned her for her lifestyle, her sister's lover, who deserted his child. There was her brilliant and eccentric lover, who had turned his back on convention and society as it turned its back on him. As romantic as their lifestyle may have seemed to Mary, it must have dawned on her that there were flaws in their paradise of equals.

When we think of 1816, many of us think of Regency romances, Jane Austen, the end of the long Napoleonic Wars. The Regency was soon followed by the stricter Victorian Age, with its repression, conventionality, and hypocrisy. Mary and her friends were, if anything, the hippies of 1816. Free love, radical politics, and the rejection of conventional religion characterized their every choice. Fiercely rebelling against the increasingly repressive establishment culture, Mary, Shelley and their friends sought a refuge in the democratic republic of Switzerland, there to live in communal sexual and political freedom, for at least a few weeks.

But it was not the sunny refuge they longed for.

In fact, 1816 was the "Year Without a Summer." The lingering atmospheric effects of the explosion of the volcano Tambora in Indonesia brought on the coldest summer in European memory. It was the beginning of a three-year climate catastrophe that led to massive crop failures and widespread famine. While Mary and her friends confronted the realities of a lifestyle at odds with convention, sorting out the sexual politics of living against the grain, the weather was nothing but terrific thunderstorms, fiery sunsets, and dark, stormy nights. On such a night, by a deep, dark lake while the thunder rolled like the voice of doom, the idea of *Frankenstein* was born.

—Sarah Stegall

Part One:

June 14, 1816

Chapter I - The Famous Daughter

> In my education my father had taken the greatest precautions that my mind should be impressed with no supernatural horrors. I do not ever remember to have trembled at a tale of superstition, or to have feared the apparition of a spirit.
>
> —*Frankenstein*, Volume I, Chapter III

S mall and quiet, Mary Wollstonecraft Godwin stood at the window overlooking Lake Geneva, called by some Lake Leman, and looked out over the misty afternoon. Here and there, sunlight shafted through a break in the clouds, picking out a wave top, a soaring bird, even a fleeting glimpse of Geneva across the water. White sails bellying in the breeze, a small boat bounced over a wave, came about slightly to the left, and passed beyond her view.

It was not them.

She sighed. Shelley and his friend, Lord Byron, had left that morning to cross the lake to Geneva; it was now mid-afternoon. Even this brief separation from Shelley made her anxious and restless.

Her son squirmed in her arms and she looked down. At six months, William was as fair as his mother and had his father's lambent blue eyes. He grunted, gasped, and then gave out a wail, pushing at her breast with one small hand.

"Is he finished?"

Mary turned. Her step-sister, Claire Clairmont, a few months older than she, lounged across a daybed paging through an old book. She glanced up, her dark eyes half-shut with boredom. "I wish Albé had let me go with them," she said.

How odd, thought Mary. In the last few weeks, since meeting the famous poet, they had moved from the formal "Lord Byron" to the use of his initials "LB" to the pseudo-Italianate pun on his initials, "Albé". Mary adjusted her dress and put William on her shoulder, patting him gently. "I do not wonder at Byron's reluctance to go anywhere with you, after the scene at dinner the other day."

Claire flipped a page so forcefully she nearly tore it. "It is his fault. He treats me like a child."

William burped gently but continued to fuss. "I think my milk may be drying up," Mary said. "I don't know if I should hire a wet nurse or wean him."

Completely uninterested, Claire sighed and turned another page. "All I wanted to do was discuss poetry with him. A perfectly normal conversation between two persons who love one another. Yet he laughed at me, in front of Shelley! And that odious Polidori laughed with him."

"Dr. Polidori always echoes Lord Byron's sentiments," Mary said, wiping her son's face. She turned him around into the crook of her arm and stepped close to the wall. The wallpaper displayed a pattern of pink roses on an ivory background. "Look, Will-mouse! Aren't the roses pretty?" She turned to look over her shoulder at her sister. "Polly can hardly do otherwise, my dear. He is, after all, merely a paid employee."

Claire snorted. "In the pay of two masters, no less. Did you know that Murray offered him five hundred pounds to keep a journal of his travels with Albé?" Her hand toyed with a pale green ribbon decorating her yellow sprigged muslin day dress.

Mary smiled. "Absurd. John Murray is far too conventional a publisher to actually print the escapades of our dear LB." She frowned. "Is Polly planning to write about you and Byron?"

Claire shrugged. "I care nothing for what John Polidori writes. Oh, look! Mary, do you remember this?" She turned the book towards Mary, holding it up to show her the illustration. In stark black and white, the image showed two small children lying flat in a bed, with their eyes closed and their arms straight out on either side of their bodies. A high window admitted a sickly yellow light, which fell on the immensely tall figure standing over the bed, looking down at the occupants with a crazed, fearful expression. Its hands were clenched in fists, thrust straight down in front of its body in an attitude of agonized anxiety; the dark shadows in its tousled hair looked almost like devil's horns. Its gaze was fixed on the occupants of the bed, oblivious to the small dog jumping at its side.

"That's my mother's book," Mary said.

Claire nodded, closing the book to show the title: *Original Stories for Children*, by Mary Wollstonecraft. "Mr. William Blake is a master of the macabre image, don't you think? Do you remember when that picture used to give us the horrors?"

Mary patted her son again. "I remember that it gave you the horrors."

Her step-sister sniffed. "No need to act so superior, as if you never got them."

"But I don't. I never have."

Claire shuddered. "And you are fortunate. To be visited by those deathly visions, to feel the breath of monsters on your face, to writhe in agony—"

"Nonsense," Mary said sharply. "'Tis only your own imagination, as I have told you often. Sister, you really must resort to reason. These imaginings are best left in the schoolroom or nursery."

"You have no feeling!" Claire said. "Truly, Sister, I do not know how you can support a life based on so … dry an outlook! At least I have an imagination!"

"Yes, a very melodramatic one." Annoyed, Mary sat down in her armchair near the window, spreading her white dress around her. She placed William in his cradle beside her chair and began to rock him.

Claire stood and strode to the window, placing a hand on one of the gold curtains. Without turning, she spoke. "Mary, I must tell you. I … I am *enciente*."

"Jane, you know I don't speak French well. What do you mean?"

"My name is Claire! Why can you not remember?"

Preoccupied with William, Mary said, "I called you Jane for sixteen years! Last year you were Clary. Now you are Claire. What will you be called next week? In any case, I do not quite take your meaning. Did you say you were … *ennuye*? Bored? The new edition of *Galignani's Messenger* is downstairs—"

"I am with child." Claire's tone was firm, but Mary saw that her hand on the curtain trembled.

Mary took a deep breath. Part of her was shocked—and yet part of her was not. "Surely you are mistaken, my dear! Perhaps you are only late? Or the exertions of our travels—"

"I have missed my courses." Claire's voice wavered a little, but she continued to stare out at the Lake where her lover's boat bobbed, somewhere in the mist.

Mary gripped the cradle hard with one hand, a deep foreboding creeping over her. "By a week, at most—"

"This is the third month I have done so." Claire turned and looked steadily at her step-sister. Her olive skin flushed as she met Mary's eyes, and she glanced away.

"The third? How is this possible, Claire? You have only been sleeping with Lord Byron for three weeks!" Mary felt her skin grow cold. "Unless ... not that I am jealous or any such nonsense, or with any idea of exclusivity, still, can it be you have been sleeping with ... with Shelley?"

Claire half-smiled and turned away. "Well, it would be within our philosophy, would it not, dear Mary? But no, I must say that Byron and I first ... embraced in London."

"In London?" Mary was stunned. "You ... when you brought me to meet him ... you had already ..." Her hands fell to her lap and twined together. "You had already been with him."

"Not yet," Claire said candidly. "Not just then. But thereafter, yes."

Mary stared, seeing that rainy day in London three months before, the elegant salon in Picadilly Square, Byron emerging from the shadows with his halting gait and his impish grin, taking her hand. "You used me." Her voice sounded flat, unlike the roiling in her head, the anger rising in her stomach. "You used me, your own sister."

Claire made an impatient gesture. "Is not utility the basis for all conduct? Of course it was no harm to you if he wanted to meet the famous daughter of the famous Mary Wollstonecraft and the famous William Godwin." Her voice held an edge. "Naturally, I expect you will fall in love with Byron, too. Have you not already?"

Mary reached for the shawl draped over the arm of her chair and gathered it into her lap. "In love with Byron? No, of course not. He is not ... not to my taste." She drew the white wool over her shoulders, seeking calm, trying to focus beyond her shock.

Claire tossed her mane of dark curls. "Well, I am not exclusive, even if you are. Despite your claims of freedom in love, you cling to Shelley like ivy to a wall. Whereas I am happy to share, in freedom and love!"

She used me. "You know I have never traded on my mother's name."

"No, of course not. No need to, when the very mention of it engages the attention of the most famous poet in England!"

"Jane—Claire, I protest. Was there no other way to win his love, but by bartering my name? My mother's name? I must declare I think this badly done."

"Badly done? Badly done? Are you now turning hypocrite on me, condemning me for what you did yourself?" Claire sneered.

Mary felt sick at the thought of a scene with Claire. She hated melodrama. "No, I—"

Claire's hands balled into fists at her side. "You cannot deny that Shelley wanted to meet you for the sake of your famous name. You will not deny that you traded on that, used it to attract him!"

Mary's eyes flashed angrily, but she forced her voice to remain calm. "Not at all, as you know. He came to meet Godwin, not me."

"Bad enough that our father has cut off all contact with us because you needs must elope with Shelley. Bad enough we have been harried throughout England, out of England, by Shelley's debts. Bad enough that I am made to feel like an extra arm or leg, useless and in the way. But now when I have found love, you condemn me? You?" She cast the book into Mary's lap. "There. Take your sainted mother's book, your sainted mother who bore your sister Fanny out of wedlock and married Godwin against her own philosophy! I am sick of hearing about her high-mindedness, and from you of all people!"

"Claire, what are you saying?"

"Nothing but the truth, I declare! Your mother went chasing after a famous philosopher, to make her name even greater. You have captured the greatest radical philosopher of the day, Percy Shelley. Yet when I lie down with a mere poet, you scorn me!"

Mary gasped. "No, you misunderstand! He does not love you, Claire! I only wish you happy—"

"You wish me at the devil, don't deny it! You are merely jealous, because my lover is more famous than yours. And some day, our child will be more famous than yours! You and Shelley have your William, Byron and I will have our son, and we shall see who is the more influential."

Aghast, Mary said, "I hardly know where to begin to disabuse you, Claire! You know that has never been our intent. You know jealousy plays no part in our—"

"Fiddle!" Claire said. "You see only what you want to see."

Mary bit back the reply, that in fact it was Claire who blinded herself to reality. In the end she only said, "But Lord Byron does not love you, Claire! I am persuaded of it! He will not support you, or the child. What will you do?"

"You are wrong," Claire said smugly. "Do not forget, he traveled all the way from England to be with me."

Mary balled her fists in her lap, willing herself not to give way to temper. "This trip to Geneva was your idea, Sister. At your insistence, we came to Lake Leman. It strikes me that rather, you have traveled all the way from England to be with him."

Chapter II - Outcasts

But where were my friends and relations? No father had
watched my infant days, no mother had blessed me with
smiles and caresses; or if they had, all my past life was now a
blot, a blind vacancy in which I distinguished nothing.

—*Frankenstein*, Volume II, Chapter IV

Mary didn't particularly like this room of the Maison Chapuis,
but it would have to do. Facing north, it endured every
draught of cold air this unseasonable weather offered. But it also
caught the afternoon sun—when there was sun—which warmed
the clammy room somewhat. Mary and Claire had done what they
could with it. The sky blue love seat and matching chairs had been
cleaned, the sideboard polished, and the curtains beaten free of as
much dust as possible. But the homely look of the worn parquet,
the black marks along the wainscoting from mildew stains, and
the general air of shabbiness always embarrassed her. Still, it
was really the only room in which they could decently receive
visitors, so she made it her afternoon retreat. She sat now on
this particular rainy afternoon with her embroidery in her lap,
watching the water run down the panes of glass. The pallid light
sloping in through the windows looked weak and ineffectual,
distorted as if in a dream.

A door slamming, the sound of boots on the wooden stairs,
and then Shelley calling her name. Mary turned eagerly to the
door just as it burst open, and her tall, wild-haired lover strode into
the room. At five feet eleven, he was above average height, slender
and strong. His light brown hair fell in waves across his pale complexion, highlighting his large, vivid blue eyes. His muddy boots
tracked dirt across the floor, his breeches dripped with lake water,
and his waistcoat was buttoned awry, but his face shone with happiness and animation. Reaching for her hands, he exclaimed, "I
missed you!" He caught her hands and kissed them, one after the
other.

Behind him, Lord Byron limped into the room, a scowl on his handsome face, his dark curls falling over his forehead. At five foot eight inches, he was shorter than Shelley, but his frame was more compact, even a trifle pudgy. His normally pale complexion flushed as he turned to his companion. "Damn those stairs! Polly, see if there's any brandy in this house!" His greatcoat flared around him like a cape as he shrugged it off, looked around for someone to hand it to and, finding no servant waiting to take it, tossed it over the arm of a chair.

Last into the room was John Polidori, a young, darkly hand-some man of neat appearance and large, speaking eyes. Also shorter than Shelley, he was tall enough that his close-fitted pan-taloons showed off a fine leg. Altogether, Mary thought, he was a fine, dark-eyed man. Right now those eyes flashed at his patron. "I am not the butler, my lord," he said peevishly. "Indeed, I am not perfectly sure whether Mr. Shelley employs one." His cravat had lost its starch, and was drooping woefully under his dark coat.

"Oh, pay Byron no mind," Shelley said. He cast himself onto the love-seat and stretched his legs out before him. "Mary, can you get us some brandy? Or tea?"

Before she could answer, Claire bounced into the room from the opposite doorway, her hands full of lace. "Oh, Mary, look! These would—oh, hello!" Her manner was as artificial as it was bright.

Byron flinched slightly, turned away, and began re-arranging some bibelots on the mantle. "Never mind the brandy," he mut-tered. "Perhaps some mulled hemlock?"

Polidori reached into his coat pocket and drew forth some letters. "When we called for the post, we brought away a copy of Mr. Leigh Hunt's *Examiner*," he said. "He has reviewed Coleridge's *Christabel*."

Claire stretched forth a hand. "Oh, let me see! Let me see!"

Polidori bowed slightly as he handed it over. "You are an ad-mirer of Mr. Coleridge's?"

"She's an admirer of anything that gives her a good scare," said Byron. "It gets her juices flowing nicely. Read her ten lines of

The Rime of the Ancient Mariner and she'll swive for hours."

Polidori frowned. "Oh, come now—"

Claire waved a hand. "Oh, I pay no attention to you when you are in this teasing mood, my lord," she said, scanning the paper. "You would insult your own mamma when you are out of sorts." Byron looked startled but said nothing.

Polidori handed the remainder of the mail to Mary. She shuffled quickly through it, pausing at one letter with hope in her eyes. But it was a letter from Fanny, her half-sister. She felt a moment of something like panic, and then straightened. She kept Fanny's letter and handed the rest back to the doctor.

"I am afraid I saw nothing from your father," he said quietly. His sympathetic smile animated his face. "I know you are looking for a letter from him."

"Perhaps tomorrow," she said, masking her disappointment. She reached for the bell. "Will you have tea?"

"Ah, tea," breathed Shelley, his head thrown back on the love seat. "Where small talk dies in agonies."

"Quite," said Byron. "So let us have large talk. Polly, you told a good story the other night, about some doctor you'd been chatting with. Let's hear it again."

Polidori looked puzzled, then flushed. "Oh, no, really, I don't think so. Not quite the thing with ladies present."

"On the contrary," Byron said. "Exactly the thing when these particular ladies are present, and we need not pretend to be cotton-mouthed. Ah, here we are!" He smiled as the maid entered, bearing a tea tray. She put it down on the low table, ducked a curtsy at his lordship and her mistress, and shuffled out. Byron's speculative gaze lingered on her.

Mary picked up the teapot and poured a cup for Shelley. She passed it to him, saying to Byron, "Don't make poor Polly blush on our behalf, my lord."

Shelley took the cup and saucer from her and leaned back again, his long legs in front of him. "Oh, by all means, do," he said, his eyes mischievous over the rim of the cup. "I haven't blushed in at least a week. I am overdue."

Byron took his cup from Mary and stood frowning down at the tray. "No sugar again?"

Claire sidled up next to him. "Oh, my dear, you know we don't use sugar, for political reasons."

"Political reasons? The worst reason in the world," his lordship said. "Sugar don't vote!"

"No, but it's produced on slave plantations," said Mary calmly. "Therefore we abjure it. May I offer you some honey?"

"And the honey bee is clinging / To the buds; and birds are winging / Their way, pair by pair—yes, I'll take some. Damn, but this is inconvenient."

"At least we are spared the nuisance of having to take it up with the fingers," said Polidori. "I had to do so at Madame Einard's a couple of weeks ago. Nasty mess it made." No one responded to him, and he looked down into his teacup.

"It is surely absurd even for you, Shelley, to allow the contents of your larder to be dictated by events half a world away," Byron said testily. "This is taking things to an extreme."

Shelley smiled. "My dear Byron, if one is to hold a principle, one must hold it all the way. Where would you have me halt my opposition to slavery? Where should I draw a line?"

"At his lordship's inconvenience?" murmured Polidori. Catching Mary's look, he flushed and looked away.

"Of course, if at any time your lordship is desirous of sponsoring a bill in Parliament, banning the importation of slave sugar ..." Shelley's eyes twinkled at his friend.

Byron bowed over the cup. "No, thank you, unless I am allowed to do it by post. I would prefer never to set foot in England again."

Claire touched his arm. "Oh, but how will you ever see your dear little girl again? Do you mean to abandon her?"

This produced a strained silence. Everyone looked everywhere except at Byron's face, which first flushed and then paled. Abruptly, Byron turned his head away from Claire and looked at Polidori, who was effacing himself against a wall. "Come, Polly. You have a story for us?"

"Yes, Doctor, let us have something amusing. And naughty!" Claire folded the newspaper and placed it on the table. Shelley immediately picked it up, opened a page, and sank into intense study.

Mary stirred her tea, looking from Claire's smiling face to Byron's frowning one. She wondered when Claire would tell him about the baby. She did not think Byron would welcome the news.

Byron sipped tea and made a face. "Well, Doctor?"

Polidori shifted his feet, glanced out the window, and then looked into his teacup again. He cleared his throat. "It was more in the nature of a medical discussion," he said diffidently. "I cannot conceive that it would be of any interest whatever—"

"Polly talked to some local sawbones about priapism," Byron cut in, a sardonic grin on his face. "His proposed 'cure' for it was something like 'more of the same'. Doctrine of signatures, I imagine, or at least of amanuensis." His laugh held a bitter edge.

Polidori looked up, surprised. "More of the same? Not at all, at least—"

"But what is this 'prepism'?" Claire asked.

"An uncontrollable erection," Byron said. "A perpetual salute. A morning glory in eternal bloom. A manly swelling that will not subside. In short, an alarm cock." Delighted with his own humor, he glanced meaningfully at Mary.

Mary raised one eyebrow but said nothing. She had long since concluded that the only way to quell his lordship's freakish sense of humor was to ignore it.

Claire giggled. "Oh, that does sound ... interesting. Do tell us, Doctor! What cure did your medical friend prescribe?"

"Yes, come, Polidori. In round, solid medical terms, tell us your friend's remedy," Byron said.

Polidori placed his teacup carefully on a sideboard, not looking at anyone. "He suggested the, ah, exertion of rhythmic manual pressure on the organ until tumescence subsided."

Byron laughed out loud, rocking back on his heel. "Rhythmic manual pressure! Oh, famous! And who, exactly, is to provide this hand-gallop? Shall I someday be obliged to pay a doctor to deflate my favorite weapon? Or shall I have Claire here trained in the art? Perhaps you could oblige with a lesson, dear Polly-Dolly?"

"You are offensive, sir!" said Polidori, his face first white, then red. "That is an outrageous—"

Claire laughed him to silence. "Oh, he is a rogue, and a damned rogue, is he not?" She jumped up and put her hand on Lord Byron's sleeve. "Come, my lord, let us be more sedate, or Polly will go off in a fit!"

"I doubt that Polly can 'go off' save in the presence of some light-skirt," sneered Byron. "He spends most of his time in the back streets when we go to Geneva." Claire giggled and he laughed with her, pleased.

Polidori stood rigid. "I protest! You know I am hunting through the bookshops!"

"Yes, but only through the naughty ones," said Byron. He turned to Claire. "He is obsessed with finding out just how vulgar and offensive the books of Europe can be. He will not rest until he has plumbed the very depths of their depravity. Why, only the other day, he dropped a book of erotic pictures on the head of an inoffensive shop girl."

"That was an accident!"

"No doubt you were distracted by the fullness of her bosom," drawled Byron. "Or were you contemplating a close examination, doctor?"

Polidori opened his mouth to retort, but catching the dangerous gleam in his employer's eye, closed it again. He turned his attention to a minute examination of an imaginary speck on his sleeve.

Byron turned to Mary. "How now, my Mary? Are you not shocked? Or were your Pantisocratic principles engaged at all?"

"Not my principles," she said coolly. "But perhaps my aesthetics. I find your laughter in rather poor taste."

The smile died on Byron's lips and his back stiffened. "Alas, I had thought you were beyond such common hypocrisy. Or am I to suppose that, having abandoned convention, you now espouse chivalry?"

"What has taste to do with either?" she said.

Polidori coughed, not meeting his employer's eyes. "Perhaps Mrs. Shelley finds it in poor taste to laugh at the deformities of others."

Byron's face hardened and his eyes narrowed to a squint. "Indeed," he snapped.

Claire stamped her foot. "Stop this! You're baiting him, Polly! And only because you have no sense of humor!" She turned to Byron, tugging at his arm. "Come, let us go play chess. Leave him to his spite!" She stomped out of the room; Byron, his eyes ablaze, bowed stiffly to Mary and hobbled after Claire, his limp more pronounced than ever.

Polidori immediately came to sit down in the chair facing Mary. "My profound apologies, Mrs. Shelley," he said. "I never know how to turn off his lordship's freaks without making them worse. I thought it were better to accede to his request, knowing that your mind is too strong to take greater offense than there was in the story itself."

Mary nodded, amused. "Well done, Polly. You apologize very nicely."

Polidori grinned, a dimple appearing in each cheek. "Thank you, ma'am. The company of his lordship affords me many opportunities for practice."

"Your dimples are quite nice," Mary said, making an effort to be friendly. She rather pitied Polidori, who often reminded her of her awkward younger brother. "They make you look rather cherubic. You should cultivate them. Do the ladies at M. Odier's appreciate them?"

Polidori blinked. "Ah. They do not have much opportunity to see them."

"Oh, for shame, doctor. You should smile more. Do you dance the waltz at M. Odier's? Do you like it?"

"I like it, Mrs. Shelley, but I am a trifle ... constrained in that company. I never know what to expect. Everyone is so informal. And yet more formal."

Mary poured herself more tea, offered the pot to Polidori, and was declined. "Every land seems to have its own peculiar manners. Here, we live so quietly, I have no knowledge of, of fine society." She sipped, and said more darkly. "Indeed, I have no knowledge of any society." She looked up at him frankly, and met his open gaze. "You know how we are pariahs wherever we go. At least, wherever there are Englishmen abroad."

Polidori nodded. "I ... I have been privy to some talk. People do not always know that I am associated with you. And of course," he said bitterly, "everyone wants to talk of Byron, Byron, Byron. I have written a play. I am a published writer. Yet I am nothing, not even a name to them. I am a star in the halo of the moon."

Mary looked pensively at the door through which her sister and her lover had disappeared. "Why is he so anxious to reinforce every prejudice the world has against him?"

Polidori shrugged. "He is a pariah, and he is proud. How else would he behave? Can you imagine him groveling for the good opinion of the world?"

Mary smiled. "I would never grovel for his, nor wish him to grovel for mine."

Polidori smiled. "And that is precisely, ma'am, why he cares for your good opinion of him, and why he so fears your censure that he anticipates it. It lets him feel as if he is in control of his reputation."

"Even if it is an evil one," she sighed.

"Very true," Polidori said. He reached for a sandwich. "Are these cucumber? How did you get them? Our cook swears they are not to be had."

Shelley threw down the paper and yawned. "Is there any toast? Where is Byron? What have you been talking about?"

Mary handed him a plate with two pieces of buttered toast. "We are discussing Albé's good opinion of me."

"He should have a good opinion of you." Shelley bit into the toast, scattering crumbs across his waistcoat. "I do, and I am not a fool."

"Has he really heard nothing of our conversation?" wondered Polidori, nodding towards Shelley.

"Oh, when Shelley is absorbed in something, you could fire cannons over his head and he would not pay you the smallest heed," said Mary. She picked up another piece of toast and began to butter it.

Shelley munched happily, sticking his hands in his pockets and sliding down to sit on his spine. "Very true. Once, in order to test my concentration, Mary stripped herself bare and—"

"Shelley!" Half-laughing, half-serious, Mary thrust the toast at her beloved. He opened his mouth like a child being fed, and bit off a piece. "I declare, you're as shameless as Byron," she said. "Without, of course, half his wit."

Shelley waggled his eyebrows at her, making her laugh, and Polidori smiled. "You two are well suited," he said, a little wistfully.

"Thank you," Mary said. "What news in the paper, my love?"

Shelley picked up the *Examiner*. "An excellent poem by a youngster named Keats. Hear:

> *... the sweet converse of an innocent mind*
> *Whose words are images of thoughts refin'd,*
> *Is my soul's pleasure; and it sure must be*
> *Almost the highest bliss of human-kind,*

Is that not wonderful? A very promising work."

"I think I have heard that name," Polidori said. He reached for the toast, but Mary drew it out of his reach and handed it to Shelley. "I think he is a medical student or some such. I fancy I may have met him at a lecture in London."

"There seems to be a very host of hybridized poets these days," Shelley murmured. "I look forward to the dawn of a new age. Chemist-playwrights writing dramas about sulfur. Musician-philosophers writing songs in the key of electricity. Oh, Mary, I am reminded: in Geneva I fell into conversation with a most interesting gentleman in a bookstore, who is an experimental philosopher. His English was very bad, and my German is, as you know, nonexistent. But we contrived, and he sold me a glass Leyden jar! I put it in the entry way."

"What an extravagance!" exclaimed Polidori. "Surely Mrs. Shelley would have preferred something more practical." He smiled at Mary. "Perhaps you should make him take it back!"

She looked at him coldly. "Shelley is free to spend his money as he pleases," she said. Inwardly she shrank a little at the thought of their bills and creditors. But Polidori's presumption irked her and she rose to her love's defense. "I shall be very interested to see whatever he wishes to show me."

Abashed, Polidori stared down into his cup. Shelley, ignoring him, rose and began to pace restlessly.

"I say, Mary, we must have Byron and Polly to dinner this evening," he said, his gaze fixed on some distant inner horizon. He ran one hand through his long hair, which fell in disorder around his collar. "The clouds were building over Jura as we came across; maybe we will have lightning tonight."

Polidori looked at him skeptically. "Do you seriously believe lightning is electric? That it is some mysterious fluid flowing to earth? It certainly does not give that appearance. I think it a very stupid idea."

Shelley shrugged his lanky shoulders. "We shall see, if we are fortunate enough to have a display. Mary? Dinner?"

Her smile was a little forced. "Of course. Doctor, will you be good enough to ask Lord Byron to step back in?"

Shelley held up a hand. "No need, my dear. I'll speak to him myself."

Polidori rose as his host exited the room. "Thank you for the lovely tea, Mrs. Shelley. It was most refreshing." He reached his hand forward. Automatically, Mary extended hers, and found it clasped in a warm, damp hand. *Arrivederci, signora,"* he said, bowing. His lips brushed the back of her hand, he raised his face to look into hers, his dark eyes looking moist. "Most kind *signora*."

Uncomfortable, Mary began to withdraw her hand, but Polidori clung to it. "I treasure these afternoons," he said in a low voice. "Lord Byron is often unpleasant. At such times, your kindness is ... a balm to me."

She forced a smile. Where was Shelley? She heard his voice in the other room, a low laugh from Claire. She pulled her hand from Polidori's. "You are always welcome, Dr. Polidori. You and Lord Byron." She emphasized the last few words. Polidori's face fell a little, the glow in his eyes abating.

"Of course," he said. His voice held an edge of bitterness. "A star in the halo of the moon." Abruptly he bowed and stalked out of the room.

Mary drew a deep breath and picked up her embroidery again. She was making a shirt for little William, and the watery light of this room was not strong enough for her to see clearly. Suddenly a pain shot through her finger, and a red stain appeared on the cloth. She exclaimed and stuck her finger in her mouth just as Shelley strode back into the room.

"Dearest!" he said, instantly seeing her pained face.

She laughed. "Oh, it is nothing. I stuck my finger with the needle. Have they left?"

"They have." He sat and took her hand in his, kissing the wounded finger. "I told them dinner would be served at seven."

She laughed warmly. "I am sure Albé took that ill."

"He did. Damned me for a country squire keeping country hours. I told him in that case, dinner would be served at five."

"Perhaps you had better warn Cook."

"Don't be absurd," he said. He released her hand and reached for the paper. "Cook knows as well as you do that Albé and Polly won't be back over here before half past eight at the earliest." He glanced at her mischievously over the top of the paper. "Of course, that leaves us ample time for ..." He glanced meaningfully towards the hall, which led to their bedroom.

Smiling to herself, she began to put away her sewing. "How odd. I find myself in urgent need of a nap."

Chapter III - Fanny's Letter

I read and re-read her letter and some softened feelings stole
into my heart and dared to whisper paradisaical dreams of
love and joy ...

—*Frankenstein,* Volume I, Chapter V

By the time Mary returned to her workroom, her son had been
put down for his nap, her lover had gone for a walk, and her
step-sister was at the Villa Diodati, transcribing some poetry for
Byron. At last, she had a moment to herself. She drew out Fanny's
letter.

Mary sat down under the window in the window seat, heedless of the chill that emanated from the glass. Below her, she could
see the small lawn that sloped down to the water, the path that
wound its way up the hill to the Villa Diodati, and the edge of its
vineyard. Trying to control the trembling in her hands, she folded
them together and pressed them into her lap, with the paper of the
letter crumpled between them. She raised her gaze to the mountains, concentrating on their piny slopes, the majestic crowns that
scraped the cloud-laden sky. She could see whitecaps on the lake,
and in the distance a fishing vessel made its slow way along the far
shore. Clouds hid and revealed the sun, leaving dappled shadows
in their wake. Such beauty, she thought, must surely portend some
lifting of the shadow on her soul.

She looked down at the letter in her hands. She knew the
handwriting, of course. Her half-sister Fanny's hand was as familiar to her as her own. Between the two of them, there had
always been a fine sympathy, if not always understanding. Fanny
inclined to melancholy, and was less inclined to books and reading.
Since the death of their mother, Mary Wollstonecraft Godwin,
Fanny had been alone, an orphan. A grieving William Godwin
had published their mother's journals and letters, naively believing
the world would be as astonished by his bold wife as he had been.

Unfortunately, what most people read and remembered was Mary Wollstonecraft's shocking sexual freedom, her depression, her suicide attempts. The world learned of her affair with an American, and the birth out of wedlock of her daughter, Fanny.

The notoriety had made Fanny the most infamous bastard in England. She lived quietly, taking on more than her share of the housework, and rarely left the house. Left behind when Claire and Mary ran away with Shelley, the brunt of the family's anger had fallen on Fanny. For this, and for Fanny's continued distress in the Godwin household, Mary felt more than a little guilt. Despite Shelley's invitations, however, Fanny had not left that household to come live with them.

Far, far more would Mary have preferred her half-sister's company to her step-sister's. She would trade Claire for Fanny any day, but the very qualities Mary loved in her sister made it impossible for Fanny to desert William Godwin.

Her mouth a taut line, Mary broke the seal on the letter and unfolded it slowly. The sodden sunlight played across its lines.

June 2nd 1816
Skinner Street
London

Dear Mary
Papa has given me leave to write to you and S—and once again he tells me that Shelley must send him money—

Mary bit her lip, anger surging through her. Money. That was all Godwin ever mentioned in her connection. No word of love or forgiveness, no word even of censure. Nothing about his namesake and grandson, William. Would nothing move him?

She resumed her reading:

—right away as he owes two hundred pounds to MK and to the assessment man. I find your letter of May v. interesting because I was so afraid there would be difficulty

with the carriages and passports, as when you were there
two years ago. France sounded so different now, with the
people so broken. Were you and S not afraid? I know Jane
was not for she would take on Wellington's army in defense
of her love.

Mary looked up, eyes clouded by anger. "Her love?" To whom
could Fanny be referring? Doubtless Fanny meant Shelley. Mary
was quite certain the family in Skinner Street knew nothing of
Jane's ... of Claire's romance with Byron. Nothing could have scandalized Mrs. Godwin more, or disturbed her father's calm more,
than knowing that one of their family had formed a liaison with
so notorious a rake. Byron epitomized everything Godwin despised—aristocratic arrogance, sexual philandering without real
feeling, support for the status quo. If Godwin had been outraged
by his own daughter's elopement with Shelley, he would have
been even more furious had he known that Claire, who was his
step-daughter only by marriage, had so betrayed his principles as
to take up with the most scandalous roué in London only a few
months ago. No, Mary, Claire and Shelley had quietly decided that
the longer this affair was kept from the Godwins, the better.

I hope that the weather has improved. In your last you
said the rain was incessant and that it seemed to be more
winter than summer. I trust little William has not taken
cold. Remember that if he is close to being weaned you
must take extra precautions regarding the disentery. Roll
several folds of flannel round the body, from the chest to the
waist. Also, give him water, in which rice has been boiled,
being very careful to strain away the husks, lest they choke
him. Although Mrs. G. used laudanum to quite her Wil-
liam when he was teething, you know I do not agree with
this. I trust you will not allow S or anyone else to dose my
little nephew with it. I wonder why Jane has not written
to me. I am worried that she may be ill because usually she
writes many letters.

Of course, Mary thought, Jane—or rather Claire—was trying to conceal her circumstances from her family. Mary hated lying to Fanny. Her elder sister had always been Mary's supporter and confidant. Yet even she could not be trusted not to betray a secret to Mrs. Godwin. Mary shuddered to remember her stepmother's red face, the screaming, the sly bullying she used to control her husband and family. It occurred to her, not for the first time, that of all the children in that wretched household, the one who had most quickly imbibed Jane Godwin's controlling ways was her daughter Claire. Mary remembered Claire's anger this morning, and saw once again her hated stepmother's face.

And she, Mary, had abandoned Fanny to that creature's mercies. Taking up the letter again, she read:

Our indoor weather has been inclement, as well—

Mary felt her stomach do a slow roll. "Indoor weather" was their phrase for the storms generated by her stepmother.

—and I do not know where I shall find shelter. I have taken on more of the household work—

Meaning, Mary knew, that Mrs. Godwin was turning her despised step-daughter into a household slave.

—and with Papa so busy in his study it is sometimes days before we speak.

No doubt, Mary thought, her father was once again hiding from his wife's wrath.

Thus your letters are very precious to me. I cannot feel at ease until I hear from you. I long to hear of little William and of Jane, and how S is walking about in all weathers in the daytime and writing revolution all night. I have written to you a week ago now, and I hope very much there is a letter from you coming to me. I have never understood and I hope you will explain why you ran away from me and if it was some fault of mine or error I beg you will tell me so that I may apologize and we will be friends again, for it is unbearable that you should be so far from me. I know that S is all your happiness now and little William but I pray that some day I may be again your dearest sister.

A tear dropped onto the paper, quickly turning the last letter to a black blob. Mary wiped her eyes on her sleeve.

I have had a letter from our Aunt Eliza. It is proposed that she and Aunt Everina, along with Uncle Edward, will visit London in August. She is full of cheerful news and congratulates me on S leaving me money in his will. But that does me little good as S will outlive all of us, I am persuaded, and I do not wish to become independent through the death of one I cherish so closely. Bid S my tenderest regards and remind him Fanny remembers him, if he does not remember her. At any event, Aunt Eliza seems no closer to accepting me as a teacher in her school than before. It seems that I am an exile, without ever having even left home, nor through any fault of my own.

Mary sighed. While it was true that Fanny had always been subject to fits of depression, Mary had to admit she was fully justified in this melancholy. Since turning twenty-one the previous year, the question of Fanny's future had been on everyone's mind. Shelley, of course, immediately proposed that she be added to their household, but Claire protested so loudly that Mary gave up any hope of compromise. Shelley then promptly offered to leave Fanny a thousand pounds in his will, but as Fanny herself pointed out, this was of little use to her presently.

The hope had always been that Fanny would take up a position in the school run by their mother's sister, Eliza. Unfortunately, once again the hand of William Godwin had interfered—after he had published Mary Wollstonecraft's letters, thereby bringing permanent scandal to the name of Wollstonecraft, Eliza had nearly gone bankrupt as parents pulled their children out of her school. It had taken years for Eliza to recover her family name and reputation: to add now to any lingering prejudice by taking in the very bastard so prominently named in those letters was unthinkable. Fanny, abandoned by all, had no future.

If ever you find yourself needing company, do but let me know and I would gladly take up the way of your life. I need not even have a Shelley to keep me, but to be living among those I love, in freedom and sunshine, rather than among these storms and frosts, would be a paradise to me. Would that I could be near you now, if only for a day or two. When you return to England, you must let me visit you often.

Mary closed her eyes. Much as she missed Fanny, and longed for her company, there could be no question of a visit as long as Claire was with them. By the time they all returned to England, Claire's pregnancy would be obvious and no hint of that could reach Skinner Street.

It occurred to Mary that her father would suspect Shelley of being the father of Claire's child. Her face went hot, then cold. He might even be right, whispered part of her mind. No, no, it could not be true. Not that Shelley would ever swear eternal fidelity, as a matter of principle. Rather, if he had been sleeping with Claire, he would take no pains to hide it. The same principles that allowed him to make love to any woman he professed to love would not allow him to be furtive about it.

Would they not?

I read over your letter to Papa the other day, which he has not read—

A pain went through Mary's stomach and she clutched the letter against her breast for a moment. "He does not even read my letters?" she whispered.

> *Your escape with S is still very much a sore point with him. S wrote him a stern letter of goodbye and no money, in which it is clear some error has been made. I either related my story very ill to S or he, paying little regard to what I might say, chose to invent a story out of his own imagination for your amusement, which you too have coloured to your own mind and made what was purely accidental, and which only occurred once in a story after the manner of Caleb Williams vis. of 'Mamma pursuing you like a hound after foxes'."*

Mary remembered the wild flight from Skinner Street at five o'clock in the morning, the closed carriage thundering along the roads, the little inn at Calais where she was recovering from the sea sickness of their crossing. And she remembered the irruption of Mary Jane Clairmont Godwin into the parlor, screaming for her daughter (never, of course, for Mary), demanding her return, threatening Shelley with gendarmes. She remembered how Claire—then called Jane—had meekly agreed to return with her mother. And then the next morning, one word from Shelley turned Claire around and she defied her mother. Mary knew that, from that moment on, it was war between her stepmother, Shelley and herself. She really had not far to look to understand her father's cold rage. No doubt he was castigated daily by that harridan, she thought. Yet surely the author of *Political Justice* had enough fortitude to hold his own against her? She remembered the charged silences, the closed doors, the tears during her growing-up years, and thought: perhaps not.

> *Regarding S, I have news that will come as a shock to you. Papa has tried to conceal it from me but Mamma was glad to tell me of it. It seems that Shelley's wife, Harriet,*

has taken up with a soldier and they are lovers. She has
left her children with her father and moved to Chelsea, or
so I gather. I do not know if S is aware of this, or even if
he would care if he did. I wrote to her two weeks ago in
the care of her father but have had no reply; I do not know
if my letter reached her.

Doubtless it was intercepted, thought Mary. Harriet's family had been angry with Shelley's separation from her. Mary closed her eyes. So many separations: Harriet from Shelley, Mary from Godwin, Mary from Fanny, Shelley from his father, Byron from his wife. Why must so much of the world intrude itself on the affairs of the heart? It was not fair. It was not just.

Mamma says there are some very bad stories being told
about you from when you thought of settling in that
neighborhood. I still think they originated with your
servants and Harriet, who, I know, has been very indus-
trious in spreading false reports against you. I, at the same
time advised S always to keep French servants and he then
seemed to think it a good plan. You are very careless, and
are forever leaving your letters about.

More injustice. Mary crumpled the letter in her fist, her vision blurring with tears. No love, no acceptance, no yielding from those who had once formed the center of her universe. She wondered if she would ever get over the shock of her father's rejection. And worst of all, that he would not even read her letters. He would not hear her. How could she reach him, how could she turn his love to her again, if he refused to hear her voice or read her words?

There had to be a way to gain his attention. She would have to think of it. Of course, there was one person whose letters Godwin would never refuse.

"Shelley ..."

Chapter IV - Eavesdropping

A new existence would bless me as its creator and source; many happy and excellent natures would owe their being to me. No father could claim the gratitude of his child so completely as I should deserve theirs.

—*Frankenstein,* Volume I, Chapter VI

The breeze off the lake was chilly as Mary stepped outdoors to go look for Shelley. She wrapped her shawl around her shoulders and made her way down the lawn to the edge of the water.

Cool and deep, it surged and lapped at the breakwater below her. What words could she use to capture the smell of water? Fresh, yet as old as time. Shadows hid the distant city of Geneva, and the wavelets made restless little sounds at her feet, as if complaining that life was too tame now that the storm had passed. Yet, over the top of Mont Jura, here came a mass of dark grey; she thought of armies marching, of the cannons that sounded so much like thunder. It was easy to see where ancient peasants got the idea of a god in the sky as lord of storms and lord of hosts. She smiled to herself, knowing what Shelley would make of the idea. On the subject of God, or rather not-God, Shelley could talk for hours.

It was a marvel, she thought, how Nature could have moods like a person. She had seen these very wavelets now lapping grumpily at her feet whirl and dash in a fury against stone and tree. She had seen these same puffy clouds driven like slaves before a tyrant wind, shredded by its violence, piled one on another as they were forced over Jura and Mont Blanc. She had seen the lightning jump from cloud to peak, from cloud to cloud. What messages were those flashes carrying? What language did the clouds speak?

I am getting to be as fanciful as Claire, she thought. She smiled a little grimly at the thought.

There was no sign of Shelley having come this way; perhaps she should look for him in the other direction. The smell of rain grew stronger, and with a sigh Mary turned to go. The path back up across the lawn looked slippery, so she chose the longer but safer route up the stone-paved walkway that ran up through the vineyard separating her house from Byron's villa. The vineyard was in full leaf, a green bower whose vines rose nearly to the height of Shelley's head. She, a head shorter than her lover, was completely dwarfed. It was like being lost in a wood, but one nowhere near as terrifying as the woods above Geneva, where their coach had broken down. Lost in memory, she almost missed the sounds ahead of her. Until one voice brought her up short.

"Again! Oh, my lord, take me again!"

Mary froze. It was Claire, and from her words, she was not alone. Mary wondered if she should go back.

"Oh, cease, woman!" Byron's mocking laughter rang out. "Here, take your stocking. I fear it is ruined."

"No, not yet! Do not go!"

"Much as I should be flattered, my dear, I really have no inclination to tumble you yet again in a damp underbrush. Nay, indeed, I am inclined, as you may plainly see, rather than at that angle that would most engage our mutual attention."

Mary felt her cheeks warm at Byron's words, but could not make herself retreat to give them privacy. Not just yet.

"Albé, I beg you, stay a moment. I must tell you something."

"If it's about dinner, yes, of course we shall come," Byron said. There were the sounds of cloth on cloth, the tick of a buckle. Mary surmised that someone—most likely his lordship—was getting dressed. "But I must really get on, I—"

"Wait." And there was something so soft and pleading, so intimate in Claire's voice that Mary actually took a step backwards, seeking to give them privacy.

"What is it?"

"My lord!" Fletcher called from some distance. "My lord, are you there?"

"It will have to wait, my girl," Mary heard Byron say. "It would be better if we were not discovered."

"I don't care," Claire's voice rang out defiantly. "Let them talk! Fletcher knows all about us!"

"Yes, but the rest of Geneva does not. Or at any event, not yet," Byron said. "I would keep it that way, for your sake at least. There are already too many tongues wagging about me and mine. I would not have you included."

"I don't care!" Claire repeated. "I love you. I care nothing for the opinions of the low and ignorant. You and I, we are alive and in love—"

"In love? Do not flatter yourself, dear girl. This has been a pleasant interlude, but do not give yourself airs!" Byron said testily.

Mary put her hand to her mouth. Claire could be a pest and a headache, but she did not deserve such low treatment. She pushed forward, determined to break through the hedge and support her step-sister. The soft pleading in Claire's voice stopped her.

"You called me your little fiend, you said we were friends of the heart," Claire said passionately. "I know you love me!"

"Peace, woman! What I say in bed is not to be taken seriously. As for being a friend, a mistress never is nor can be a friend. While we agree, we are lovers, and when it is over, we are anything but friends."

"Think you that I am as weak willed as all the others?" Claire said. Mary felt heat go over her. "All the other women I have read about? The men I have heard whispered about? Your own wife?"

"Take care," Byron snarled. "I do not take well to slander."

Claire was not discouraged. "Women have failed you and failed you, have they not? Because they are mired in the ignorance of our age, that holds that men and women cannot be equals."

"You are not my equal!" Byron nearly shouted.

"I am as intelligent, as passionate, as any man. As you yourself, Albé. You know—"

"You cannot compare yourself to me, child," Byron said.

"You care so much for rank?" A note of contempt crept into Claire's voice. "I had not thought you so ... so poor-spirited."

"I am not your Shelley or your Godwin," Byron said in a hard voice.

"But do you not fleer at convention, at what the ignorant and close-minded say you must be, should be? You, who could be any genius—"

"As always, you misunderstand," Byron broke in. "Let me make it plain to you, madam. I am a nobleman. You are a commoner—"

"Oh, that matters nothing between two who ... who love one another—"

"Think you that we live in isolation? Claire, I do not live on an island, at least, I no longer do. I do not live in a remote forest or a mountain top, nor do you. We live in a world that is hostile to us, to you. Think you that your innocence or your ideals will protect you from scorn?"

"My father cares nothing for the small-minded world—"

"The more fool he," Byron said. Mary heard exasperation in his voice. "Shelley may think him a genius, I think he is a dangerously naive fool."

Claire gasped. Mary shook her head; although she had suspected Byron of conventional notions, this was her first confirmation of it. Well, it was to be expected.

"Albé." Claire's voice was soft, caressing. "Here, your cravat is crooked...."

"I can dress myself, I thank you," his lordship said testily.

"Stand still," Claire said. There was silence, while Mary imagined Claire's quick fingers tying her lover's neckcloth. Mary recollected how often Claire had assisted her father in this way. "There. Even Fletcher will not find that completely disreputable, I fancy. Albé, I ... I really must speak to you about something important."

A long, deep sigh from Byron. "Child, I already know."

Mary blinked. He knew? Claire echoed her thought. "How do you know?"

"Any fool can see what you want," Byron said. "You want me to be Shelley to your Mary. It cannot be. I will not live that way."

"But you have had mistresses, lovers, you surely cannot care what people say!"

"God!" Byron's voice was tight. "Such unworldliness. Claire, how do you live? I declare Shelley and Godwin both have much to answer for."

"Why are you angry? What do you care? I know that I, for my part, care nothing for what people say of us." Claire's voice took on the familiar defiant quality.

"Of course you do not." Mary heard Byron draw a long, shuddering breath. It sounded as if he was close, as if she could reach through the hedge and touch his sleeve. "Claire, you do not know what it would be like. You are unknown, and I pray God you stay unknown to the world. A connection with me will bring you more notoriety than any lifetime can hold. You say I care nothing for gossip; you are mistaken. I care. I cannot help but care. And there is nothing, nothing I can do. Do you know what is said of me in the drawing rooms of London? Do you know that they—"

There was a choked silence, and a rustle of leaves. Then Claire's voice, soft and low. "Here. Let me hold you. I know it hurts, what they say. They are jealous, and they are liars. And I know there is nothing behind your words, Albé, nothing but despair. They have hurt you, but I will not. I will never hurt you." There was the soft sound of a kiss, and Claire's whisper. "My love."

Mary stepped quickly and quietly backwards the way she had come. There were soft murmurs in the vineyard ahead of her, and perhaps a sob, though she could not tell whose. Her foot came down on something hard and she stumbled—Claire's shoe lay in the path. She left it there as she continued backing away. When she was far enough down the path, she turned and hurried back to the house.

It was not until she crossed the threshold that she realized there were tears on her cheeks.

Chapter V - Domestic Interior

William, the youngest of our family, was yet an infant, and the most beautiful little fellow in the world; his lively blue eyes, dimpled cheeks, and endearing manners, inspired the tenderest affection.

—*Frankenstein*, Volume I, Chapter I

M ary hurried into the house, distraught. Should she tell Shelley what she had overheard? Should she speak to Claire? Should she say nothing? The latter seemed the wisest course, at least until she knew Claire's mind better.

Under all the worry, irritation. Claire was, once again, the source of drama and conflict. Why, oh, why must she always be part of the household, always clamoring for the center of attention, always, always shrill and demanding?

Mary entered her parlor, which was also her work-room. As much as she would have liked to settle in with a book or to write in her journal, there were too many pressing duties. And she had too much to think about to write, anyway. Better, she thought, to occupy her hands, do something useful.

She took out a basket and cleared her work-table. Carefully she laid its contents on the table. Then she sighed and straightened, pressing her hands against her back. She let out a deep sigh. Rubbing her eyes with her hands, she looked down at her handiwork. Spread across the cheap deal table was a collection of scraps of bleached muslin, some lace and some ribbon snipped from an old dress. Somehow, she would contrive to assemble these into a new dress.

She glanced critically at the issue of the women's magazine lying open at one edge of the table. The dress portrayed in it had too many ruffles for her taste, and a ridiculously restricted hemline that made the term "walking dress" a joke. But she could adapt it. She hummed to herself, working out seams and sleeve attachments, pondering the placement of lace. She picked up half the bodice, which she had just finished piecing, and held it up to her chest. Turning, she assessed the affect in the full length mirror behind her.

She would have to adjust the bust line, that was immediately apparent. Since William's birth, she had been slow to regain the slender figure Shelley had loved at first sight. One of the reasons she was making a new dress was that she could no longer let out her older dresses. Besides, those girlish fashions, so reminiscent of the schoolroom, no longer fitted her self-image of motherhood. Her gaze met her own hazel eyes in the mirror as she thought about her future.

Would Shelley leave her? It was the fear always at the back of her mind, so devastating that she dare not give it voice lest that give it reality. He had left his wife for her. He had left his children for her. Would he leave her? Would he leave William? She despised herself for this fear. She was her mother's daughter. She was not a slave to be bound to some man. She had thought that she could make her own living somehow, as her mother had done, but now with the care of an infant, she was not so sure. The nagging doubts about the purity of her mother's motives dissolved as she recognized that, having once experienced the difficulty of raising a daughter on her own, Mary Wollstonecraft had opted for compromise when she realized she was pregnant again. She had married William Godwin as soon as she learned she was pregnant with Mary.

Mary looked at her reflection. How far could she compromise? What future did she have, if Shelley left her? She could not return to Skinner Street, to the father who rejected her, to the stepmother who despised her. She thought about being under Mrs. Godwin's rule again. She shivered. Laying aside the fabric, she took up her shawl. Immediately, its comfort calmed her.

She had never known her mother, the famous writer who had died mere days after her birth. On nights when her stepmother raged and Claire quarreled, Mary could wrap herself in the soft cashmere and imagine her mother's arms around her. Her mother had worn it when the portrait of her that hung over her father's desk had been painted. She had worn it the night she had birthed Mary. She had worn it as she died. Her grieving father, who worshiped the memory of Mary Wollstonecraft, had wrapped his infant daughter in her dead mother's shawl.

Mary remembered one year, the anniversary of her mother's death, when her father had brought her into his study and opened the locked drawer of his desk. With her mother looking down on them, he had laid the shawl in her hands, saying nothing. Mary knew whose it was, even if she had not seen the tracks of the tears on Godwin's face. And when she left her father's house, she had taken the shawl with her, sole memento of her mother.

Mary sighed again, contemplating the varied scraps and bits of muslin scattered across the table. Perhaps she should piece them together, she thought. Too bad one cannot patch together a life. How could she stitch herself back to her father? How long would she and Shelley be joined? Forever? Or until tomorrow? He loved her, she was sure of that. But he had loved Harriet, his wife, too. Though he professed to love her no longer, Shelley had written to Harriet, urging her to come join him, Mary, and Claire in Europe. We should all live together, children, dogs, everyone, thought Mary. It would be like Byron's menagerie of animals and birds, an ill-assorted lot that traveled around with him. Oh, how she longed for a home, Mary thought suddenly.

She remembered her father's household on Skinner Street: two adults and five children, where no two children had the same parents. Like her basket of scraps, she thought, stitched clumsily together into a family. And that fabric tore so very easily. In fact, she had been able to unstitch herself from her stepmother, but only at the cost of bringing along Claire.

Sadly, she remembered that though Claire's mother wrote to her, Mary still had heard not one word from her father.

"There you are!" Claire came in, her hair mussed. "Cook has quit."

"What? Why? When?" Mary pulled her shawl tighter.

"Just this minute. Cook told Elise and Elise came to me."

"Elise should have come to me. She knows I have worked in here every afternoon for the past three days."

Claire scowled. "Why should she not come to me? No one said you were the head of this household. She has as much reason to tell me of household affairs as—"

"Oh, let us not quarrel," Mary said suddenly. She sat down abruptly on a stool, clutching the shawl around her shoulders. "What was Cook's reason?"

"Oh, as you would imagine—sheer laziness. She says she cannot cook to please so many demands."

Mary closed her eyes. "Demands. Yes, I can see that. Shelley is a vegetarian, yet Dr. Polidori will insist on meat at every meal."

"Usually the most expensive cuts," Claire sneered. "But what angered Cook was when I told her that Byron would only eat potatoes with salt and vinegar. He told me yesterday that he is on a reducing diet again. Although truly, I think he looks just as—"

"I must go down and speak to her," Mary said, standing up again. She felt tired, bone-weary, not so much with physical fatigue but with a deep, sad longing inside her, which drained off her vivacity and energy. She unwound the shawl and dropped it on the table.

"I do not think it will do any good," Claire said. "Cook has already left."

"I thought you said this has just happened."

"I heard her slam the door of the pantry as she left. It took Elise a few minutes to find me, and I couldn't find you for fully a quarter of an hour. By now, Cook is halfway to Geneva."

Mary took a deep breath. "Well, we must contrive. Perhaps we can order a cold collation?" She glanced at the window. "It's light yet. I will send Shelley to order—"

"Shelley is still on his walk," Claire said, avoiding Mary's eyes. Their morning quarrel, unspoken but still felt, simmered between them. Both women refused to acknowledge it. "I do not think he will be back very soon."

Knowing Shelley's ways, Mary agreed. "What's to be done?" she asked of no one in particular. She ran down possibilities in her mind. Borrow from a neighbor? They all shunned her and her family. Cook it herself? On such short notice, not knowing what was in her own larder, it seemed impossible. Finally, she said reluctantly, "There is no recourse. We must cry off."

Claire looked shocked. "Dis-invite Byron? He would be mortally offended."

Mary's mouth set in a firm line. "It seems uncommon easy to offend his mighty lordship."

"Oh, come now. That's too strong, Mary. He is a good friend to all of us, if a mite touchy. He feels things, you know."

Remembering his casual dismissal of Claire's declaration of love only an hour past, Mary's mouth quirked up. "And we do not? No, we mere mortals must acknowledge his superior status as well as his superior sensibility. No, no, do not argue, Claire. You are correct, he will find it offensive, but there is no choice, really. In this calamity, even the lord of Picadilly must bow to the inevitable. Shall you walk over with a note?"

To her surprise, Claire looked away. "No. No, I ... I fear I have some other ... I ... no."

"I will send Elise," Mary said. "And we must ask her if she knows someone who can take Cook's place. Although from what I have seen of the peasants in this neighborhood," she said bitterly. "We will be fortunate not to be fed solely on black bread and cheese for the rest of our stay here. And whatever excuse I shall make to his lordship, I have no concept."

Claire shrugged, looking sullen. She rubbed her cheeks with her hands. "Tell him ... Oh, say what you will." She turned away and stared out of the window, towards the Villa Diodati.

Mary started to turn to her, to comfort her, but Claire's rigid back and stiff shoulders told Mary that comfort would not be welcome. "I'll be back directly, then." She walked out, composing a note in her head. Perhaps a touch of humor ...

Mary was halfway to the cellar, still searching for her errant servant, when someone knocked at the front door.

"Elise!" Mary called.

The knocking again. Exasperated, Mary opened the front

door herself. Lord Byron's manservant, Fletcher, stood stolidly on the threshold. Beefy, with a shock of receding red hair, he was England incarnate in this foreign land. Valet, servant and baby-sitter, he had been with Byron all of Byron's adult life. Now he extended his hand; it held a note. "From his lordship," the man said dryly.

Mary stepped back, inviting him in. Fletcher shook his head and took one step back. "Thankee, miss, but I'm to go back anon, with an answer."

The note was addressed to her, in Byron's crabbed handwriting: *Come to supper at the ungodly hour of eight.*

She glanced up at Fletcher. "When did he write this?"

The man shrugged. "About an hour ago," he said.

"How did he know our Cook had left us?" Mary demanded.

"Our Lucille, what does the chamber for us, she seen Cook going down the road and ran out to speak to her. His lordship swore and says as how his friend Shelley should not dine on barley-water tonight."

Mary felt heat shimmer over her, shame and humiliation mixed with relief. She drew herself up with dignity. "My compliments to his lordship, and thank him for his kind invitation. We shall surely be there."

Fletcher nodded, touched his forehead, and shambled away. Mary closed the door, feeling a cold wind on her face.

Hearing steps behind her, Mary turned. "Well, we shall not go hungry tonight," she said as Claire came down the stairs. "Lord Byron has invited us to dinner. Is that my mother's shawl you are wearing?"

Claire went pale. "Albé has invited us to dine? Today? I must change." She turned, one hand on the banister.

"Not to dinner, to supper. At eight. And that is my mother's shawl, Jane! Give it back."

Claire stared at her, a storm in her eyes. "You will not lend me one moment's comfort? Not one moment's warmth?" Her pale fingers clutched the shawl around her. "Oh, cruel, Sister!"

From the nursery above, a fretful wail started. Mary felt the tingling in her breasts, the milk letting down in automatic response. Anxiety prickled her all over.

"Jane. Claire, rather. Please, I cannot manage this now. William needs me—"

"Yes," Claire sneered. "William needs you. Shelley needs you. Even Byron needs you. But I, I am supposed to need nobody. I mean nothing to anyone. Not to you, to Shelley, to Albé." She turned suddenly and fled up the stairs.

At that moment, Elise opened the door at the far end of the hall, leading to the kitchen. "Madame, the baker's boy is here. What shall I tell him?"

The wail from upstairs arced across Mary's nerves. The pressure in her breasts increased, and she felt the sudden wet surge of milk. She suddenly felt very young, very unsure of herself. No cook, Claire in one of her moods, and now William waked early from his nap. "Tell him I will come directly," Mary said. Elise ducked back into the kitchen.

Mary ran lightly up the stairs to the second floor nursery. William lay in his cot, cheeks red and wet, sobbing. Mary lifted him quickly in one arm, unfastening her dress with the other. The child's mouth was open, pink and howling; she lifted him to her left breast and he immediately latched on. The silence was broken only by the sounds of contented suckling. Mary sagged as the feeling of peace and love flowed over her, the feeling that always infused her when nursing little William. How could anyone not love this, she thought. She lowered herself into the flowered chair next to the cot.

Rocking back and forth, she hummed a little tune. William's baby fist curled around a lock of her hair. Eyes closed, he tugged on it, and she smiled.

Shouting from below stairs, a crash of crockery. Claire no doubt taking command of the kitchen, Mary thought. She imagined the angry baker's boy, the insulted Elise, the sulks and sullens that would pervade the atmosphere of the house. She should go down and sort it all out, as she always did, in her quiet, calm way. But who, she wondered, would be quiet and calm for her?

She looked down at her son, now drowsy and content. Here in this cocoon of mother and son she was safe, she was able to love and give love without distress or restraint. This was how it should be, she thought. She herself had never known her mother's breast, had never known the soft comfort of a mother's arms. She ached within, eager to be to William what no one had been to her—a source of love and care.

And then she thought of Claire, pleading with Byron in the garden only an hour ago, and she clutched her son more tightly to her bosom. And Byron's cruel words: *a mistress never is nor can be a friend.*

Not true, she thought. Shelley was her dearest friend, and she was his. "And in any event," she said, gazing down at her son. "I refuse the title of mistress. Companion. Yes, I will be friend and companion."

She thought of Claire, of the child growing inside her. Mary remembered Shelley's joy and delight on learning of her pregnancy. She did not think Byron would react the same way to Claire's news.

Mary hugged her son more tightly to her, rocking, thinking.

Chapter VI - Mary Writes to Her Father

I waited for my letters with feverish impatience: if they were delayed, I was miserable, and overcome by a thousand fears; and when they arrived, and I saw the superscription of Elizabeth or my father, I hardly dared to read and ascertain my fate.

—Frankenstein, Volume I, Chapter II

O nce again Mary sat at the writing table, but this time the ink dried on the quill as she nervously picked at the paper. She had intended to write in her journal, to settle her thoughts with an essay on the spectacular scenery or her thoughts on the republican politics of Switzerland. Instead, she found herself obsessed with the same question: why would Godwin refuse to read her letters? Always, he had read every word she had written, praised and supported her, encouraged her in every way to become a woman of letters like her mother. And now, when she lived most like her mother, this stifling silence. For him, of all people, to shun her was the worst of all.

She should write to him. But nagging doubt paralyzed her fingers, stifled her mind. It had always been the same way with him: the cold silence, the distance, the back turned in contempt when he wanted to punish her. Then the slow thaw, like glaciers reluctantly melting. He would look out of those pale blue eyes, always calm, always composed and serene, and he would shake his head slowly, and then would come the words. He was good with words, better than most men, and for him they were toys and weapons and friends and tools all in one. He would begin to build a vindication, slow argument after argument, breaking down every opposing view, ruthlessly destroying any of her assertions or feelings.

In the end she would be crying and begging for his forgiveness, promising never, ever, ever to do it again, whatever it was. Her friends thought her family was progressive and strange because her father never beat her or her siblings. What they didn't know was that William Godwin's silences were worse than any beating, and his "discussions" were worse than any scolding. They were as cold and solid as stones, and more inert. Tears would not move them or wear them away.

Now she sat, bewildered and confused as she had been since the first time they returned, she and Shelley and Claire, from their elopement two summers ago. Elated by her adventures, flushed with pride that she had finally stepped into her mother's footsteps and dared to live as she believed, as Godwin had taught, she had returned to Skinner Street only to find the door barred and The Silence in place. Godwin would not hear her, would not see them. He refused her letters and wrote only to Shelley, and then only to demand money.

Because the money must continue. That was a separate consideration. At first she had taken that for granted, as she had taken it all her life. It was part of his creed: that money belonged to whoever needed it most. It was revolutionary, dangerous, exciting. It changed everything, that creed. It meant that Godwin had every right to ask a rich man like Shelley to support him, only because philosophers needed to be supported in order to contribute to the betterment of mankind. Naturally, since Godwin was the chief progressive philosopher of his age, he deserved to be supported. Naturally, Shelley was to provide that support.

She took up her pen, dipped it in the inkwell, scratched a few times on the blotter. Finally, she began.

My dear Father,
I cannot understand how all this time you have continued
to shun me for that which you yourself taught

She scratched furiously at the paper, blotting over her line. No, that would not do. She knew what happened if anyone presumed to question or reprimand William Godwin. Perhaps he would respond to a reminder of her love for him, of her devotion to his fame and principles.

My dear Father,
I do not understand why you have turned your back on us. I
have named my son for you, your own grandson. Will you not
see him? He is the sweetest child

Again she scratched out what she had written. An appeal to sentiment was the last thing Godwin would pay attention to.

My dearest Papa
We are now well situated on the shores of Lake Geneva,
across from dark frowning Jura, behind whose range we
every evening see the sun sink, and darkness approaches
our valley from behind the Alps, which are then tinged by
that glowing rose-like hue which is observed in England.

Yes, she thought with satisfaction. That was the tone to take with
her father: distant, formal, objective, logical. Appeal to his reason; unlike Shelley, the last approach that would gain his attention would be an emotional one. She set out to remind her father
of how alike they were, how much they shared—that she could
write as well as he, tell a story as well as he, make words a powerful weapon as well as he. In this, she knew her father saw her lost
mother in her. In this, she excelled over all the other children of
that household. Let her only remind him of her mother, and his
heart might soften.

There is more equality of classes here than in England. This
occasions a greater freedom and refinement of manners
among the lower orders than we meet with in our own
country. I fancy the haughty English ladies are greatly
disgusted with this consequence of republican institu-
tions, for the Genovese servants complain very much of
their scolding, an exercise of the tongue, I believe, perfectly
unknown here. The peasants of Switzerland may not
however emulate the vivacity and grace of the French.
They are more cleanly, but they are slow and inapt. I

*know a girl of twenty, who although she had lived all her
life among vineyards, could not inform me during what
month the vintage took place, and I discovered she was
utterly ignorant of the order in which the months succeed
each other. She would not have been surprised if I had
talked of the burning sun and delicious fruits of December,
or of the frosts of July. Yet she was by no means deficient in
understanding.*

Mary dipped her pen in the inkwell and sat thinking. How to
word the next part? By now her father would be, perhaps, nodding
in unconscious agreement, imagining her among the benighted
peasants of the Alps, painting pictures in his head of their household. How to draw in his sympathy?

*My only fear is that my William, who of course is named for
you, should feel the neglect of education which is so pervasive
here.*

Ah, yes, that was it. A discussion of the education of the young
would always catch her father's eye.

*You know how strongly I adhere to your principles of
education, and how important it is that a young mind be
formed quickly in life, and directed into the proper paths.
For his education, I could ask no better teacher than you
yourself, and I look forward to the day when you may meet
your grandson, and see that he is like you in so many ways.
Not least of these is his mind, which is already bright and
alert. You will see in him perhaps my mother's round face,
and in his eagerness for learning an echo of his mother.
How sad it would be if, through discord between us, a discord that lies primarily in my adherence to the principles
you yourself taught me, he should lose the opportunity to
live and learn in England, rather than in foreign lands.*

There, she thought. That ought to strike home. Her father held foreigners, save for a few French revolutionaries, in contempt. Having traveled Europe far more than William Godwin, she now knew how narrow and unreasonable his prejudices were, but this was not the time to argue them. Having now gained her father's full attention, she advanced to her final plea.

I do not understand this shadow that lies between us, nor whence it comes. My mother's shade, were it here, would stand beside me in mute astonishment. Did she not love you as I love my Shelley? Did she not scorn the world's opinion as I do? Did she not bear me in disdain of common prejudice? She thrust away the chains of tradition, eschewing the enforced prostitution of marriage for most of her life. You celebrated her life to the world, yet when I betake the same path, for the same reasons, I am cast forth. I entreat you to reconsider your position, both for my sake and the sake of your grandson, who will need your firm hand and seasoned wisdom as he grows up. Write to me, father, and tell me that you embrace me once again, that you hug your Mary to your bosom as of old. Do not let me languish out here in the outer darkness, alone and bereft of my only parent, my only father. You created me, and you answer me now with only silence. Fanny writes to me. Mrs. G writes to Jane. You write to Shelley, but never to me. Why? Write me, and tell me that I may always be Your Mary.

By the time she had finished, the paper was dotted with tears and inkblots. She considered rewriting it in her best hand, and then decided to let the honesty of those tears speak for her as eloquently as her words. She folded the letter and was addressing it when Shelley strode in, his greatcoat flaring behind him.

"That was a capital walk, along the lake side to the east. That country is all Rousseau. Have you seen my copy of *The New Heloise?*" he said. "I was sure I had it with me in the—here it is, on the table." He picked up the book, glancing at Mary. "Here, now! Are you crying?" He knelt beside her, as Mary furiously dashed tears from her eyes and cheeks.

"It is nothing, sweetest. I was writing to Godwin."

Shelley's hand squeezed her knee. "You have heard from him?"

Mary shook her head, unable to speak. She held the unsealed letter out to him, trembling. He took it from her slowly, his eyes on her face. Tenderly, he stroked her cheek, leaned forward to kiss it. "You wish me to post it, my dear?"

She nodded. "If you would ... seal it up in a letter of yours. Then he will be sure to see it. And once he has it in his hand, and sees it is open, he will read it ... oh, I cannot bear it, Shelley! To be cast out—" She flung her arms around his neck, and his arms came around her, guarding and enfolding her.

"Mary, my Mary," he murmured into her hair. She felt his hand between them, heard the rustle of paper as he thrust the paper into his greatcoat pocket. "My own, we do not need him, do we? Do we not have one another? Do we not have love, sacred love, to hold us to one another more surely than any other tie?"

She nodded, sniffling into his shoulder. "But he is my father!"

She felt him nod against her hair, and tuck her head under his chin. She knew he liked her to nestle against him like that, contrasting her petite form with his long and lanky one. His Dormouse, he called her. Now she folded up gratefully against him, knowing he would not find an excuse to shut her out or walk away, but would stay. "Mary, Mary," he crooned, rocking a little. "So fair, so young."

"I do not understand it," she said, sniffling. "Why, why does he not follow the obvious bent of his affection and be reconciled to us? Oh, I know what it is. It is that woman, my stepmother— I will not, will not call her Mamma ever more! She plagues my father out of his mind, all for spite against me. Oh, if only I could see him, talk to him...."

"But am I not enough, my Dormouse?" He drew back, kissing her forehead. "And our Will-mouse? Need we the approval of anyone other than ourselves? Are we not following the obvious bent of our affections? And how other should real people act, if they are ever to act in accord with their true natures?"

She laughed. "Only you, Percy Shelley, would read a weeping woman a lecture in philosophy!"

"Ah, but the reason I love you, Mary Maie, is that you listen to, and understand, my lectures in philosophy." He kissed her.

"Oh, Shelley, am I greedy?" she sighed when he released her. "I want my father's love. I want your love. I want William to love us as well. I even, sometimes, want Jane's—Claire's love."

He laughed. "Yes, you are greedy, my tyrant." He leaned backwards, and she gave a little squeak as he pulled her with him, and then he was rolling over on the floor with her, his big boots tangled in her muslin skirts. "See how I pay tribute to my little empress," he laughed. She laughed back at him, her tears forgotten.

He kissed her smile, and then kissed her again, and the kiss went deeper and then her hands were in his hair and his hands were all over her, and before long Mary had lost all thought of her father, or her letter, or any other thing than the man in her arms and the sound of rain against the window.

Chapter VII - Shelley Learns the Truth

God, in pity, made man beautiful and alluring, after his own image; but my form is a filthy type of yours, more horrid from its very resemblance. Satan had his companions, fellow-devils, to admire and encourage him; but I am solitary and detested.

—*Frankenstein,* Volume III, Chapter VII

An hour later, Shelley, disheveled and half-dressed, drowsed next to her on the carpet. She did not want to get up and attend to chores, or even to little William. She wanted to laze away the day with her lover, reading and making love and talking about the perfectibility of man.

What she did was get to her feet and adjust her gown. "Come, dearest, it is the afternoon. We must not idle away the day."

"Why not?" he said, smiling. He reached a hand up to her but she evaded him. "Oh, come, my love. 'Let us not to the marriage of true minds make impediment'."

Shaking her head, Mary backed away. Shelley groaned and got up, looking like a heron unfolding its long legs. He picked up the greatcoat where he had discarded it and shoved Mary's letter into the pocket. Mary fussed with her bits and pieces of dressmaking, a smile on her face.

"Where is Claire?" Shelley said, yawning.

"I believe she is changing," Mary said. She told him what had happened with the cook.

Shelley only shrugged. "Ah, well, I leave it in your good hands, my dear. Would you wish me to speak to Byron about a new cook?"

"Why do you imagine he would take an interest? Or be able to assist us?" Mary asked. It peeved her a little that Shelley was so unworldly about domestic matters. Doubtless, she thought, it came of being raised as the heir to a title, with servants to worry about such mundane things. Shelley may have thrown off his family, but he would never be able to throw off his upbringing.

Shelley picked up two of her cut pieces and held them up to the light. "How do these go together? I cannot figure it. Why, Byron has several servants, perhaps he has a spare cook he can lend us. In any event, as long as we have bread in the house we shall sup. We do have bread?" he said hopefully.

"It is of no consequence at the moment," Mary said, taking back the pieces. She told him of Byron's dinner invitation.

"Very good," Shelley said absently. He stood at the window, gazing out over the lake. "The clouds are building up. It may be quite rainy in the evening. You must take your shawl."

Mary did not answer. A thought had occurred to her: after the passage between Claire and Byron, and knowing as she did now about Claire's pregnancy, the potential for disaster in the coming evening loomed large. Should she wait for Claire to make the announcement to Shelley?

And a little, dark voice in her wondered if Shelley would be surprised, if Shelley would claim it as his own?

Since when has Claire ever waited on my convenience? Mary asked herself. She drew a deep breath. "Sweet Elf," she said, using her nickname for Shelley. "I have something important to tell you."

Shelley turned, and the light behind his head turned his hair into a nimbus of glowing chestnut.

"Claire is with child," Mary said.

He looked at her blankly a moment. "Claire? Our Claire?"

His stunned surprised made Mary's heart rise. He could not be so amazed if he'd had congress with her step-sister, she thought. "None other," she said calmly.

"By whom? Or does she know?"

"Byron, of course. You know that they have been sleeping together—"

"When we arrived here—"

"Since March," Mary said.

"But that was but a few days," Shelley said.

"We conceived the very first time we made love, if you recall."

"Ah, my Maisie-girl. Yes, that sublime and wonderful night."

He strode forward, grasped her hands and kissed them. "You made me so happy. I have since that day thought of it as my true birthday, the day I was reborn in love, all due to you." He bent and kissed her passionately.

Mary almost forgot her topic, until he pulled away. "Oh. About Claire. Dearest Shelley, what shall be done?"

Still holding her hands, Shelley said, "Byron will not be gladdened by this."

"Quite an understatement, my love. He has only two months since left behind his child and wife. He will be.angry."

"We must make him see reason."

"Pray, how?"

"I am sure he cannot be so unfeeling as to turn away from her, with Claire right here in from of him," Shelley said confidently.

"You sound so certain. What would you have Byron do?" Mary said.

"He must provide for Claire, as well as the babe."

"And raise it?" Mary said, growing irritated by his breezy nonchalance. "I cannot see Lord Byron as the doting parent. Nor, judging by his actions, does he."

Shelley scratched his head. "Will you suggest to him that Lady Byron take it in? And perhaps take Claire as well?"

Mary looked at him skeptically. "You cannot be serious. Albé is not of our persuasion in such matters. He adheres to custom, at least, he claims to, whatever his actual conduct."

Shelley looked puzzled. "But he has room enough, and money enough, to support Claire and the babe. Why would he not?"

"Why would he? I have known Byron only a short time, and I respect him in many ways, but Shelley, he is as untamable as a waterfall or avalanche. He will never be domesticated."

Shelley stuck his hands in his pockets and strode up and down the room, thinking. "He will support it. I will persuade him. And Claire must raise it, of course. She is part of our family."

Mary felt a sinking feeling in her stomach. If she did not head Shelley off, Claire would be stitched to them forever. "Is that in her best interests, though? You will recall that she was living an independent existence when she met with Byron. If he will not live with her, perhaps he can set her up in some house, her and the child."

"Well, of course, if he does not want to live with her," Shelley said firmly, "he is not obliged to do so, you know."

"Perhaps not for Claire's sake, but what about the child? Will you let him abandon her and it as well?"

"No, no, no. You know me better than that. If necessary, we can adopt it."

"Adopt it?" Mary put down her scissors. "You will let the world think that Claire's child is yours?"

His blue eyes were wide, innocent. "What do we care what they think?"

I care, Mary thought, but refused to admit it aloud.

He looked away from her. "I can make provision for it," he said. "For Claire and the child, both."

Mary felt her fingers grow cold. "You mean in your will," she said. She hated his mention of this document. Shelley had already altered it to provide for herself and William. "But in order for Claire to receive this money, you would have to die," she said. She felt a sudden constriction in her chest as she said this, as if a hand had squeezed her heart. "No one wishes that."

Shelley made a slow fist, staring at it. "The damned entailment. My father will not see reason."

Mary nodded. Shelley's father, Sir Timothy, had refused Shelley's proposal to break the entail on some of the property he had inherited from his grandfather, and settle it on his female relatives. Sir Timothy's outrage had extended to cutting off his son and heir from all but a pitiful stipend. "A terrible waste, to be sure. Godwin would have railed against it."

"He is correct, of course. Money should belong to those who can use it to forward the bettering of society," Shelley declared passionately. "And what better use to make of it than the education and upbringing of children? Let them only be brought up in Godwin's principles of justice and fairness, with love and care, and the world will be changed in a generation!"

"We have, I fear, strayed from the difficulty," Mary said. She was all too familiar with her father's philosophy of utilitarianism, having been raised in it. "What shall we do about Claire?"

"I take it she has said nothing to Byron?"

"No, I do not believe she has. We must wait until she does so. Pray do not tell her that you know. We must see how matters go forward at dinner. Perhaps she will tell him tonight."

"In any case, we must be sure that Claire is provided for, one way or the other," Shelley said firmly.

Mary fought down a spurt of anger. "Must we? Is Claire really our responsibility?"

Shelley turned and their eyes met. In that candid blue gaze, as always, Mary could detect no hint of subterfuge. Would she never stop worrying about his ties to her, to their child? "You speak of responsibility," Shelley said. "Will you not speak of love? Do we not love Claire, our sister?"

"Perhaps," she said. "One thing must be clear: Godwin cannot know of this."

"Why not? We have made no secret of our situation, of our son."

Mary nodded. "No, we have not. And I am at home with that position, and all the infamy that it brings us. No, you must, you really must admit that our liaison has brought us nothing but condemnation."

Shelley stared down at the table, one finger pushing at a heap of fabric until it fell over, unraveling across the floor. "No, you are correct, dear Mary. But why would we care? Indeed, I vow that Claire herself is more in favor of our principles than we are!"

"You are right," Mary said. "And for that reason, she must be protected. She does not reason, she does not understand what will happen to her, without a protector."

"She should not need one!" Shelley declared forcefully. "It is a damned outrage that a woman cannot live her life as she pleases."

"You know that my sentiments match yours in this, dearest, but that is not to the point. Claire will have to live in this world.

She will be judged on appearances; no one will care for who she is on the inside."

He sighed and came forward. Stooping, he laid his forehead against Mary's. "I will speak to Byron, when the time comes. There must be some way to persuade him. Until then, I shall keep silent about Claire's condition. Should we ask Doctor Polidori to examine her?"

Mary shook her head. "No. He would tell Byron, and such news should come to him from ... someone he respects."

Shelley chuckled. "And who might that be, Mary?"

She smiled a tight smile. "A conundrum, to be sure."

Mary backed away and began gathering her sewing together and putting it in its box. "It is getting late, Shelley. If we are to make it to Byron's at a reasonable time, we had better change."

Shelley looked at one of his coat cuffs, then the other. Both had been made by a famous tailor in London; all of Shelley's clothes were of the finest materials, the best workmanship. He took it as his due that he should be well dressed, as a gentleman. Mary had never bothered to point out to him the incongruity of his fashionable wardrobe in contrast to his egalitarian principles. At least he made up for it, she thought, by the way he dressed so casually, so carelessly in those fine clothes. "Must I really change into a claw hammer coat and breeches?" he mused. "Byron does not even wear a cravat."

"He out-Brummels the Beau himself," Mary said. She came forward, flicking pine needles off the shoulder of his coat. "Come upstairs and I will have Elise brush your coat. And pray remember, do not let on to Claire that I have told you her news."

He dropped a kiss on her head and drew her hand into the crook of his arm. Mary glanced around and said, "What has become of my shawl?"

But Shelley tugged at her, and she gathered her skirt and went out with him into the hallway. Time enough to find her mother's shawl later.

Chapter VIII - Dinner at Byron's

My food is not that of man; I do not destroy the lamb and
the kid to glut my appetite. Acorns and berries afford me suf-
ficient nourishment. My appetite shall be of the same nature
as myself and will be content with the same fate.

—*Frankenstein*, Volume II, Chapter IX

R ain clouds were smothering the sun when Fletcher opened
the front door of the Villa Diodati to Mary, Shelley and
Claire. The stolid servant accepted Shelley's great-coat and flung
Mary's cloak over one arm. "His lordship be in the parlor, sir," he
said. Fletcher always preferred to address Shelley, and avoiding
speaking to the women when he could. "Dinner will be served
forthwith."

Mary wondered, a little fearfully, what manner of collation
an eccentric like Byron would serve them on short notice.

Byron stood in front of the parlor fire, jabbing at it with a
poker. He wore a dark blue coat of superfine, cream colored buck-
skins, and well-polished Hessians. As always, his shirt lay open
at the collar, revealing his strong neck and giving him an air of
studied simplicity. Carefully disordered, his curls fell over his forehead in the manner he had made fashionable two years before. He
frowned at the fireplace. "I cannot get this cursed chimney to draw
properly. Is there no one in Switzerland who can build a reliable
chimney? Shelley, good Shelley, come and fix my fire."

With a nod, Shelley strode over and seized the tongs next
to the fireplace, while Mary sought out an armchair and collapsed
into it, without waiting for an invitation. Even a few days in his
lordship's company had taught her that Byron's manners were as
informal as his dress.

Claire strode quickly over to Byron and took his arm. He
frowned, and for a moment Mary thought he would cast her arm
from his. Then he sighed as she laid her head to his chest. He
murmured something and a half-smile appeared on his handsome

face. Perhaps they will come to agreement, Mary thought. Her heart misdoubted her.

John Polidori strode into the room, formally dressed as always. His cravat was neatly and modestly tied, his broadcloth coat well cut, his waistcoat a sober burgundy with a single watch chain. His high collar was well starched, rigid and immaculately white. He suddenly turned his head and his eyes met hers: dark, so different from her Shelley's sky-blue, open gaze. She felt a slow flush of embarrassment climbing her cheeks, at the same time that she realized that it was more than just embarrassment. Young Polidori was a very handsome man.

Then Polidori stopped next to Byron, and it was as though the sun had gone into eclipse. Against the classic features, lively eyes and carefully disordered nonchalance of his lordship, the young doctor almost disappeared. There were few men on earth who could hold a woman's gaze when Lord Byron was in the room, Mary thought.

The flame in the fireplace roared to life, and Claire clapped her hands. Shelley smiled absently, replaced the fire tongs, and bowed to Byron.

"Thank you, Shelley. You have saved my life. I was perishing of damp," Byron said.

Shelley nodded absently, his eye having been caught by a new book lying on the mantel.

Polidori bowed to Mary and Claire, and said to Byron, "I am told there is no meat at dinner tonight."

"With three guests at my table who abjure it, it would be an unfriendly act to offer it," Byron said. "And you know I eat it only rarely myself."

"It is most unwise of your lordship. You have favored me with the guardianship of your health. I must insist—"

"No, you must not insist. I beg of you, no arguments tonight, Polly. The thunder alone is enough to induce the headache."

Fletcher appeared at the door and bowed. "My lord."

"It appears dinner has been laid," Byron said jovially. "Naturally, since you have just got the fire going so splendidly, we will leave this room and dine in a colder one. Shall we?"

Claire laughed. "Oh, let us be mad, and eat in here. Can the table not be moved into this room, and dinner laid?"

"Rather unusual," Polidori said stiffly. "But if it means there will be meat—"

"Most unusual," Shelley said, laughing. "Rather, let us eat on the terrace!"

"In the rain?" Claire said, eyes dancing.

"If we eat on the terrace, half of Geneva will take to the water to watch the most notorious Englishmen on the continent eat beets," Byron said. "No, we shall be only slightly unconventional tonight. Come."

Shelley helped Mary to rise, but carried the mantel book in one hand. Claire clung to Byron's arm, glowing, a half-smile on her face. Polidori followed, alone and aloof.

"You will appreciate this, Shelley, my democratic friend," Byron said as he led the way into the dining room. "Behold, a Table Round, suitable for an Arthur or a Lancelot."

And indeed, the heavy rectangular table of yesterday had been replaced by a round one, now bearing soup tureens, platters and a central candelabra.

"But where shall we sit?" Claire said. "Where do you sit if there is no head of the table?"

Byron strode to a high backed chair and flung out an arm dramatically. "Sit where you like. This is an exercise in democracy, no, anarchy. Call it an expression of utilitarian principle!"

With a quick, light laugh, Claire said, "Wherever you sit, Albé, I shall sit at your right hand."

"What, so conventional?" Byron cried. "No, no. In this brave new world of social anarchy, I must have my philosophical guide at my right hand. Shelley, if you will." Byron indicated a chair facing the window. Fletcher nodded to a footman, who stepped forward and pulled out the chair. Shelley bowed but stepped to hand Mary into the chair to Byron's left. Only then did he allow himself to be seated. Fletcher held the chair for his master. This left Polidori and Claire standing rather awkwardly, until Claire put her hand on the chair next to Shelley.

Polidori sprang forward to pull it out for her. "Allow me, Miss Clairmont."

"Thank you." Looking troubled, Claire sat and Polidori adjusted her chair. He then took the one next to her, sending a fulminating look at his employer.

Byron, so far from noticing, was staring at Shelley. "You have brought a book to my table, sir?"

Shelley glanced down. "Yes. I found this copy of Coleridge above your fireplace. *Christabel; Kubla Khan: A Vision; The Pains of Sleep*. Leigh Hunt has given it a good review, you know."

"Ah, yes," Byron said lightly. "Murray, the publisher, sent it to me in the post recently. It is only out since May. Most intriguing."

"We must have a reading after dinner," Mary said politely. She wished Shelley would put the book down, but he paid no attention to the company, his nose buried in the pages.

Byron signaled to the servants to begin serving. Mary smiled at him. "We are indebted once again to your lordship. I have no notion where I am to replace my cook."

"I do not envy you the task," Byron said. His smile was as dazzling as sunlight. "A cook who can accommodate so varied a menu will be a rare find, indeed. Fletcher, do make sure that the good doctor has his fair share of the entree." This last remark was in the nature of an irony, as Polidori was known to hold vegetables in distaste.

Fletcher served Byron, but a single footman served the rest of the diners. The fare was as unusual as the seating arrangements: no mutton, no turbot, no poultry dishes. Rather, in respect of his guests' principles, his lordship had decreed a vegetable repast. The soup was followed by asparagus and peas rather than a meat dish, and that was succeeded by mounds of boiled potatoes, along with a dish of beets prepared with mustard.

"I do hope that this conforms to your politics," Byron said, leaning towards Mary. "I believe I have covered your avoidance of meat, sugar and celery. Unless in the last hour you have also forsworn root vegetables? If so, the kitchen will be sorely taxed, but we shall make some effort to oblige."

"Your lordship is very kind," Mary said primly. "You set a very fine table. Thank you."

"More than kind, he is wise," Shelley said, looking up from the book. "Our diet should be that of the earliest men, I am persuaded. The depravity of the moral and physical nature of man originates in his unnatural life and diet. The sooner we return to eating as nature decrees, the sooner we will turn from vice to folly."

"Surely meat is the natural food of man," Polidori said. "We are hunters, after all."

"By design, not at all," Shelley said sternly. "Where are your fangs, doctor? Your claws? With what weapons do you kill and rend your meat? None at all. Indeed, you cannot even eat meat as nature presents it."

"I beg your pardon?"

"It is only by softening and disguising dead flesh by culinary preparation that it is rendered susceptible of mastication or digestion, and that the sight of its bloody juices and raw horror does not excite intolerable loathing and disgust." Shelley took a roll from the footman and began to butter it. "No, doctor, our natural diet is clean, honest, and devoid of that violence that must attend on the destruction of our fellow creatures for food."

"What would you have us eat, then?" said Polidori stiffly.

"Vegetables, with as little cooking as possible, and bread." Shelley flourished his roll.

Polidori admonished his patron. "My lord, you really should eat more than a mouthful of potatoes," he said to Byron as his lordship passed up the *soup de bonne femme*. "It is unwise of you to tax your strength in this manner."

Byron cocked an eyebrow. "I have said, I am on a reducing diet. I can hardly fit into my waistcoat."

Claire laughed. "And how long will you continue to eat nothing but biscuits and soda-water?"

"And wine," murmured Mary, as she watched Fletcher refill Byron's glass.

"Only as long as you continue to notice it, my little fiend," Byron said with a mischievous twinkle in his eye. For a moment, some warmth shimmered between Claire and Byron. Mary began to hope there might be some substance to their feelings, despite Byron's careless rejection of her earlier that day.

"Oh, nonsense," Claire said."You are looking positively underweight, Albé. The doctor is right, you should have some bread, at least." She patted his lordship's hand. Byron frowned and drew his hand away.

"I cannot, Shelley has eaten all of it. I say, Shelley, leave a crumb for us." Byron gestured for Fletcher to fill his wineglass again. "Shelley? Oh, someone poke him."

Shelley, absorbed in the book, heard none of this until Claire leaned over and touched his arm. "I beg your pardon?"

"You interest me, Shelley," Byron said, pushing a potato onto his fork. "I abjure most meat to keep my figure trim. You, however, reject it through principle. Tell me, which approach is more likely to find favor with our fellow beings?"

"Surely the principle of mercy outweighs even vanity," Shelley said, smiling.

"And where shall our fellow-beings learn this principle? You will have to shout rather loudly to be heard over the butchers and cooks of the world." Byron took a tiny bite of potato and washed it down with a healthy swig of wine.

"Our Shelley is the new Prometheus," Claire said, raising her glass to Shelley. "Like the godling, he will use his gifts to persuade mankind. Surely you have read *Queen Mab*, my love?"

Byron shrugged. "I have. The notes bid fair to outweigh the poem. Good my Shelley, next time pray confine your notes to a separate volume, so that I may more easily avoid them." His cheek dimpled in a disarming grin.

Shelley flushed but returned the grin.

"I was quite in earnest. Shelley-Shelley, my Shelley-savior, what Madonna will bring forth this Messiah who will lead the masses to enlightenment? Shall it be my Claire, here, virgin when I first took her?"

Polidori gasped and swung round to stare at Byron, who paid him no mind. "Or shall it be fair Mary and her son, another Christ? Or even you yourself, Shelley? Perhaps you are our new Shiloh."

Claire cocked her head to one side. "Shiloh?"

Byron put his elbows on the table and rested his chin in his hands. "Ah, I forget. I am among the heathen, here. Have you none of you followed the news of Mistress Southcott, of Exeter? She who claimed to be a prophet, and to be bearing the new Messiah?"

At their blank stares, he shook his head. "And here, Shelley, was your golden opportunity, had you but known it. She prophesied that her son would be the new savior, and would be named Shiloh. You could have stepped up and claimed the title! You would be honored! Feted! Followers would flock to you, and your harem could expand fivefold!"

Shelley laughed. "What fantasy is this, my lord? A Shiloh?"

Polidori coughed. "'Tis true, Mr. Shelley. Two years ago, I believe. She was a lay preacher who claimed to be bearing the new, er, Messiah. Instead, she died, I recall."

"Or was taken up in a whirlwind," said Byron gaily. "Or swallowed by the earth! Either way, as I say, Shelley, you should take up her now-bereft followers as your own! Be the new Messiah, and lead us all to a paradise of free love, reason and virtue!"

Shelley's expression had faded from amusement to stone. "Your lordship will have his jest," he said formally. "But you know I am an atheist, and would never try to deceive men into virtue by reference to that which does not exist."

His tone sobered Byron, and Mary caught a fleeting glimpse of a hurt, embarrassed schoolboy under the Satanic brows. Then Byron looked down and shifted his feet. "Ah, Shelley, don't be offended. My Shiloh, my own savior, you are more like to be the new Prometheus than the new god. More like to be torn by a vengeful god, than ascend to his throne."

Any reply Shelley might have made was cut short by the servant who removed his empty plate. Byron threw down his napkin and rose. "I propose that we dispense with the formalities—"

Claire laughed gaily. "What formalities have we observed so far?"

"—And retire, all of us, not just the ladies, to the fire our Prometheus has so lately brought to life. Come, Claire." Byron extended a hand to Claire, who rose and took his arm. Gazing merrily up at him, she allowed him to lead her away into the parlor.

Polidori coughed into his hand. "Well. It seems we are to amuse ourselves. Mrs. Shelley, may I have the honor?"

Mary allowed him to raise her from the chair. Shelley sat staring absently into space, toying with a biscuit. "My love?"

"Ah." He came to himself with a start, and rose from his chair. "Of course. I shall join you directly." He shoved the biscuit into a pocket, picked up the Coleridge book and wandered through the door to the hallway. Mary started to call him back, but shrugged.

Polidori drew her hand through the crook of his arm. "We shall have to excuse him. He will come back."

He will come back.

As she allowed Polidori to lead her away from Shelley, the words echoed coldly in her mind.

Chapter IX - Shelley's Experiment

> Our family was not scientifical, and I had not attended any
> of the lectures given at the schools of Geneva. My dreams
> were therefore undisturbed by reality; and I entered with the
> greatest diligence into the search of the philosopher's stone
> and the elixir of life. But the latter obtained my undivided at-
> tention: wealth was an inferior object; but what glory would
> attend the discovery, if I could banish disease from the
> human frame, and render man invulnerable to any but a vio-
> lent death!
>
> —*Frankenstein*, Volume II, Chapter I

The fire had died down only a little, but the parlor had not warmed appreciably during their dinner. Rain hit the windows fitfully, in a sullen rhythm. Cold fingers of wind played with the drawing room curtains. Their heavy velvet surfaces were damp here and there with rain that had been driven in through cracks in the window jambs, evidence of some neglect.

Polidori bowed Mary into a chair and then, at Byron's order, went to fetch the mail and a newspaper from the library. Claire whispered with Byron, who seemed in a playful, if sardonic mood.

Mary drew her chair closer to the fire, but still a shiver went through her. She wished she had been able to find her shawl. It worried her that she was so distraught lately that she may have mislaid something so precious to her. She picked up her reticule and drew out her embroidery.

"Ah, Shelley," Byron said, hailing his friend. Shelley had managed to find his way back to the parlor, still clutching the volume of Coleridge.

"I say, Albé, this is a remarkable poem, this *Christabel*. We must have a reading."

"And we shall, but not at this instant. Come, I've had a letter from Leigh Hunt. Let us see what he has to say about my *Parisina*." The two men leaned over the missive, searching the crabbed handwriting for mention of Byron's latest poem.

"More light, Sister?" Claire leaned close with a candle in a silver holder. Without waiting for Mary's answer, she touched the flame to a candelabra on the table beside Mary, lighting all six candles.

"Surely I do not need so much light," Mary said, half smiling. It disturbed her that Claire assumed so many of the duties of a hostess in Byron's house. Yet, what could she say? It was for Byron to object, if he did.

His lordship, however, was across the room, deep in conversation with Shelley. Polidori lounged carefully just to Shelley's left, clearly hoping to join the conversation. He was, however, ignored as always.

"I have always preferred this room," Claire said. She sat down on the settee next to Mary. Her rose muslin dress caught the light from the fire and cast highlights on her olive skin and dark eyes. "So much more elegant than the dining room. I have suggested to Albé that he have it redone in Empire blue. Since that was Napoleon's favorite color, he favors the idea." Her eyes sparkled.

Mary glanced at the dusty white moldings, the faded grandeur of the green watered silk wall coverings, the white woodwork marked here and there by mildew. The entire room looked like an aging grande dame, hanging on to its memories of the cool rationality of the Enlightenment. "It would be most expensive," she said. "But it would be very elegant, I am sure. I did not know that Napoleon's favorite color was blue."

Claire leaned close, whispering. "I don't know that it was. I merely said it was. Albé didn't know, either, so he believed me."

Mary was a little shocked, but not at all surprised, to learn of Claire's lie. Perhaps, she told herself, it was unimportant to someone like Byron whether his ladylove told the truth or not. She herself could not imagine lying to Shelley. "Did you bring your embroidery?" she said, changing the subject.

Claire shook her head impatiently. "No, of course not. But how can you sit here and pay no attention to what's going on out there!" She flung a hand towards the windows, which at that moment were lit by a distant flash of lightning.

"It is too damp for me out there," Mary said. "And you know you would not endure it for a second. You would cry when your dress was ruined by the rain."

Claire stared at her. "Of course not. How little you know me." She rose abruptly and walked boldly over to where the men stood. "Byron! Shall we have a game of chess? Or make it backgammon, if you would win this time!"

Byron turned, and Mary was relieved to see the amusement in his face. She wanted Byron to love her sister, now more than ever. "What, and disgrace myself in the good doctor's eyes? He would never forgive me if I lost a game, any game, to a mere woman."

Startled, Polidori objected. "Why, no, my lord, I would never—"

"Oh, you are an old woman, Polly-Dolly," Byron said. His tone was so affectionate, however, that even the prickly doctor subsided.

"Let us have some news of the outside world, instead," Shelley suggested. He picked up the newspaper lying on the sideboard.

"Yes," Mary agreed. "What new revolutions are brewing? What new popes have fallen or arisen? What new wonders has science birth'd in the last two weeks?"

"What new plays have opened?" Polidori contributed, his gaze darting from Byron to Shelley.

"And most important of all—" Byron spanked Claire smartly on her rear, forcing a surprised gasp from Polidori. "Who is swiving whose wife in Mayfair this summer?"

"More likely, the world has come abroad to Geneva," said Mary. "If the number of telescopes trained on this house during the luncheon hour are any indication, we are the toast of Europe. Or at least, its most favored destination for idlers, gawkers and fools."

"What's this?" Byron said, his dimples deepening. "Something has touched a nerve in our Mary." He turned to pour a brandy.

"My fault, I believe," Polidori said. "I was in town last night, as you know, at Madame Odier's. Many of the guests do not know that I know you, so they spoke rather more freely than otherwise. I told Mrs. Shelley that the prevailing rumor in town presently has it that the tablecloths Fletcher and the maids hang on the balcony every morning are, er, the petticoats of her and Miss Clairmont!"

Byron threw back his head and laughed. Claire beamed and put her hand on his arm; he covered it with his own. "We must make sure to lay out some stays and corsets in the morning. Or perhaps we could hang my trousers beside them in the name of equality. What say you, Shiloh?"

Shelley laughed, and turned to gather Mary in to his amusement. Their eyes met, they smiled, and for a moment, for Mary, there were no other people in the room. Then he strode over to her, newspaper in hand. He bowed gallantly. "Dearest, you are always the light in my firmament. May I also ask you to be the light of my newspaper?"

She smiled and shifted to give him room next to her, closer to the candelabra. "What news of the fettered and corrupted world, then, my love?"

The settee was small enough that his shoulders rubbed against hers. Subtly, she arranged herself so that, beneath her white muslin skirts, her leg lay along his long one. In his forest green waistcoat and dark brown trousers, polished boots, and wildly disarrayed hair, he could have passed for a woodland creature himself. Dropping a warm smile on her, he opened the pages. "Ah. An item to interest our good doctor. A bookseller in Chatham announces the publication of a treatise on the diseases of India, with special reference to a recent spate of dangerous fevers in Madura, Dindigul and Tinnivelly."

"Madura, Din-digul and Tin-ni-vel-ly! Madura, Din-digul and Tin-ni-vel-ly! Shiloh, do those syllables not sing, absolutely sing to you?" Byron said gaily. He struck a theatrical pose and his fine baritone rang out. "Ma-du-ra—"

"Din-digul and Tin-ni-vel-ly!" Claire added her soprano in a descant, laughing so hard she could hardly keep the tune.

Together, she and Byron repeated the phrase several times, varying the notes, their voices winding together like a braid of song. Mary smiled to see them happy together.

She felt Shelley stiffen beside her. "Oh, this is unfortunate," he muttered.

Byron and Claire broke off their impromptu concert. "Bad news?"

"Richard Sheridan is ill, perhaps dying." He turned a page. "His friends are requested to aid him."

"Short of money, no doubt," Byron said shortly. His face lost its happy expression, becoming closed and shut off. "He has never been the same since they released him from debtor's prison."

Mary shuddered at the mention of the shadow that fell so near her own father. Shelley looked up and locked glances with his friend. "We should write to him. I can write my solicitors. Perhaps a subscription—"

"He would not accept it," Mary said in her soft voice.

Byron looked at her. "You know this? How?"

"Do you not remember, how the Americans voted him twenty thousand pounds once, for trying to stop England fighting their secession? Yet he refused it. A man that proud, he will not accept charity even on his deathbed."

"I fear you are right, dearest," said Shelley, folding the paper back.

Byron gazed at Mary with a dark look in his eyes, as though seeing her clearly for the first time. "You know Sheridan so well?"

Claire answered first, sitting down on the opposite settee and patting it suggestively with her hand. "Indeed, yes, B. He was ... is ... a friend of our Papa's, is he not, Mary? He has been an admirer of Mr. Sheridan's for almost all his life."

"Not, perhaps, as much as he used to be," said Mary. "Remember that they quarreled rather publicly over the French Revolution."

Byron raised an eyebrow. "I had always imagined Richard Brinsley Sheridan to be a supporter of reform," he said. He studiously ignored Claire's obvious attempts to get him to sit beside her.

"He was," Mary said. "He is. But he was a man without a fortune. He could not afford the luxury of political dissent, when he had a living to earn." Her gaze met Byron's and locked, despite the hauteur creeping into Byron's expression. "Not every revolutionary is born to wealth," she said. "Rousseau, Voltaire, Sheridan ... men of principle but without means."

"Which makes it ever more incumbent upon those of us with means to be the means of revolution," Shelley said heartily. "What say you, my lord? Shall we form a company of charitable revolutionaries? Shall we use our money to shove the powerful and tyrannical off their thrones?"

Polidori snorted. "You cannot be serious. Why, for his lordship to fund a revolution would be a remarkable inconsistency."

Byron looked coldly at his doctor. "I have no consistency, except in politics; and that probably arises from my indifference to the subject altogether." He turned to Shelley. "Even so, and though I approve your theories in theory, so to speak, I am not persuaded that they will bring us anything but misery. Do away with aristocracy? No, sir. If we must have a tyrant, let him at least be a gentleman who has been bred to the business, and let us fall by the axe and not by the butcher's cleaver."

Claire winced. "Government by the corrupt and idle? Do you not see what is happening in the world, in England? B, how can you close your eyes to such tyranny?"

"Perhaps, as a member of the peerage, his lordship finds it inappropos to see what he is not supposed to see," Mary said acidly.

"It is easy enough to peer through the window into the counsels of the mighty, when they lock you out," Byron said, frowning. "I am an accident, my feral little fox. I was never supposed to be a member of the peerage."

"How not?" said Polidori, taking out a snuffbox. At Mary's frown, he put it away again.

"I was destined for hell, and got diverted into another delivery," said Byron. His tone was light but his frown was dark. "When my cousin got himself killed in the wars, they had no choice but to dump the peerage—and the debts—on me. Why, the damn fool could not even wait until Waterloo to die."

Shelley said, "That hardly makes you a revolutionary, though."

"No, merely an outsider, which is worse. To the *ton*, I am an upstart, a hanger-on, an oddity and a monster. The last time I attended a ball, they stared at me in horrified fascination, as if I were an exhibit in a raree-show." Byron bit off his speech suddenly, turning away.

"His lordship does not demur his title enough to forswear his state," muttered Polidori. Mary looked sharply at him. It wasn't that she disliked his opinions—far from it—but that he was so cowardly about them. He would only mutter them, not speak them aloud as Shelley. But then, she thought, what poor man has the luxury of free speech? Even as the thought crossed her mind, an image of her impoverished father came into her mind, steadfastly writing his revolutionary tracts despite government censure. She smiled at the thought.

"And what amuses my Dormouse?" said Shelley in her ear. He rattled the paper, holding it up as a screen between the two of them and the rest of the company, which was getting up a quarrel.

I love my father, and you, and all free thinkers, she wanted to say. What she said was, "Do something quickly, lest open war break out in Byron's best drawing room."

"And I am a man of peace," he said. He patted Mary's hand and opened the paper. "I say, Byron, shall we go for a sail on the night tides?"

Byron, interrupted in mid-tirade against Polidori, paused. He lifted an eyebrow. "You are careless of your life, Shiloh, but I value mine. Have you not heard the thunder all evening?"

"Oh, but how magnificent, to bare our breasts to the storm, to feel its full fury on our faces and know that Nature's most powerful forces are arrayed against us!" Shelley cried.

Byron shook his head. "Not even for the opportunity to see Mary's breast bared to the storm. There is too much danger of lightning."

"Danger? I should say opportunity! Why, we can even advance the progress of science," Shelley said.

Mary looked up in alarm. What had started as a diversion threatened to turn into something more dangerous. "Shelley—"

But Shelley shook the paper practically in Byron's face. "See here, where a fellow in Milan claims that all this un-summer-like weather—cold, storms, all of it—is the consequence of introducing Franklin's lightning rods into Europe! Can you imagine a thing so absurd!"

Polidori shrugged. "But it makes sense to me, Mr. Shelley. If I put up a lightning rod, am I not inviting lightning? Why be surprised if we experience more of it?"

"Hah. I perceive that you are unfamiliar with the works of Dr. Franklin. He actually discerned that the inclement summer of 1783 was caused by a volcanic eruption in Japan! It was not lightning that brought storms, nor the lightning rods that brought the lightning! The dust from the eruption entered the air and shielded us from the sun's rays."

Polidori shook his head. "I do not wish to be impolite, but surely that is nonsense! How could a volcano in Japan affect weather in Boston?"

"It would have been in Philadelphia, actually. But do you not see the majesty of it? The magnificence of it? Byron, surely you can see how stupendous an idea it is, that Nature erupts on one side of the world and causes rain on the other side!"

Byron shrugged and picked up a poker to jab at the fire. "I am not so enamored of Dame Nature as to assert that she works so subtly. Come, we must have a game of whist or chess."

But Shelley threw down the paper and strode up and down the room, his gaze on his feet and his hands in his hair. "I have it! Byron, it is splendid! We can use this very storm to disprove this Milano! Let us set up the Leyden jar and draw down some of the electrical fluid! It will show that Franklin's rods are not the cause of all this intemperance."

Polidori looked alarmed. "What? There is no electricity in lightning! Lightning is fire, not an electrical fluid."

"No, doctor, it is surely formed from the same substance as the etheric upper atmosphere," Shelley said. "My teachers, my books, they agree that the etheric fluid is surely converted by some subtle means into electrical fluid. I have myself felt it!"

Polidori and Byron both looked at him. "You have felt it?" Byron sounded curious.

"Oh, yes," Shelley said. He stopped in front of Byron, his hands waving wildly. "When I was at Oxford, I used to conduct electrical researches. There is one device—I can build it again in no time!—whereby a wheel is turned, and electrical fluid is generated out of thin air! And by touching a rod, it may be conveyed to the person. I have used it to thrill my sisters, and on one occasion made my sister's long hair rise up into the air!"

Claire giggled. "Like the time in London when we went out in the thunderstorm, do you remember? And your hair was standing out around your head like a halo! I called you Saint Shelley!"

"Yes, of course," Shelley said excitedly.

"And a saint you will surely be, or at least the first martyr to science," Byron said. "You cannot be serious, Shiloh! I will not have you struck dead on my very lawn!"

"Nothing of the kind. I have worked with these substances many times. Come, Polidori! Surely, as a man of science, you will help me in this! Let us read the heavens in their own light!"

Polidori drew back. "I have ... I have seen men who were killed by lightning. In Edinburgh, at my medical studies. I would not see that again."

Mary rose to her feet, her embroidery falling to the floor. "Shelley, no!"

Shelley looked from one to another. "None of you are wise enough, or brave enough, to look your Dame Nature in the face?"

"I will," said Claire. "I know where the Leyden jar is. I will send Fletcher for it." Without waiting for an answer, she darted out of the room.

Chapter X - The Storm

I eagerly inquired of my father the nature and origin of thunder and lightning. He replied, "Electricity;" describing at the same time the various effects of that power. He constructed a small electrical machine, and exhibited a few experiments; he made also a kite, with a wire and string, which drew down that fluid from the clouds.

—*Frankenstein,* Volume I, Chapter I

Mary put a restraining hand on Shelley's arm, but he shook it off, gently. "Come, my Mary. There is nothing to fear."

Byron chuckled. "Indeed, I begin to think not. Consider it, my dear Mary. Should Shelley, the notorious atheist, be struck down by fire from heaven, thus giving triumph to his enemies? That would require Heaven to have a sardonic sense of humor, and I am persuaded that God does not know how to laugh. Shelley, what will you require of us?"

Too afraid to speak, Mary stood trembling as the men readied their experiment.

"We must have a kite, some silken string—Mary, we shall commandeer your embroidery threads. Oh, and a kite. Oh, damn, where shall we find a kite?"

Byron's face went slightly pink, and he looked down at the fire. Mary was startled—he almost looked shy. Byron cleared his throat. "I am ... tolerably good at making kites." His glance slid sideways to Mary. "Mayhap I can press some silk petticoats into service—"

Shelley laughed. "Famous! Yes, we must have some silk. Mary? You will oblige?"

Mary's first instinct was to slap Byron for his impudence. She made fists of her hands and put them behind her. "I think not, dearest. And I must urge you against this course."

Shelley was not listening. "I have it! A shirt, your lordship. Mine is muslin, it will hold too much water."

"Albé's shirt is silk," Claire said, and giggled.

"Ah!" Shelley cried. "Come, Byron. Sacrifice your tailor to the needs of science!"

Byron, reluctantly, unbuttoned his waistcoat. "If I am to sacrifice my wardrobe, I absolutely require lightning in a bottle. I shall toast you in it."

"To be sure!" Shelley cried. Helplessly, Mary watched as her lover stripped the feathery plumes from an array of dried reeds, then tied the stems into a large X. "Polidori, please hold this."

Polidori held the X shaped frame, and Byron quickly tied the thin shirt onto it. Soon he held a clumsy but functional kite.

As he worked, Mary noted that Byron's chest was pale but well-muscled. Most of all, she noted the goosebumps on his skin. Byron looked at the kite carefully, then drained his brandy glass. "It might fly," he said. "It is nearly as elegant as a pregnant camel, but perhaps it can become airborne. Indeed, in this wind, the pregnant camel might fly."

Claire returned at that moment, followed by a panting, dripping Fletcher. Fletcher carried a two foot high cylinder of glass. The inside of the lower third of the glass was lined with copper foil; a cork stopper closed its throat and a long wire ending in a ball of lead emerged from the cork. He set it down carefully on the small sideboard and stepped quickly away.

Polidori caught up the water carafe from the sideboard. "You will need this, or so I am told."

Shelley shook his head. "Not at all. That is an outmoded conceit, thoroughly discredited by Dr. Franklin in his researches."

Looking offended, Polidori backed away, still holding the carafe.

Byron cocked his head as he regarded Shelley. "You do not need water to contain the electrical fluid?"

"On the contrary. The fluid is captured in the metal of the inner lining, I believe." Shelley busied himself with the jar, tightening the lid, rattling it to hear the chain inside tinkle against the glass. "Yes, all is in order."

Mary caught Shelley's hand in hers. He looked at her, startled, then his smile softened his face. "I cannot allow myself to fear," he said softly to her. "How will Dame Nature respect me, if I let her bully me? You will see; all will be well."

"I cannot lose you!" she said. Images of his burned, blackened body danced in her imagination. Without him, where would she go? How would she and William live? "Have you thought about what it will mean if something goes wrong? If there is some accident, how will I live without you? I cannot bear the thought!"

His fingers tightened around hers, and he raised her fingers to his lips and kissed them. "My love, I go out on the lake every day. That is far more dangerous. More men drown than die from the lightning-strike. Would you have me cower?"

Before she could answer, he was turning away. Claire was ahead of him, flinging open the French doors with a laugh. The rain struck him in the face as he stepped through, and Shelley laughed.

"This is madness," said Polidori angrily. "I will have no part of it, my lord. It is detrimental to your health."

"Then if I am struck by the fire of heaven, I shall not owe you this month's salary," Byron said testily.

"Albé ..." Mary said. "Can you not stop him?"

He caught her look, held it, and shook his head. "Too late, my dear," he murmured. Byron stayed long enough to catch up the Leyden jar into his arms, then he limped out after Shelley.

Thunder cannonaded through the mountains on the other side of the lake, their peaks outlined by the flicker of lightning. As the party descended the terrace and crossed onto the sodden lawn, the wind whirled through the vineyard, causing the leaves to dance in a satanic frenzy. Ahead of Mary, Shelley's tall form strode along, with Byron hobbling behind as fast as he could. Ahead of them both, Claire laughed and twirled down the aisles between the vines, her dark hair haloing around her head. Lightning strobed, illuminating her as if she were in a theatrical show—the light now starkly blue-white, so bright that Mary squinted, now black as a windowless dungeon.

And always, the singing of the wind. Mary clutched her arms around herself. Here, near the shore, it was beating the waves to a froth, but overhead she heard the deep groan of high altitude tempests shaped by the peaks of Mont Blanc and Jura. Rain beaten to mist by the blast gusted in her face and then was flung elsewhere, so that she was alternately ignored and taunted by the rain.

Ahead of her, the trio halted near the little beach. She could see them only by intermittent flashes; torches or lanterns were out of the question in this cyclone. As she approached, placing her feet carefully on the slippery grass, she saw them as a series of images caught in succession: Shelley taking the Leyden jar from Byron, the two of them placing it on the sand, Shelley uncoiling the silk, and Claire dancing about with the kite in her arms, laughing in near-hysteria.

"... need a key, such as Franklin used?" Byron was asking. Coming close, Mary could see water running off his bare back and shoulders.

"No," Shelley said. He was tying her embroidery silk to the wire leading from the Leyden jar, his movements quick and expert. He tossed his limp, wet hair impatiently over his shoulder. "I have a refinement on that technique. We must set a wire from the jar's outside metal band into the ground. This will draw off the more dangerous electrical vapors. What we must avoid at all costs is contact with the silk, once the kite is in the air."

"Oh, no, Shelley!" cried Claire. "I want to hold it! I want to feel the wind tugging at it, begging it to fly from my fingers!"

"More likely it will strike you dead," Shelley said prosaically. "Once the kite is launched and the silken cord is wet, it will suck the electrical fluid from the sky. If you are touching the silk at that moment, you will be killed."

"Oh, Shelley, this is too dangerous!" cried Mary.

He looked up at her just as the levin flared again, and she caught his impish grin. "Not at all, my dear, if we follow some simple precautions. You will see. The rain will wet the silk line so that it can freely conduct the electrical fluid into the Leyden jar, capturing it. Then we can take the electrical fluid indoors, where we may kindle other electrical fires, or—"

A white-hot bolt of lightning zigzagged across the sky, and at the same moment, Claire tossed the kite heavenward. The wind sucked it out of her hands, carrying it aloft in seconds. Thunder cracked overhead. Byron shouted something, but Mary could not make out the words. Shelley stepped quickly away from the jar at his feet, pulling Byron with him. "Don't stand too close!" he shouted. "Claire, come away!"

The skies opened up with an angry hiss, and suddenly Mary was drenched with icy rain. The wind slapped her sodden hair into her face. "Shelley!" she cried. "Come out of this!" Lightning flared again, winked out, and blue circles danced before her eyes in pitch darkness.

When her sight cleared, she saw Byron with his face turned to the sky, laughing, his mouth open. Water ran off his chest and hair. Beside him, Shelley crouched down to stare at the Leyden jar, then craned his neck to follow the string up into the darkness.

Somewhere in the night, Claire shrieked and laughed. "Come dance with me! LB, come and dance!"

This was madness, Mary thought. Her heart pounded. Were they all to be killed out here, dancing with the lightning? She shivered, and felt hot tears on her cold cheeks.

Across the water, lightning flickered again and again. By its light, she saw Claire run up to embrace Byron, who pushed her away, eyes intent on the jar. Shelley pointed to the kite string, which now glowed with a dim and unearthly blue glow. She followed the glow upwards, along the kite string. Far above her head, eyes squinting in the rain, she could just make out the blue outline of the kite, bobbing madly in the gale. Then it plummeted suddenly, dipped, plummeted again, and fell into the heaving lake. The blue glow snuffed out.

Shelley clapped his hands. "Famous! Come, Byron, help me get it back into the house."

"Don't touch it!" Mary cried, but already Shelley was lifting it in his arms.

Byron helped, laughing. "It weighs no more than it did before. You are hoaxing us!"

As they carried the jar past her, Shelley winked and said to Byron, "Indeed not. Bring the good doctor, and I will show you a miracle!"

Claire danced past Mary, her soaked gown clinging so closely to her skin that she looked as if she were dancing naked. Her dark hair hung dripping around her face, and her eyes flashed with dark fire. "Is it not wonderful, Mary?" she cried as she followed Byron and Shelley. "Is it not the very pinnacle of feeling? To have captured lightning!"

The trio disappeared into the house. Mary turned to follow, shivering and unhappy. Surely nothing good could come of this.

Chapter XI - Re-animation

... my candle was nearly burnt out, when, by the glimmer of the half-extinguished light, I saw the dull yellow eye of the creature open; it breathed hard, and a convulsive motion agitated its limbs.

—*Frankenstein*, Volume I, Chapter IV

When she returned to the drawing room of the Villa, Mary found Shelley and Byron lifting and carrying tables about. Claire stood in front of the fire, wringing out her hair and her gown. The fire shone through the thin, sodden fabric, showing dark nipples underneath. Claire seemed completely unconcerned.

Mary shut the door behind herself and immediately the sound and fury of the storm abated. She drew a deep breath, shivering. At that moment, Dr. Polidori appeared in the doorway carrying Claire's shawl. He stopped when he saw Mary. "Mrs. Shelley! You are also soaked! This is most unwise. I pray you come by the fire. I have asked Fletcher to make up a toddy for Miss Clairmont; I shall ask for one for you. My lord, will you not put on a shirt or jacket? Mr. Shelley?"

Shelley and Byron ignored him, intent on re-arranging their table near the fire. Claire twisted a handful of her skirt, scattering drops on the floor.

"There," Shelley said, standing back from the table. On it the jar sat looking exactly as it had before the fires of heaven had touched it. Mary sighed inwardly. Perhaps Shelley's experiment had failed. Perhaps there was no danger in the ordinary glass and metal contraption before her. Still, she noted that Shelley was careful to keep everyone away from it.

In short order, candles had been placed around the room, a space had been cleared next to the jar, and Fletcher had arrived with a round of hot toddies for everyone. Mary sipped hers gratefully, feeling the warmth curl through her. Shelley refused his drink, murmuring comments to Byron as they discussed the upcoming demonstration. Mary sat in front of the fire, spreading her skirt out to catch its warmth. Beside her, Claire tossed her half-dried hair across her shoulder to allow it to fall down her back in a black waterfall. "I declare, this is the most exciting evening we have had at Villa Diodati," she said to Mary.

"By far," Mary murmured. She was still apprehensive, but the warmth of the fire and the effects of the unaccustomed rum were rendering her mood pleasant and agreeable. "Shelley, won't you—"

"As you can all see, there is no water inside the jar," Shelley was saying to Byron. "Most experimenters are persuaded that the electrical fluid must itself be stored in a similar fluid. I agree with Doctor Franklin, however, that the electrical substance is finer than that, perhaps as fine as any alchemical substance."

"Alchemical!" Polidori snorted. "Really, Mr. Shelley. Will you produce the Philosopher's Stone next, I wonder? Are we to be treated to a demonstration of the 'magic' of Cornelius Agrippa and Paracelsus?"

Mary scowled at Polidori, but the young man was not looking at her.

"You misunderstand, as usual, Polly," said Byron. He sloshed more brandy into a glass; the tang of it reached even where Mary sat. "Mr. Shelley has obtained the very elixir of life from the heavens. He has brought down the very fire of God." Mary wondered if she was the only one who heard the irony in Byron's voice. "He seeks not a stone, but a fire. Like Prometheus, he means to steal fire from the gods."

"He will burn himself, then," said Polidori testily. "I have seen what this 'fluid' can do to flesh and bone. You will want to spare the ladies—"

"Oh, bother," said Claire, tossing her head. She strode across the room, reaching her hand towards the jar. "No one need spare me—"

"Stop!" Shelley grabbed her arm and pulled her away before she could touch the jar.

Byron bent over, giggling. "Maenad! Madwoman! Would you walk over a cliff in sheer defiance?"

Shelley put Claire behind him. "I will demonstrate, but you must stand back a little. Mary, I fancy my gloves are under that newspaper? Thank you."

"Is it dangerous?" Mary asked, handing the leather gloves to Shelley.

"Not if you know what you are doing," Shelley said. He pulled on the gloves carefully and picked up the poker from the fireplace. She noticed that his hair was standing up all around his head, as if he were a saint with a halo. Nothing could be farther from his religion—or lack of religion—but Mary found herself fighting both amusement and fear.

Wearing the gloves, Shelly held the poker out from his body as he advanced on the Leyden jar. His feet assumed the *en garde* stance of a fencer, one foot forward and one back. Byron, chuckling and rubbing a hand through his wet hair, backed against the side cabinet, his eyes on his friend.

"Mr. Shelley, I urge you to desist," Polidori said. Mary thought that his earnest expression was completely negated by his pompous form of address. Really, was the man made of starch?

The tip of the poker approached the wire at the top of the jar. Suddenly there was a loud snap, and a tiny bolt of lightning leaped from the wire to the poker. Claire shrieked and jumped at Byron, who caught her with an oath. Polidori cried out something in Italian. Mary hardly noticed—her heart leaped in her chest, her skin went cold all over. But Shelley stood, cool and poised, in the center of the rug. "Don't worry," he said. "It is completely tamed, as long as one takes precautions."

"Oh! It was so loud! So bright!" Claire squealed, pawing at Byron.

Byron shoved her away, carelessly, his eyes on the jar. "Can you do it again, Shiloh?"

"I can do better than that," Shelley said. "Tell me, Byron, have you a carcass of a chicken about?"

Byron raised an eyebrow. "You propose to revive a chicken? It is not enough to abjure the eating of animals, now you must resurrect them?" Nevertheless, he touched a bell. Fletcher walked stolidly into the room. "Fetch, O Fletcher, a chicken from the store room. Or if we have no chicken, a turkey or a duck or a pigeon. Anything with wings, in fact, that is dead. Should you discover a heavenly angel, however, you must hide it from Shelley and bring us something else."

Fletcher nodded stoically. "Yes, my lord." He went away.

Polidori frowned. "I fear I have some idea of what you plan to attempt. I saw something like it myself, in Edinburgh." He glanced around at Mary and Claire. "I, er, fancy the ladies would want to retire. The experiment, if you conduct it as I saw, would be most disturbing—"

"Oh, nonsense," Claire said. She put her hands to her hair, re-arranging her curls. "We have heard it discussed often, have we not, Mary?"

Shelley turned to look at Mary. "You've seen a chicken revived?"

Mary sat down again, her hands clasped tightly in her lap. "Not quite. We live ... we used to live near Newgate prison. One of our father's friends witnessed the exhibition there by Mr. Aldini. He came to dinner, and told us all about it afterward."

"Oh, and how we screamed, didn't we Mary?" Claire laughed. "I declare we did not sleep a wink all night! So delicious!"

"It was horrible!" Mary squeezed her eyes shut. "Mr. Aldini inserted metal rods into the mouth and ear of a hanged felon. I can never forget what he told us. 'The jaws of the deceased criminal began to quiver, and the adjoining muscles were horribly contorted, and one eye was actually opened. In the subsequent part of the process the right hand was raised and clenched.'" She opened her eyes. Byron was staring at her in fascination, while Shelley carefully wound a thin wire around the knob projecting from the jar.

At that moment Byron's manservant walked back into the room, carrying a plucked chicken on a plate. "Your chicken, my lord."

"Put it here," Shelley said, directing him to a clear space beside the Leyden jar. But Fletcher eyed the jar suspiciously, reluctance in every line of his body. "Oh, here, give it to me," Shelley said impatiently, and jerked the plate out of the man's hand. He slid the plate onto the table, grasped the wire in his gloved hand, and touched it to the cold corpse.

The headless body jerked once.

Claire screamed and clasped her hands to her face in delighted terror. Byron stared, then drank the rest of his brandy in one gulp.

The naked wings and thighs spasmed erratically. Mary stood frozen in shock as the headless creature twitched as if alive, as if trying to regain its feet and totter blindly out of the room. "Shelley ..."

Her lover glanced over at her, his eyes cold and remote, off somewhere, far away from her. She felt a chill creep up her back.

"By God, sir!" cried Byron. "But this is amazing! You are bringing it to life again!"

Claire shrieked and covered her face with her hands, then immediately peeked through her fingers at the chicken.

Fascinated, Mary stepped closer. Was it possible? What would a headless chicken be able to do? Could it stand? Walk? How could it direct itself, with no head?

Claire pushed past her, clutched at Shelley's arm. "Oh, let me! Let me touch it!" She reached for the wire in Shelley's hand. Byron grabbed her from behind and shoved her aside.

"Idiot woman!" he said.

Shelley glanced over at Claire, amused. "If you touch this wire, my dear, you will dance indeed. And you will not like it." He touched the wire to the chicken again. The whole body flexed, one leg jerking convulsively. Fletcher, staring, put his hand to his mouth and ran from the room.

"By God, sir, you could make this pullet dance!" Byron said, waving his empty glass. Half-drunk, he tottered backwards, colliding with Mary. "Oh, beg pardon, my dear."

Mary disentangled herself from his lordship, pushed him towards Polidori, who caught him with a sound of distaste. "Your lordship is a trifle disguised," she said. "Perhaps you should sit down."

Shelley, paying no attention to the others, bent closer to the Leyden jar, adjusting something with his gloved hand.

"What, sit down?" Byron bellowed. "And miss the greatest amusement I have had since coming into this country? Why, I want to see that chicken cluck and fly and dance! Shelley, how dare you dance with my chicken, you ... you vegetarian!"

Mary glared at Polidori. "Can you do something with him?"

The doctor merely shrugged helplessly. Byron staggered upright, weaving slightly now. Claire promptly came to his side, and he leaned on her. "I say, Shiloh, this is damned peculiar of you. You, who will not eat a chicken, now abuse its helpless corse? I would not have thought it of you."

Shelley ignored him. He picked up a pair of tongs from the sideboard and inserted the joined ends into the hollow carcass. "Pour me some brandy," he asked of no one in particular.

Byron was leaning on Claire and Polidori was dithering, so Mary stepped forward to the brandy decanter. She poured a half glass and handed it to her lover. Leaning in, she said, "Shelley, my dear, this will frighten Claire no end. You know how susceptible she is to disturbances. And in her delicate state ..."

His blue eyes met hers, but his expression was distracted, as if he were far from her. "Thank you," he said mechanically, and drained the glass. He handed it back to her. "Best step back, my love."

Seeing what he was about to do, Claire released Byron, who staggered sideways.

"Damn you!" his lordship cried.

But Claire clapped her hands together. "Oh, famous! Do it again!" she cried breathlessly.

Shelley touched the wire from the Leyden jar to the ends of the tongs. The result was startling. The entire carcass convulsed violently, then shivered for several seconds. The wings and legs jerked and flapped spasmodically, and the stump of the tail flittered.

Claire squealed, then burst into screams. "Oh, horrible! Horrible!"

Byron clapped his hands over his ears, glaring at Claire. "Stop it! Stop it at once!"

John Polidori stepped between him and Claire, shielding her at the same time from the sight of the spasming corpse. "Don't look, Miss Clairmont! Turn away at once!"

A faint tendril of smoke rose from the body of the convulsing chicken, along with the smell of cooking meat. Dispassionately, Shelley removed the wire, then touched it to the tongs again. The chicken convulsed so violently it flipped off the plate onto the table. To Mary, it looked as if it were trying to escape the torture of the wire.

"Enough, Shelley," she cried.

Shelley took the wire away. "Keep watching," he said.

Byron and Mary leaned closer. The chicken lay inertly on the table, but then a faint twitch started in one wing. Another leg jerked once and stopped. A shiver went through the entire corpse.

"But you are not touching it with the apparatus!" cried Byron. "Why, man, you have revived it! You have brought it back to life!"

Mary put her hand to her mouth. The chicken shuddered once and then lay still. Shelley reached over and detached the wire from the Leyden jar. "Have you really?" Mary whispered.

Shelley looked at her, and this time it was her Shelley, her lover, the sweet natured poet was back. "Have I what?"

Mary swallowed. "Have you ... restored it to life?"

Byron laughed. "Of course he has! What better act for one who will not eat a chicken, than to give it back its life! Oh, Shiloh, you threaten the livelihood of every butcher in Europe!"

Claire screamed and collapsed on the sofa. Polidori drew a bottle of smelling salts from an inside pocket and waved it under her nose.

Mary's gaze was locked with Shelley's. "Can you do it?" she whispered. "Can you bring the dead back to life?"

In her mind's eye, she saw the narrow lodgings in Nelson Square, the cold room with a small fire, the cradle holding its lifeless bundle. Her firstborn, her premature daughter, dead two weeks after birth. "I thought she was sleeping," she whispered, lost in the memory. Shelley took her hands. "Our little one, our first. I thought she was asleep, so I did not suckle her. But in the morning, I knew she was dead. And the doctor said she died ... of convulsions." The tears started behind her eyes; her hands shook. Shelley gripped them firmly. "Of convulsions ..." Mary stared down at the quiet carcass on the table.

Shelley drew her into his embrace. "Don't think of it now, my dear. She is gone, we have our Will-mouse."

Mary pushed herself out of his arms. "But don't you see? If we had known, if you'd been there, maybe with your ... your jar. Maybe you could have revived her, maybe you could have saved her." She kept her voice low, but it was not low enough.

"I don't know," Shelley said. "I don't think it would have worked. She was too frail, my love. Too early."

Polidori came up behind Shelley. "Mrs. Shelley, is there anything I can do?"

Hiding her tears, Mary shook her head and turned away. Polidori cleared his throat, embarrassed, and turned away.

"I say, Mr. Shelley," he said. "Do you know, I read in *Galigiani's Messenger* that the authorities are so enamored of this new electricity, they are setting up rescue stations along the Thames."

Byron limped up. "Rescue stations? For what?"

"For drowning victims," Polidori said. "The idea, I perceive, is to attempt to revive drowned persons who are pulled from the water."

Shelley gazed at him in fascination. "And does it work?"

Polidori shrugged. "I do not know. I have not read of any trial of it yet."

Byron laughed and clapped Shelley on the shoulder. "Well, Shiloh, my love. We have here a lake, suitable for drowning. We have your Leyden jar. On whom shall we experiment?" He bowed at Polidori. "Doctor, will you assist the advance of science, and volunteer?"

"Oh!" Claire shrieked. "You are all of you horrible and mad!" She shrieked again and ran from the room.

"Damn it!" Byron said. "There she goes again. Shelley, we

must find her before she damages the furniture in her hysterics."

Shelley carefully laid down the wire, removed his glove and laid it on the table. "Of course." He followed Byron out of the room, following Claire's loud shrieks and groans.

Mary stared at the jar, at the wire. Carefully she picked up the leather glove and slipped it on her hand. She reached for the wire, but another hand caught hers.

"No." John Polidori's dark gaze met hers. "No, Mary. It is unsafe. It is ... unnatural."

"And death is natural, so it is acceptable?" But Mary made no further attempt to touch the Leyden jar.

"This is death, not life," Polidori said, and pulled the glove off of her hand. He held it in his. "He plays with death. He thinks of it constantly. But you ... you are a mother, a woman. The very essence of life. You should have no part in this."

Mary pulled her hand away. A mother, yes. And then was not one, only a woman who had given birth to a corpse. She remembered the tiny body wrapped in a blanket, remembered how she rubbed her baby to warm it, would have held it to her breast had Claire not gently taken it from her and left her bereft, her arms empty.

She looked away from Polidori's earnest gaze, and saw the pale-fleshed corpse of the chicken lying in a puddle of grease on the table top. As she watched, it gave one final quiver, as if dying all over again.

Mary's hand rose to her throat; she clutched at her collar. "I ... forgive me." She rushed from the room, stumbling blindly into wall and door, nearly clawing her way through it to get away from that twitching horror on the dinner plate.

Chapter XII - Gallery

... when I destroyed his hopes, I did not satisfy my own desires. They were as craving and ardent as before. Still I desired
love and fellowship, and I was still spurned.

—*Frankenstein*, Volume II, Chapter XVIII

Mary fled along the corridor, hurrying away from the sounds
of Claire sobbing. She came to a staircase; her choice was
to run upstairs or take refuge in the servant's quarters. She was
unfamiliar with the kitchen area, so she caught the banister with
one hand and hiked her skirts with the other. Running lightly up
the stairs, she turned left at the top and entered a large receiving
room. It was unlit, and the curtains had not been drawn. Clutching her elbows, Mary went to stand in the window overlooking
Lake Geneva. Lightning flashed across the lake, and thunder
rumbled through the room like a tiger growling from the shadows.

She felt wetness on her cheeks and thought at first the window must be open, but when she drew her fingers across her face
she realized they were tears. For whom? She wondered. For little
Clara, her dead daughter? For her own step-sister, about to be re-
pudiated by Byron? For herself, doubting her own lover? Or even
for the long-dead felon whose body had been given over to exotic
experiments?

"Mrs. Shelley."

She turned and found Polidori standing in the doorway. He
carried a candlestick with a lit candle in one hand.

Mary turned back to the window to hide her tears. "You have
a soft tread, Doctor. I did not hear you approach."

She heard his feet now on the hardwood floor, saw her shadow cast onto the glass by the approach of his candle.

"I regret that that demonstration caused you any distress,"
Polidori said. His voice trembled a little, as did the candle in his

hand. "If I may say so, Mr. Shelley does not always consider your feelings as he ought."

"No, he does not," she whispered.

A gentle hand on her arm, and she turned, to be presented with a snowy handkerchief. This act of simple kindness caused the tears to flow more freely, to her chagrin. "Forgive me," she said, trying to recover herself.

Instead, she found herself pulled against a warm shoulder clad in fine wool, with an arm firm around her shoulders. For a moment, she let herself relax into John Polidori's embrace, seeking safety and solace.

It seemed that she had been seeking those very things forever, ever since fleeing her father's home with Shelley. From England, across Europe, back and forth in the wake of Shelley's whim, on the run from debtors and Shelley's waking frights. One child lost, another carried from country to country like baggage. She felt so tired, so tired.

Polidori's hand came to rest on her hair. "My dear Mrs. Shelley. Or, more truly, Miss Godwin. He does not treat you well. I know he is precious to you, but ..." He stroked her hair. "My dear, he cannot love you, not truly, if he neglects your feelings as he does."

He cannot love you. The words sent a chill down her spine, echoing her very thought of a moment ago. But now she felt her whole being rise in revolt at the thought. She pushed herself out of Polidori's arms.

"You forget yourself, Doctor," she said primly. And realized how absurd it was to be saying that to the man trying to comfort her, who had given her his handkerchief. "I apologize. I am ... distraught. The demonstration, well, it would unsettle nerves of granite."

"But you are not so frail, I am persuaded," Polidori said. In the candlelight, his dark Italian eyes glittered, and shadows aged his face beyond his twenty years. "I warrant you have strength he does not see. You carry all of your family—your sister, Shelley, your son. Who carries you?"

Mary shook her head and looked away. "I do not need a man to take care of me," she said. "My mother taught the world that women could stand equal to men."

"Doubtless," Polidori said. He stepped closer; she could smell soap and damp wool. "But it is not a sign of weakness to want to be respected. He does not respect you." He caught her elbow, turned her to face him. "You can assuredly do better. He has defiled your name, and given you nothing. Not even his name."

"He cannot," Mary said. "Nor would I—"

"Of course he cannot," Polidori sneered. He was so close Mary could feel the heat of him through the fancy waistcoat. Something in her wanted to relax against him again, wanted to sink into comfort and not question the source. "He is a fool. A man of honor would never have taken a virgin girl from her father's house when he still had a wife and child at home. What kind of man dallies with one woman while committed to another? You deserve better."

All desire for comfort vanished. "Better?" Mary stepped back swiftly. "What 'better' would you propose, Doctor?"

"Call me John, I beg you," Polidori said. "We are friends, are we not?"

"Perhaps," Mary said, a hard edge creeping into her voice. "But what are you saying?"

Polidori hesitated, fumbling at the last moment. In a trembling voice, he said, "You must know my feelings by now, Mary. Surely you are aware of my deep regard, my—"

Panic rose in Mary's breast. Don't let him say the words, she thought quickly. "Doctor. John. You mustn't—"

Fervently, Polidori seized her hand. His palm felt damp against her fingers. "Mary, come with me. To me. I will protect you, cherish you. I can take you to a quiet place, a retired country house where no one will know of your name or shame. Oh, let me—"

Mary jerked her hand away. "Shame? You speak of shame?"

"You know what they say of you, in the village, in London, everywhere. That you are Shelley's whore, even Byron's mistress.

The world condemns you, reasonless. What you have done, it was not done wantonly, but for love. The world will never understand, but I do. Mary. You are sweet and ... and kind, you deserve better than this. Let me show you how I feel."

And before she could protest, he had seized her shoulders, drawn her to him, and laid his mouth on hers. His lips were warm, wet, and trembling. He tasted of strong brandy.

Shocked, Mary thrust her arms against his chest, breaking his hold. She stepped backwards, ending with her back against the cold window glass. Thunder muttered over her shoulder. She wiped her hand across her mouth. "Have you taken leave of your senses?"

Polidori's eyes glittered black in the wavering light. "Mary— Let me spare you from this shame."

"You do not understand. Shame? There is no shame in love. There is only shame in forced prostitution, in slavery. Do you know nothing, have you learned nothing from our conversations? You know my principles."

"Yes, and what have those principles bought you?" Polidori burst out. "I see you. I hear you. I see you unhappy, unhappy with Claire, with your situation, unhappy with him." He pointed at the door, in the direction of the rest of the house, of Shelley. "Like it or not, Mary, he shames you. I would shield you." He took another step towards her. "Come with me. I can marry you. I can give you a name, a home. I will raise your son as my own. Let me love you, Mary Godwin."

It was the last word, the repetition of her father's surname, that broke any idea in Mary of agreement. "I cannot be with a man who does not respect my mind. And if you do not agree with my principles, if you reject the very foundation of my mind and life, I cannot agree to be with you. I'm sorry, Doctor. John. I cannot. I see that you mean well, but you truly do not understand what it is, this between Shelley and me."

"Will you abandon every decent principle for that man?" Polidori demanded. "Will you share him with your sister, with his wife? With the next woman to catch his eye? Will you demean yourself so far as to be a cast-off mistress with a child, one day?"

Stung by the echo of her own fears, Mary slapped him across the face, reflexively, without thinking. Then her hand flew to her mouth. "Oh, no. I should not have done that. I ... I'm sorry. But you don't understand."

Slowly, Polidori touched his cheek where her blow had landed. "No. I do not understand. I do not think you know what love is. But whatever it is you think you feel, it cannot be love."

Mary shook her head. Useless to argue with the man. She stepped around him and headed for the door. "I am going home now."

"Mary ..." There was heartbreak in his voice.

Against her will, she stopped and turned. Framed against the window, lit by flashes of light, Polidori stood with hand outstretched.

"He will abandon you, in the end," Polidori said. There were tears in his voice, but his silhouetted face showed nothing but shadow. "He will leave you. And you will be alone."

Because he voiced her own deepest fear, because she would not, could not tolerate the thought, Mary Godwin turned and ran from the room.

Stumbling blindly down the stairs, clutching the handrail, she felt cold all over. Without Polidori's candle, the hall was dark, the boards popping and creaking under her slippers. When a hand suddenly shot out of the shadows and grabbed her arm, she shrieked.

And found herself struggling in Lord Byron's arms. "Hush, Mary, hush!" he said softly.

Mary struggled to catch her breath. "You frightened me, my lord."

"Evidently," he said. There was amusement in his voice, and he released her arm only to catch her hands in his. "You are chilled through, my dear. Come down to the fire."

Behind her, a floorboard creaked, and they both glanced back into the darkness at the top of the stair. Was Polidori lurking there, with his wet mouth and grasping hands? Mary shook her head. This was absurd. "I am overtired," she said. "I must go home."

Byron pulled her hand through his bent elbow and turned her towards the end of the hallway. "Of course. I will order up the carriage, if you want. The night is foul."

She walked with him, finding assurance in his calm presence. She smelled him, a combination of cheese and lavender-water. "Did you find Claire?"

"I believe Shelley is comforting her now," Byron said. Something in his tone made Mary stiffen.

"Comforting?"

"But yes," he said, pausing to open a door. Beyond lay light and warmth. "She did not go far. In fact, I believed she relished the chase less than the capture. As I discovered last January." His voice was grim.

"You owe her some measure of respect," Mary said. "She came to you in love."

"Do you call it that?" Byron closed the door behind them, and dropped her hand from his elbow. "I call it no more than lust, dressed up for company."

"Is not love the great object in life?" Mary said. Surely this poet of the ages could understand that.

Byron was silent again, then said, "The great object of life is sensation, to feel that we exist, even though in pain."

"Do you love no one, my lord?" she asked.

There was a longer silence, as Byron led her down another long hall, this one papered in fading pale orange wall paper that showed damp stains here and there. A draft caught at Mary, making her shiver; Byron in shirtsleeves, and more than a little tipsy, seemed to feel it not at all.

Finally, at the door to the parlor, Byron laid a hand on the handle and turned to her. His face was pale, with lines she had never seen before etched in it, eclipsing the famous dimples. "Love." He said it as if considering a new mathematical concept, a new concatenation of rhyme or meter in a poem. "Love." There was such empty despair in his voice that Mary drew back.

In a low voice, staring past her, with sad eyes, he spoke. His voice was so low that she had to lean in to hear him.

> *For he through Sin's long labyrinth had run,*
> *Nor made atonement when he did amiss,*
> *Had sigh'd to many though he loved but one,*
> *And loved one, alas! Could ne'er be his.*

Without looking at her, he went through the door. Mary followed him.

Chapter XIII - Utilitarianism

... my country, which, when I was happy and beloved, was dear to me, now, in my adversity, became hateful. I provided myself with a sum of money, together with a few jewels which had belonged to my mother, and departed. And now my wanderings began, which are to cease but with life.

—*Frankenstein,* Volume III, Chapter XVII

In the parlor, Shelley was helping a shivering Claire into a chair before the fire. Byron strode past all of them, making straight for the brandy decanter. Mary wondered where Polidori was. Did he still brood in the room with the bared window, overlooking the storm over the lake? How would she face him tomorrow?

Coming close, Shelley leaned down to rest his forehead against Mary's. "I am tired, love."

"Dancing with lightning, how can you be?" she asked drily.

"Take me home. Take me to bed," he murmured.

Mary glanced over to the fireplace. Byron stood staring at the fire, drinking. As she watched, Claire's hand crept into his. Byron did not shake her off.

"Yes," Mary said. She straightened, her sturdy figure straight and strong in the dim light. "We will go home."

They clasped hands and walked to the door, leaving Byron and Claire in their tableau by the fire.

Mary had no idea where Polidori had gone. She did not care.

Outside, Shelley absently offered her his arm. She took it gratefully, feeling the damp even through her slippers. Mary drew the edges of her cloak about her.

"Shelley," she said in a low voice. "Polidori tried to kiss me tonight in a room upstairs in the villa."

"Did he?" Shelley's voice held amusement. "And did you enjoy it?"

She shook her head. "He does not ... appeal to me in that way." She felt a hot flush along her cheeks as she remembered the shock of Polidori's mouth on hers, her sudden and unprepared reaction.

"I would say he is handsome enough," Shelley said, his voice tinged with that hint of distance he always got when speaking in abstracts. "Do you want to sleep with him? I can sleep in the boat, if you prefer. And as a medical man, he might even be able to introduce you to—"

"Will you be serious!?" Mary hissed furiously. "Do you not care that his ... his approach was uninvited, unwanted?" She despised herself for wanting him to leap to her defense like some hero out of a novel by Walter Scott. He was a philosopher, not Lancelot, she told herself. "You would not care if I slept with him!"

"Why, no, Pecksie-girl," he said, honestly surprised.

"Stop! Oh, *why* must you...?" She stopped looked down at her feet, struggling to control her breath. *Why can't he want me, just me?*

As always, it was as if he read her thoughts. "You know my mind on this, love. I thought you shared it. Love is free; to promise for ever to love the same woman is not less absurd than to promise to believe the same creed; such a vow in both cases excludes us from all inquiry. You are free to act on your feelings, as I am. We are not chained by custom."

She swallowed. Yes, of course. This was the creed she had heard all her life, first from Godwin and then from Shelley, her father's most ardent disciple. And in her mind, yes, she agreed. But in her heart, where the fear of abandonment lived, it was another story. "I choose to act on my feelings, then," she said. "I ... I do not care for Polidori in that way. I will not sleep with him."

Shelley patted her hand where it lay on his arm. "Well, I applaud his taste, if not his—"

"Oh, do be serious," she said, half laughing. The wind blew damp mist at them, curling over the path.

"But I am serious," Shelley said. "We must not feel bound to one another, except by chains of love."

Mary wanted to ask him what happened when those chains fell away, or held only one of a pair. Instead she took his arm and walked with him through the floating fog towards the lights of their temporary home.

The house was warm and welcoming after the damp mists. "Have you seen my shawl?" Mary picked up a cushion from the divan, then looked under it.

A cry from the staircase, and then Elise was at the door with a wailing bundle in her arms.

Mary sat in the chair. "Bring him to me," she said authoritatively. "You may come back in half an hour."

The nursemaid curtsied and handed over the crying child. Mary unbuttoned her gown with practiced ease, ignoring her lover's bright gaze, and put the baby to her breast. Immediately he quieted, giving all his attention to his task. Shelley rolled over on his stomach, propping his chin on his hands and waving his feet in the air like an overgrown boy. "A feast for the gods," he murmured.

Mary raised an eyebrow. "Which would make you ... Father Zeus?"

At that moment, thunder growled distantly. Shelley grinned. "Behold my thunder!" he said.

William, preoccupied, said nothing. Quietly, the three sat before the flickering fire, hearing the thunder roll across the lake, seeing the flashes of lightning at the windows. Finally, Mary laid her son on her shoulder to settle him.

Shelley lay prone on the floor, head propped on his elbows, staring at his son. "He has grown. I vow he was half that size last week."

Mary laughed. "If he takes after you, he will be taller than me in a month." William burped, and then Mary set him down on the floor in front of his father. The two looked at one another curiously.

"Watch. He imitates me." Shelley slowly rolled to his side. Baby William grunted, and then slowly rolled to his side as well. "Well done, little man."

"I thought I was wearing that shawl this afternoon. I declare, things walk off by themselves," Mary said irritably. Unable to find the shawl, she sat on the divan and watched her lover and son.

"Perhaps Elise took it," Shelley said absently. He waggled his fingers at William. William blinked round eyes and drooled a bit. Shelley rolled onto his back, looking up at Mary. "Why are you all the way up there, Maie?" he said, using his favorite pet name for her.

As always when he was in this mood, Mary found hers matching his. She felt a giggle rising in her, and scrunched her skirt around her knees. She knelt next to Shelley, then stretched herself on her stomach. Baby William, confronted with two parents side by side, cooed.

"He is a very fine baby," Shelley said soberly. "Almost as fine as I was."

She looked at him critically until she caught the twinkle in his eye. "Oh, I have no doubt you were spoiled to an inch of your life," she said. "Servants to wait hand and foot on Sir Timothy Shelley's heir. A different nurse for Sundays and regular days. A gold-mounted baby carriage."

Shelley laughed, and baby William echoed him with a gurgle. "Not at all. But I did have a pony when I was three. Shall we get Will-mouse a pony, my love?"

"He's a trifle young."

"He'll be a big boy, like me," Shelley said. He rolled up into a sitting position, scooped up his son, and lifted the child over his head. William squealed in delight. "Won't you, my son? We shall teach you to ride a pony, and sail in boats, and—"

"And swim," said Mary firmly. "And tie his own shoes, and read Greek and Latin."

Shelley brought the child closer to his face and nuzzled him. "He's a little young yet for Catullus."

"But not too young for a bedtime story." She reached in vain for William, as his father swung him out of her reach.

"We shall be pirates!" Shelley cried to his son. "Adventurers! We shall sail the seven seas, my son and I! We shall climb all the Alps, and see every river's source. I will teach you chemistry, and we shall unlock every secret Nature hides!"

She laughed. "Will you make him a philosopher?"

"One of the Peripatetics! Like his father!" Shelley said, tossing his son in the air. The boy giggled as Shelley caught him again. "We shall go a-roving! We shall visit the Indies!"

"With tuppence in his pocket, like his mother and father," Mary laughed. "How much did I have with me when I ran away from Skinner Street to be with you?"

Shelley smiled at her, his look warm. "My fearless Mary! I think you brought five pounds with you?"

"Not even so much," she said. "I brought you only myself."

"And Claire," he reminded her.

"And Claire," she said, making her voice neutral.

"When we get to Italy, we will buy a house with a sunny garden." Shelley nuzzled his son. "Shall we live on the coast or in the countryside? No, Will-mouse, you bust dot pull by doze 'ike dat. Ow."

She thought of the narrow, cramped house in Skinner Street in London where her father had moved the family when she was a child. She thought about the noise of the crowds a few streets over at the execution grounds, cheering the death agonies of the condemned. She thought about the stench of the nearby slaughterhouses, and how they had had to keep the windows tightly closed in a vain attempt to keep it out. She remembered the noise of carriages on the cobbles at all hours, keeping her awake.

"A house in the country," she said. "With a window I can open."

"It shall be a temple to the Lares and Penates," he declared, tickling William. "They are innocent deities, and their worship neither sanguinary nor absurd. Their shrine shall be good wood fires, and a window frame entwined with creeping plants. Their hymns shall be the purring of kittens, the hissing of kettles, the long talks over the past and dead—no, William, ouch!" He disentangled William's small fist from his long locks. "We shall have the laughter of children, the warm wind of summer filling a quiet house—in Italy, perhaps? And the pelting storm of winter struggling in vain for entrance."

Mary laughed, glancing at the window. "With that last, we have had too much experience of late!" She watched as Shelley cuddled the boy, head bent to head, the gold of William's hair contrasting with the sun-dappled brown of his father's. It was a fine picture he painted, but she remembered that they had lived in four different homes—or was it five?—since she had eloped with Shelley two years ago. "A home. Yes," she said. But it came out in a whisper.

Shelley did not hear her, or perhaps did not want to. "Ho!" he addressed his son. "Shall we build a boat and set sail for the North Pole? Or we will sail to Virginia and look at the red men!"

Useless to dream of a fixed home, when Shelley embodied the very wind itself.

Elise, the nursemaid, appeared at the door, apparently unconcerned to see her employers romping on the floor like children. "Madame," she reminded Mary in her heavily accented English. "Eet ees time for the boy to be in bed."

Mary glanced at the clock on the mantelpiece. "Yes, it is. Shelley, hand him over."

"But we are going to sail to the Indies and sing under a hot sun!"

Mary took the baby from her lover. "He shall do all that tomorrow," she said. "But now, he goes to bed."

William protested, but Mary kissed his fat cheek and handed him to Elise. "I shall be up presently to sing to him." Bobbing a curtsy, the young woman left, with William's cries floating behind.

Shelley lay face upwards on the carpet, hands behind his head. "My father never played with me."

Mary plopped down beside him, spreading her skirts around her. "Mine, neither. Maybe you must be a boy as much as a man to do such a thing?" She leaned over and kissed his nose. He smiled. "You are an experiment in fatherhood."

He raised an eyebrow and drew her down into a passionate kiss. His mouth was soft but demanding, and Mary felt the familiar warmth seeping through her that his kisses always brought. She brought her hands to his face, then slipped them into his hair, so silken against her fingers. She felt his mouth smile under hers, and then he rolled, taking her with him, until he lay atop her on the hard wooden floor. His mouth left hers and traveled down her neck.

"Mary, Mary ..." he murmured.

She pressed the back of his head, clasping him to her shoulder like William. She longed to shout, to scream, to tell the world of this man, this special and intoxicating man who saw into every corner of her soul. What she said was, "Shelley, Elise may be back at any moment...."

"I don't care," he murmured. His fingers danced down her side. "How does this come off?"

"Shelley!" she protested, half laughing. "You are shameless!"

"With you, always," he said, his voice filled with gloating. "My Pecksie girl ..."

Half-laughing, half-protesting, she squirmed out from under him. "Shelley! At least wait until we are back in the bedroom!"

"Women." He rolled onto his back again, sighing. "Byron does not hide his amours in his bedroom."

Mary stood, smoothing her skirt. "Assuredly. Which is why he is the scandal of Europe."

"But I'm a scandal too!" Shelley complained. "In my own minor way. Mary ..."

She smiled and held out a hand. He got to his feet, clasping her hands in his. "My Mary ..." He kissed each cheek softly. He twined his fingers in hers, tugging gently, and led her out the door. But instead of turning left to go to their bedroom, he turned right.

"Shelley?"

He shushed her with a finger to his lips, entering the short hallway. His greatcoat lay across the small receiving table; he caught it up and handed it to Mary. Still silent, he opened the front door and guided her through.

The night was overcast, with the smell of rain on the wind. The clouds scudded before gusts of wind, revealing and then concealing the dilapidated garden around them. It was not as cool as Mary had feared. Still, she shivered a little as she slung the coat one-handed around her shoulders. It smelled of Shelley—sweat and crushed grass and shaving soap. She clutched it close around her as her lover led her down the short steps to the walkway and out towards the little dock where his boat was moored. Faintly, she heard the lapping of waves against the low retaining wall.

"Shelley, what are you doing?" she said, her voice low.

"We have had hardly any time alone," he whispered back. "May I not have a moment with you, just us together?" His voice sounded a little plaintive.

She wanted to ask him why, if he wanted her to himself, he insisted on dragging Claire with them everywhere. What she said was, "You will catch a chill."

"No, but thank you for reminding me." He turned right, heading for the bottom of the little garden. "Ah." Despite the dim light, he unerringly found the small box he had nailed to a tree near the waterline. He opened the hinged front of it.

"A thermometer reading? Now?" Mary was half amused, half frustrated. Her mad love had once again set out on one course and diverted himself to another. Straight lines were anathema to Shelley.

"I neglected to do it as usual, at sundown." Shelley busied himself taking the large mercury thermometer out of the box. He turned it this way and that, trying to catch the light strongly enough to read the markings. "Sixty degrees? On a June night? Remarkable! Alas, I have nothing to write with—oh, wait. Look in the pocket of my coat."

Obediently, Mary thrust her hands into the pockets of the greatcoat. As usual, they were full of an odd assortment: bread crumbs, a flower, a smooth rock, coins. Her fingers encountered paper and drew it out: a letter. "Here—" Then her eyes fell on the inscription and she froze. Her father's handwriting was as familiar to her as her own. She stared down at the letter, blinking. "What … .how?"

Shelley looked up, and even in the dim light spilling from the upper windows of the house, his face looked pale. "Oh. I didn't mean for you to see that."

Mary thrust the paper towards him. "Dated a week ago. And you didn't tell me."

He turned from her and slowly placed the thermometer back in its house. He closed the door and placed his hand flat on it. "I didn't want to worry you."

Her hand shook. The papers rattled. "Do you think I am a child?"

He looked at her, his eyes looking larger than ever. "Maie, I ... no, you are not a child. But you are my happiness, and if you are made unhappy, then I am made unhappy, and ..." He trailed off, biting his lip.

"What did he say?"

Shelley sighed. "He asked for money."

"Of course," she said bitterly.

"He wants five hundred pounds."

Mary closed her eyes. The book shop, the demands of a large family, and her father's illnesses, all contriving to make him a constant borrower. Except that William Godwin, in line with his philosophy of utilitarianism, did not consider it borrowing. "Money belongs to whoever needs it the most," she quoted softly.

"Exactly," Shelley said, his voice lighter. "A sentiment with which I am, as you know, completely in accord. And I am quite happy to use my coin to succor the revolutionary, the reformer, the man who will make mankind better. But ... but I am afraid, Mary, that that man may not be your father."

Oddly enough, her bitterness against her father vanished in the face of this criticism. Feeling her whole being growing cold, she said, "You called him the greatest man of the age."

"Yes. And I meant it. But, Mary, I have given him so much ... lover fifteen hundred pounds! And it vanishes!"

"He has so many calls on his purse, and his creditors beset him constantly." Even to her, her defense sounded less than forceful.

"I understand. But whatever I give him, it is not enough. I gave him over a thousand pounds two years ago. Another five hundred this spring. And now he writes demanding more. Yet I see nothing from him that improves anyone's lot but his—no new books, no society for reform, nothing. He merely spends it and asks for more, as if I were a fountain of gold. Mary, dearest. Is it not prudent to consider whether this is the best use of what little money I have?"

She was silent, her heart wrung. Shelley was right, and yet, and yet. Godwin had never needed her; now she could help him. Now she could earn his love back, perhaps. "He is my father," she said softly. "For a long time, he was my god."

Shelley sighed and ran a hand through his hair. The effect made him look like a startled ostrich. "I thought when my grandfather died, it would all settle itself out. But the allowance from the estate is so small, and much of it goes to Harriet...."

At the mention of Harriet, Mary felt a pang. Should she tell him the contents of Fanny's letter? Honesty compelled her. She had never lied to Shelley. And yet ... she would spare him that news awhile longer, as he had spared her. She bit her lip. "So. Are you going to refuse Godwin?"

Shelley hunched his shoulders and stared up at the clouds covering the waning moon. Its light shone feebly behind its veil. "I don't know. Would it not be better spent on ... other causes? An orphan, perhaps. Or that organization for women's education your aunt wrote to Fanny about. Or Claire. She will need money for the baby."

At the mention of Claire, Mary's jaw tightened. "Surely that is Byron's affair."

Shelley looked at her, a long silent look. She read in it sympathy and cynicism, an unusual combination for the ebullient Shelley. "And you really think Albé will make provision for what he will call a bastard?"

"So you would rob Godwin to pay Claire," she said angrily.

"That is unjust. As your father has said, money belongs to those who require it."

She knew it. It didn't matter. The paper crumpled as she made a fist. "Claire comes first," she spat. "Always. I know that."

"No! Mary—"

She flung the letter at his feet. "Pay them both, then. Leave nothing for me and your son."

Shelley's look hardened. "Would you have me deprive a child of food and clothing, to satisfy you? Would you have me cast a child off? Would you have me cast Claire off?"

As always, he had penetrated to the heart of her, to the fear that coiled around her soul. "Shelley ..." Her voice pleaded, heavy with the words she could not say. *Don't leave me. Don't desert me. Don't cast me off.*

In one long stride he was in front of her, catching her up against him. His long arms wrapped themselves around her. "Oh, let us not quarrel, Dormouse. You know I will give up everything for you. I will do anything for you, my love. I will buy your father's love for you, even if I must do it in installments. I will write tomorrow to my solicitors."

She slipped her arms around him, holding his solidity and warmth against her. He was here, she thought. Not Godwin, not the father who had cast her off only for doing what he had advocated. Hypocrite, her mind said, but she closed her eyes and turned away that thought. To question her father on that principle was to bring into question everything she and Shelley had done in the name of his philosophy.

And it was far too late for that.

Chapter XIV - Brides and Lovers

... let us only cling closer to what remains, and transfer our love for those whom we have lost to those who yet live. Our circle will be small, but bound close by the ties of affection and mutual misfortune. And when time shall have softened your despair, new and dear objects of care will be born to replace those of whom we have been so cruelly deprived.

—*Frankenstein,* Volume III, Chapter V

Returning to the house, Mary waited while Shelley secured the doors. This was one of the facets of her life with Shelley she loved most of all: going up to bed. In the sober and staid routine of locking up, checking that drapes were drawn, assuring that the fires were out or dying, Mary felt grown-up and responsible.

The domesticity of it soothed her, reassured her of her place with Shelley, of her entry into the world of women and competence and agency that her mother had once known. She was not quite sure whether Mary Wollstonecraft had enjoyed putting out all the candles but one, to light her way upstairs with her beloved. It was, nevertheless, a connection to her mother in that bond of housekeeping. For Mary Godwin, it was the rituals that they carried from place to place that made their household a home; the dwelling itself changed every few months, so it was more important to her that the evening ritual be got through, than that the sofa was sagging or that the cushions were worn.

Shelley followed close behind her on the stair, his hand on her hip. Warm and full of promise, it rested lightly; she was intensely aware of it as she rounded the turn and started up the last flight. At the landing, she glanced over to see that Claire's door was closed. Doubtless she would stay the night at the Villa with Byron. For once, Mary had a night to herself with Shelley. With an inward sigh of relief, she opened the door to her sanctuary.

Their bedroom was small, and since Claire had taken the room in front, she and Shelley had made do with the rear, where there was no view of the lake. Still, it was theirs and they could close the world out, and Mary was glad of that. She set the candle on the table beside the big four poster bed. She heard the creak of the single chair next to the door and Shelley sat down to pull off his boots.

"We should see about a new cook in the morning," Shelley said. A boot thumped to the floor.

Mary opened the latch and swung the shutter wide. Above them, clouds roiled and churned, the moon not yet risen but beginning to limn the slopes to the east. "It must be past one," she said.

"Aye," said Shelley. The other boot hit the floor. "And I needs must rise at dawn for another reading."

Mary laughed softly. "Another thermometer reading? Are you scientist or philosopher?"

"Both," he grinned. "And lover." He stood and slid his braces off his shoulders.

Mary stepped to him and placed her hands on his. "I will do it," she said. This was another ritual, one she also carried from place to place in their wanderings. Behind the closed door, she and Shelley were not mother and father to small children, or philosopher and writer, or even political radical and revolutionary. They were merely man and woman, beloved and familiar.

This was her time, Mary thought. Not Claire's or Byron's or the world's. Hers.

So Mary made her movements slow, drawing the silk shirt from his waistband. He stood still, tall and bushy haired, saying nothing. But this close, she smelled the rain on him, smelled wild night air and warm male skin. She leaned in and rested her forehead on his chest.

"Mary ..." His voice was soft and warm. He threaded his fingers through her hair, pulling hairpins, letting it fall in a cascade down her back. "Mary."

She slid her hands up under the shirt, feeling his skin against her palms, slipping her hands around his waist. This was how she had first touched him, that night in the St. Pancras churchyard.

They had met there, as usual, at her mother's grave. As usual, they discussed her father's writing. And as usual, they had inched closer and closer to one another, aware of the tension building between them.

She remembered how she had thrilled when his hand first sought hers, first traveled up her arm, first cupped her chin for a shy kiss. And then the night he had, with fire and trembling and passion, laid her down on that grave and taken her childhood. Did he remember that night, the girl trembling in his arms with passion and joy and surprise?

Mary stretched up on tiptoe, and Shelley bent down, and his mouth found hers in the semi-dark. Warm, as his mouth had been that first time, but no longer shy. She slid her hands back around, up his chest, feeling hair tickle her palms, feeling his flat nipples rising under her fingers. Against her belly, he rose hard, pressing against her through the thin muslin of her gown. His arms came around her, stroking her back, combing her hair through his fingers. They moved together, and now Shelley was unbuttoning her, divesting her of gown and petticoat and chemise, letting them all drift silently to the floor like foam around Venus rising from the waves. She shivered a little as the cool air struck her skin, but then he skimmed a hand down between her full breasts and she felt heat flood her body. For a man who lived in his head, his hands could be remarkably expressive.

"My love," she whispered. He dipped his head to kiss her again. She broke the kiss to help him slide his shirt over his head and arms, a wifely moment, and quickly folded his shirt across the chair. Shelley might think nothing of flinging her garments to the floor, but Mary knew washerwomen came dear. When she turned from the chair, he had already kicked his way out of his pantaloons and smalls, so that the dim light of the candle gilded his bare skin. Naked, the gangly wild man who slouched his way through Europe became an elegantly framed man, long of limb and torso, proportioned as an athlete. His long walks had given him the silhouette that Byron could only hope for, lean and graceful. And at this moment, highly aroused.

The poet-philosopher held out one large hand, inviting her. Gathering her close, he molded her to him with hands and lips, sealing them together through thigh and hip and shoulder, her breasts pressing into him. He whispered her name into her hair, trailing hands above and below, now circling her waist, now stroking her shoulders. His hand slid between her thighs and she became liquid fire. Mary threw back her head, moaning.

"My girl, my Mary ..." He bent suddenly and picked her up in his arms, lightly as a child. She felt the flex of muscle under her hands as she grasped his shoulders. He took one stride forward and flung them both, half-intertwined, onto the bed, muttering,

He reared his shuddering limbs and quelled
His gasping breath, and spread his arms to meet
Her panting bosom ...

"Oof! You quote from your own poem? Oh, vain!" Mary laughed as he landed on her, his weight bearing her down into the feather mattress. The support ropes holding it up groaned as Shelley, on hands and knees, leaned over her, kissing her neck, down her chest, from one soft breast to the other.

"Her panting bosom," he whispered. "My Mary."

She clutched his head in her hands as he kissed her stomach, threaded her fingers through his light chestnut curls, caressed his ears. His mouth teased her, his hands possessed her, his heat seeped through her. Under him, she sank into the feathers, as if falling into a sea of down. She shifted, parting her knees, felt him fall between them. "My heart," she murmured, and felt his hands on her thighs.

Then he was kissing her deeply, sliding into her, filling her and she felt that tension growing in her belly, felt it spiraling through her center, as he rocked into her over and over. His hands caught hers, pressing her down, almost smothering her. But she felt liberated, knowing at this moment that she owned him, he was completely and only hers. The knowledge percolated through her, even as thought fled and feeling took over, until her arms and legs were wrapped around him, holding him close, closer. Shelley, damp with sweat, cried out and surged into her, and Mary met him halfway as she herself crested at the tide they made between them. She screamed into his shoulder as he bellowed into the feather mattress, arms braced, head down.

Then the quiet fell over them, as he subsided and they gently twined together, melting in afterglow. She smelled him again, that unique combination of rain and man and sweat that locked itself in her brain and said, "Shelley" to her. She could have found him by that scent blindfolded, in total darkness.

"I know that poem, too," she whispered into his shoulder: "Then, yielding to the irresistible joy. / With frantic gesture and short breathless cry / Folded his frame in her dissolving arms." She giggled. "Although, my arms are not quite dissolving ..."

He chuckled into her breast. "Now blackness veiled his dizzy eyes, and night / Involved and swallowed up the vision."

"Go to sleep, dearest."

Wrapped in his arms, his breath warm against her neck, Mary let herself slide into sleep.

Part Two:

June 15, 1816

Chapter XV - Polidori the Gossip

... when I became fully convinced that I was in reality the monster that I am, I was filled with the bitterest sensations of despondence and mortification. Alas! I did not yet entirely know the fatal effects of this miserable deformity.

—*Frankenstein,* Volume III, Chapter IV

At breakfast, Shelley had a book in one hand and toast in the other as Mary came down.

"Has Claire come home?" she asked.

Shelley dipped the toast in his tea and shook his head. "Elise tells me she came home at dawn. I suspect she may be out of sorts today. And in her condition ..." He shrugged, as would a man so well experienced with pregnancies. "It appears to be clearing, my love. Would you care to take a walk with me?"

"I would, but I must feed William. Perhaps this afternoon we may walk down to the village."

"Hmm." Shelley closed the book he was reading and beamed at her. "You look lovely, my sweet. I have an agreement with Byron to shoot with him this afternoon, if the weather holds."

Mary nodded. "Then I shall take our son out for some sunshine." She leaned over to kiss Shelley's cheek. "Do be back by noon."

"Assuredly!" Shelley swept out of the room.

After her breakfast, Mary called the nursemaid to bring William. "Have you seen my mother's shawl?" she asked, when Elise brought her baby.

"No, Madame," the girl said. "Eet ees that white one, no?"

"Lamb's wool, white, with fringe," said Mary. "It was my mother's. I cannot conceive where I may have left it. Oh, very well, fetch me the dark blue one in the parlor."

The girl handed over William, already fussing. Mary carried him to the small lawn between the house and the lake. She sat on a low stone wall with her back to the breeze and opened her dress.

The lake was a million shades of blue in the bright sunlight; the mountains loomed above it like remote and majestic guardians. Mary wondered who lived on those wooded slopes, what kind of man it would take to survive on those craggy heights. A strong man, she thought, one whose nature was closer to the animal nature than that of the men she knew. Perhaps one of the denizens of Rousseau's works could survive there, she thought. Elise came out to wrap the blue shawl around her shoulders, then returned to the house.

The chill breeze whipped Mary's hair against her face; with her hands full of her son she could not put it back but was forced to endure it. She turned a little, so her back took the full force of the wind, and faced more directly into the sun. How warm it felt on her face! At her breast, William suckled contentedly, his eyes closed. Mary smiled down at the perfect lashes lying along his chubby cheek. Softly, she sang to him:

> *Lavender's blue, dilly dilly,*
> *Lavender's green*
> *When you are King, dilly dilly,*
> *I shall be Queen.*

She broke off. "Not quite the thing for the son of a republican," she murmured. William paid no attention, his whole being given over to the bliss of the moment.

"Would I could do the same," his mother whispered. She looked out over the small terrace, with its rock retaining wall above the tiny lawn that fell down to the enclosed cove below. The clouds above Jura were huge, gray, massive. Though she sat in bright sunshine, even as she watched, their shadows flowed ominously down the mountainside, headed for the shoreline, the lake, her. She treasured this moment in the sun with her healthy baby, and didn't want to go in just yet. But soon. If William took a chill ...

A step on the path above—Shelley? Mary peered eagerly over her shoulder, but it was John Polidori. She adjusted her shawl to cover her exposed breast but otherwise made no effort to hide herself.

"Mrs. Shelley." His posture was stiff and formal. He was meticulously dressed, in a dark suit with a cravat so fiercely starched Mary decided it could probably stand in a corner on its own. "I am first commissioned by his lordship with an invitation. He proposes to sail over to Geneva again this morning, and asks if you and Miss Clairmont would care to come along."

"That would be delightful," Mary said. "Tell him we shall join him at the dock at his convenience."

The doctor nodded absently, his gaze fixed rigidly over her head. "Thank you. I shall convey your compliments to his lordship. And now, on my own poor behalf ... I ... I owe you a most sincere apology," he began. His face paled, then flushed, and he clasped his hands behind his back. "I cannot conceive what came over me last evening. I pray you will find it in your generous heart to forgive me for such a—"

Mary waved a hand. "Oh, do sit down, Polly," she said.

He stopped with his mouth open, blinked, and then shut his mouth with a snap. He seemed offended at her easy forgiveness. "It was really quite—"

"Oh, I know you could not have meant those things you said. Indeed, you rather reminded me of William, when he gets caught with his hand in the cookie jar."

Polidori looked at the child in her arms, confused. And perhaps insulted, by the expression on his face.

Mary smiled. "Oh, I meant my younger brother, William. He's at an awkward stage, do you know. Thirteen, and unsure of himself and how to behave around girls."

Polidori's mouth tightened. "Indeed. I am an adolescent, to you. How very amusing."

Mary soured inside. She had no patience for this self-involved man's constant sulking. "I meant it as a compliment, Doctor. I am fond of my younger brother; I only meant that you remind me of him."

"I am older than you are," he said stiffly.

She sighed. "Oh, do let us be friends," she said. "Pray be seated, and let us enjoy this fine morning before the rain arrives."

Polidori fidgeted with his waistcoat button, touched his stiff cravat nervously. Finally he relented and seated himself on a low stone wall. "The child seems well."

"Yes, thank you. He feeds quite lustily."

The doctor smiled, and stretched his legs out in the sunshine. His polished boots shone. How closely he mirrored the dandy who employed him, Mary thought.

"There has been no fever or chills?" Polidori asked. "He sleeps as usual?"

"Yes, he seems to be fine. No ill effects from the vaccination. Shelley and I are grateful for your care, Doctor," she said. "It was kind of you to arrange for the procedure."

Polidori nodded. "I am glad. At least here is one patient his lordship cannot throw in my face," he said.

Mary raised an eyebrow but said nothing. For some reason, Polidori always chose her to unburden himself to. "You have quarreled?"

Polidori waved a hand, but his cheeks turned a little pink. "Nothing, nothing at all, I assure you, Mrs. Shelley. As for the vaccination, I am glad to find you and Mr. Shelley so ... advanced in your thinking."

"We are not burdened with superstitions about vaccinations, at any account," she replied. William broke off his nursing and fussed a little. "All finished, my Will-mouse?" She shifted him, threw the shawl onto her shoulder, and put him up to pat his back. As she did so, her shawl slipped a little, exposing her bare breast.

The doctor glanced quickly away, his cheeks even pinker. "I, er, brought the book by Tasso I spoke of earlier." He stood and faced away from Mary, gazing out over the lake. "Your Italian is coming along very well."

Mary listened with only half her attention. William fussed more, his little legs kicking. The shawl slipped completely off her shoulder and fell to the ground. Holding the squirming infant in one arm, Mary struggled to fasten up her bodice. William's flailing foot caught her on the chin. "Be still!" She bent to retrieve the shawl, but the boy slipped, and at the last moment she had to catch him with both arms before he fell. Defeated, she sat back against the sun-warmed wall and cradled her son.

Polidori, oblivious, stared across the lake at the darkening vista. "I daresay his lordship would say mine is insufficient, despite having been raised in both Italian and English." His tone was of brooding offense. No doubt he had been rehearsing it all morning, Mary thought.

Mary's temper snapped. "Oh, do stop feeling sorry for yourself and help me, Dr. Polidori!"

Surprised, he turned, assessed the situation, and immediately stooped to gather her shawl. "Would you like me to hold him?"

She promptly handed the kicking baby to the doctor. "By all means, if you can contrive not to drop him. My shawl ... thank you." Grateful for its woolen warmth, she settled it firmly across her shoulders, finished fastening her gown, and held her arms out for her son. Polidori, holding the infant with careful concentration, handed him back. William protested, his little mouth opening with a wail, his feet kicking. His sock fell at Polidori's feet. "Oh, I say ..."

Polidori was looking at William closely. Mary felt her heart give a little lurch. "Doctor? Is something wrong?"

Polidori blinked, his black eyes looking sheepish. "Oh, not at all. I was thinking of something his lordship said the other day, about how his mother caused his deformity by binding her stays too tightly. You will forgive me if I observe, er, that neither you nor Miss Clairmont, er, wear stays. Speaking, of course, strictly as a medical man." He seated himself again, this time very close to Mary. "I applaud you on your forward thinking."

Involuntarily, Mary glanced at William's feet. They were perfectly formed, with five fat pink toes on each straight foot. She looked up at met Polidori's look. "A mother cannot help but feel for him," she said. Mary wrestled her son's foot into his sock, then set him firmly on her shoulder. She patted his back. "No, my lack of stays is my mother's doing. She refused to confine herself with such unnatural bindings, and when I became old enough to throw off my, my stepmother's medieval restrictions, I abandoned them as well. Not for William's sake but for mine." She looked at Polidori. "Forgive my curiosity, doctor, but ... have you seen Lord Byron's foot?"

"Indeed I have. It is on his mind day and night, I assure you. If there is ever the least little twitch or pang, we must retire for him to consult me."

"It seems so strange to think of him as ... imperfect." Mary said. "He is so ... in so many other respects he is ..." She could find no words to finish her thought.

Polidori raised an eyebrow. "Oh, I understand. His lordship's physical beauty transcends all bounds. I have lost count of the women who have cornered me in balls and salons for a private chat about Lord Byron's person." His mouth twisted bitterly. "They are very disappointed to learn that he does not have a cloven hoof."

Mary smiled. "I did not suppose he had. But he never mentions it, never makes apology for it."

"That does not mean it is not far from his thoughts."

"You make it sound as if he considers himself some kind of, of monster."

"He does," said Polidori bluntly. "You may think it is society's scorn for his ... behavior that forces him into exile. I think in his heart, however, it is his foot. He has never been comfortable among society. He is extremely sensitive, and never allows anyone but me or Fletcher to see him unshod."

Mary looked up from burping her baby, startled. "No one? Not even ..."

Polidori's posture grew stiff. "This is not really seemly conversation for a ... a lady."

Mary chuckled. "Not even a lady with a child? And do not forget, Claire is my own step-sister."

"Yes, but he—" Polidori bit his lip, looking off towards the lake. A slow flush climbed his cheek. "His lordship is free enough with his tongue where it concerns me," he said in a low, tight voice. "Why then should I adhere to strictures he does not?" He turned towards Mary. "He does not even undress when he ... with ladies. Not even with Miss Clairmont, so I gather from ... from his remarks." He looked very uncomfortable.

Mary found his shyness amusing in a medical man. "Really, Doctor, there is no need to spare my blushes. My questions come from a mother's concern, not morbid curiosity." She looked down. "You may not know that William is not my first-born."

Polidori's face went blank. "Not ..."

Mary felt the old pain, the one she always felt when she thought about that thin, frail creature born on a cold winter night. "Last year, in February. She was ... the doctor said she was two months early. They did not expect her to live. She lived eleven days."

Suddenly she buried her face in William's hair, inhaling the sweet baby-smell of him, hiding her tears.

Polidori stammered, "I-I had no idea. Please accept my condolences. What a sad loss."

"I still dream of her," Mary said. "I dream of rubbing her beside a fire, reviving her. Do you think, Doctor, that such could have worked? Could we have revived her? Would she be alive today if...?" William squealed, and Mary realized she was holding him too tightly.

Polidori put out a hand as if to touch her. "Mrs. Shelley ... Mary ... I am sorry. I do not think anything could have been done. Born so soon before her time ... no." He shook his head regretfully.

"It struck me ... eleven days. Do you know, that is exactly the length of time my mother lived, after I was born?" She adjusted William's wrap. "I am bracketed by death, Doctor," she said bitterly. "My mother lived eleven days, my daughter lived eleven days. Perhaps I have inherited the touch of the Death Angel. I fear that everything, everyone I love will die." She looked down at William. So perfect. So precious. Tears formed in her eyes. "Compared to the touch of death, what is a club foot?" she whispered. "Can such a thing be inherited?"

Polidori shook his head. "I do not believe in a 'touch of death'. As to the club foot, however, there is room for doubt."

Unbidden, an image of Claire entwined with Byron, his long hair in his eyes, his lazy smile, his strong arms around Claire came into Mary's mind. She thought of Claire carrying Byron's child, of what their child might look like. "Then is it your medical opinion that such things as his lordship's foot can be ... inherited?"

Polidori was silent, looking out over the water. "Pardon me, Mrs. Shelley, but I suspect you have a more than intellectual interest in the question."

Mary looked down at her son, and adjusted her skirts. "Of course, I do not wish to invade his lordship's privacy—"

"Miss Clairmont is with child by Lord Byron." He stated it as a fact, not a question, still not looking at Mary.

Mary cleared her throat. "She has not told him. I pray you will respect her wishes."

He nodded. "I guessed it. Her volatility, the flush on her cheeks. And this morning, when I rose, she was in Byron's bedroom, vomiting. I believe the midwives call it 'morning sickness'."

"Has Byron guessed?"

Polidori laughed shortly and turned to meet her look. "By no means. She could doubtless give birth in front of him and he would be none the wiser. His lordship looks seldom beyond his own interests."

Mary took a deep breath. "Do you think her child might inherit Byron's deformity?"

"Possibly. But I doubt it. And even if it was born so, there are modern remedies. His lordship was born with his foot turned under, and he received no competent medical attention as a boy. As a result, he was teased and tormented about it. Now he hides it in shame, as though it were some kind of punishment."

"Is there nothing that can be done?"

"Not now. As an infant, certainly. Hippocrates himself describes a treatment that might have worked: repeated manipulation, bandaging, and overcorrection. Had his lordship been treated when the limb was young and pliable ..." He shrugged. "Now, I doubt there is any remedy."

"His father and mother did not care enough to seek proper help for him?"

Polidori shrugged. "He saw very little of his father, who abandoned him as a child. His lordship says there were doctors." He made a face. "Quacks and charlatans, as near as I can tell."

Mary thought about Byron, his beautiful face, his straight back, his excellent form when riding. She thought of his halting step, how slowly he climbed hills and stairs. "I wonder if he has ever had the joy of running," she murmured.

Polidori toyed with a pot of blue flowers on a pedestal beside him. "No, but ask him about his swim across the Hellespont, a few years ago." He brushed at a fly buzzing in front of his face, and squinted as the sun suddenly broke through the clouds. "He even swims in pantaloons, to keep his foot hidden."

Mary looked down as she patted her son. "Albé has a daughter in England. I only wondered if she was similarly ... afflicted ... and whether he had arranged for, as you say, competent treatment."

Polidori stroked his chin. "I think if she had been born with her father's disfigurement, he would have mentioned it."

"Or perhaps not," Mary said. "He is very proud."

"Oh, proud, yes. The very pride of Lucifer himself." A bitter smile twisted Polidori's handsome face. "Pray that it does not presage a fall."

Mary shifted William to her other shoulder. "Still, it is ironic, do you not think? That a man widely considered the most beautiful man in Europe thinks of himself as a monster."

Polidori poked a toe at some grass growing between the cracks of the pavement. "Beautiful on the outside, but not on the inside."

"Would it be preferable, do you think, to be born beautiful on the inside and ugly on the outside?" she asked.

Polidori shrugged. "Surely virtue outweighs mere physical appearance, in the larger scheme of things."

Mary looked askance at the young man. "You cannot mean that, Doctor. Come, let us be rational. Look around you. The most shocking debaucher on the Continent can do nearly as he pleases, merely because he has a title and the face of an angel. Yet there may be an actual angel, perhaps in some village here, who looks like a devil and is treated as such. Do you really think the world is perceptive enough to look past the surface?"

Polidori coughed. Clearly he wanted to disagree, but was too polite to do so. "Perhaps it is as you say," he said. "In any event, his lordship will act according to his will, and never according to the dictates of the world. To some, so I perceive, that makes him a monster."

Chapter XVI - Sailing to Geneva

I took the boat, and passed many hours upon the water. Sometimes, with my sails set, I was carried by the wind; and sometimes, after rowing into the middle of the lake, I left the boat to pursue its own course, and gave way to my own miserable reflections. I was often tempted, when all was at peace around me, and I the only unquiet thing that wandered restless in a scene so beautiful and heavenly.

—*Frankenstein*, Volume II, Chapter X

The sun was playing hide-and-seek behind the clouds when Mary, Claire and Shelley climbed into the little sailboat. Byron was already aboard, restless and abrupt. Claire leaned over him, presenting her cheek for a kiss, but Byron turned his head. "Sit down and don't rock us all into the lake," he said.

Shelley helped Mary into the boat. "Don't worry," he whispered into her ear. "It's a fair day for a sail. Nothing to worry about."

The first time Shelley had persuaded her to sail in a boat, Mary had been deathly afraid. Remembering the terrible seasickness that gripped her every time she sailed, she had braced herself for a horrible experience. To her delight, however, the calm surface of the lake had held no such terrors in store, and now she was able to relax and enjoy the soft lapping of the waves against the side of the boat.

Byron's servant Fletcher handed in a basket that clinked glassily, then clambered in and threw off the tie.

John Polidori was already in the boat, manning the oars. Despite the cooling breeze, his forehead was shiny with sweat already. As soon as Mary was seated, he pushed off from shore. "Mayhap we can raise the sail?" he muttered to his lordship.

Byron lay against a gunwale, head back, eyes closed, soaking in what sunlight flittered through the clouds. "Quiet, Polly," he said. "I shall raise my mast when I am ready."

Polidori snorted and leaned into the oars.

Shelley had not sat down, but leaned against the mast, looking out over the water. The sun broke through the clouds for a moment, and he raised his face to it and sang:

Oh! had we some bright little isle of our own,
In a blue summer ocean, far off and alone,
Where a leaf never dies in the still blooming bowers,
And the bee banquets on through a whole year of flowers;

Claire, who had been sulking in the stern near Polidori, looked up and smiled. In her lovely soprano, she joined him in the next verse of Thomas Moore's song:

Where the sun loves to pause
With so fond a delay,
That the night only draws
A thin veil o'er the day;

Byron opened his eyes, squinted, grunted, and hauled himself up into a sitting position. He reached under a blanket and brought out a bottle of brandy. Pulling the cork with his teeth, he took a long draught of it.

Shelley and Claire, singing together, continued the song:

There with souls ever ardent and pure as the clime,
We should love, as they loved in the first golden time;
The glow of the sunshine, the balm of the air,
Would steal to our hearts, and make all summer there.

Mary, watching Shelley smile fondly down at Claire, who laughed and sang at him, felt a pang go through her. She looked away from the happy pair and found herself caught in Byron's gaze. For a moment, his guard down, she saw rage and anger and sorrow mixed in his face, saw the despair he hid behind brandy and sarcasm and irony. He held her look, and a chill passed over her, and a wave of sadness. Then his mouth turned up in a sardonic smile, he raised the brandy bottle in a toast to her, and muttered,

Still must my song my thoughts, my soul betray:
Still must each accent to my bosom suit,
My heart unhush'd—although my lips were mute!

He turned away, staring past Shelley to the far shore, where the mountains loomed over Geneva in dark majesty. Mary lifted a hand to touch his, halted, and drew back. Byron seemed somehow remote, closed in, as if wrapped in a cloak of isolation. Mary wondered if he was thinking about his wife back in London, his little daughter. She had inwardly scorned him for abandoning them, but now, seeing the naked grief in his eyes, she wondered if she had misjudged him.

Claire and Shelley finished their song, and Claire clapped. Her mood more buoyant now, she stood and picked her way over to Byron. He ignored her as she settled in next to her. Mary scooted closer to where Shelley still leaned against the mast, peering ahead. She reached up and took his hand. Absently, he squeezed it, glanced down at her, smiled, and looked off across the water again.

She closed her eyes against the sun, settled herself against Shelley's knees, and allowed herself to drift into a half-sleep. With William safe at home in Elise's care, she had no other thought than to spend a morning with her beloved. She felt Shelley's fingers winding absently in her hair; over her head he spoke to Byron.

"... the lairs of dragons," Byron was saying. "Until Wordsworth, anyway. Yet even Wordsworth cannot aspire to mountains such as these."

"No," Shelley agreed. "I do not think there are any mountains, anywhere, that can compare to Mont Blanc. Or Jura, master of thunder. But then, you have surely seen greater mountains, Byron. What about Albania? Greece? Have you not gazed upon Olympus himself?"

A grunt from the middle of the craft, where Polidori pulled at the oars. Mary felt sunshine on her face and knew the craft had turned in the wind.

"Olympus! Well enough, I suppose, as mountains go. But not at all in the line of the Alps," Byron said lazily.

"These heights take away the breath," Shelley said. "Indeed, they take away my sight. I cannot believe what I see. How can mere men climb such ramparts?"

"'Tis easy enough," Polidori puffed. "Put one foot in front of the other, so I am told."

"Peace, fribble," said Byron. "And steer a bit to port—that's to the left. We're going to miss the docks otherwise."

"You might lend a hand," said the doctor. No one answered him.

Shelley turned and sat, shielding Mary from the sun.

"I wonder what it would be like to stand on the very top of Jura," came Claire's voice.

Mary shifted, turning her face away from the warmth of the sun. Without asking, Shelley lightly set her hat on his knee so that the brim shaded her face. Opening her eyes, she looked up and saw him smiling down at her.

"I think it would be windy," said Byron.

"But sublime," said Shelley. "Imagine the sweep of Nature below, the works of man made so tiny by distance."

"As they should be," murmured Mary. Her gaze took in the opposite shore, where verdant mountains plunged steeply almost to the edge of the lake, as though they had been tumbling into the water in some distant era, and been frozen in mid-motion.

"Why so?" said Polidori. Mary heard the creak of the oarlocks, felt the puff of cool breeze on her face. She glanced at Byron, who lounged against the gunwale, brandy glass in hand, surveying her with his usual sardonic look of amusement.

"The works of men are the work of the mind and the hand," she replied. She closed her eyes, feeling the breeze on her skin. "Nature is the realm of feeling and art, the kingdom of the heart. Only in her bosom can we find real truth, real beauty, not covered up and distorted by human minds."

Shelley clapped his hands together. "Hear, hear, darling Mary!"

"Amen," said Byron. Mary heard the clink of glass, the gurgle of liquid. Even on the other side of the boat, she could smell the brandy. "Here's to great nature and her bosom!"

Claire sat up suddenly, her dark curls dancing around her face. Her eyes lit with mischief. "Oh, but you have stood atop Jura!" she said to Byron, then: "He who ascends to mountain-tops—"

Byron scowled. "Be silent, wench! I did not give you leave to quote me."

"No, you did not," she giggled, squirming out of reach. She grinned at Mary. "He gave me those lines to copy out, two nights ago. I have them by heart already:"

> *He who ascends to mountain-tops, shall find*
> *The loftiest peaks most wrapt in clouds and snow;*
> *He who surpasses or subdues mankind,*
> *Must look down on the hate of those below."*
> *Is it not a perfect description?*

Byron was not pleased; Mary saw the way his mouth made a taut line, the way his fist tightened on the glass. He said nothing, looking away, his chin thrust outward in sullen resentment.

"Most excellent," Shelley said, oblivious to his friend's discontent. "Is that a new addition to *Childe Harold?*"

When Byron made no answer, Claire said, "We have several dozen lines of it already. One can almost see the mountains in his words:"

> *There they stand, as stands a lofty mind,*
> *Worn, but unstooping to the baser crowd,*
> *All tenantless, save to the crannying wind,*
> *Or holding dark communion with the cloud.*

"I like the line about 'unstooping to the baser crowd.' Surely, on such peaks as these, only the most sublime thoughts can survive!"

"Or the man of nature," Shelley said. "Rousseau's natural

man might live there, unimpeded by the shackles of custom and restraint."

"Or good taste," said Byron.

Mary sat up, setting her hat firmly on her head. "You are both of you in error," she said. "Rousseau says that man in a state of nature, such a one as might live alone on these mountaintops, is only a product of his upbringing. Man of himself is neither good nor bad, but only as he is taught. He has neither justice, as we know it, or good taste."

Byron saluted her with a glass. "Well said, my Mary. You show considerable wit for a female. One might almost be persuaded that the education of women is a good thing."

Mary cocked an eyebrow. "One might almost be persuaded of the same, of aristocrats."

Byron guffawed, his hair blowing into his face as he tipped his head back. "Oh, madame, I am undone!"

Shelley chuckled. "Touché, my love. Yet to be serious a moment, do you not agree, Byron, that man in a wild state of Nature, untouched by so-called civilization, is infinitely to be preferred to the over-bred, disconnected man of today's cities and towns?"

Polidori stopped rowing, his black curls plastered to his forehead with sweat. "Oh, poppycock!"

All turned to look at him. "The good doctor has an opinion on philosophy?" Byron's lip curled dangerously.

Polidori glared back at him. "This is nonsense. There is nothing special in Nature. It is a thing to be subdued, a thing to tame. Left alone, your precious Nature will kill us all." He let go his oars, looking at his reddened palms. He unbuttoned his waistcoat, shrugging it off. "Science is the sworn enemy of Nature and I am a man of Science. Therefore we are allies against your 'Nature'. We are both devoted to her conquest."

Shelley's blue eyes widened a bit. "But is not Nature the first ally of the physician?"

Byron laughed bitterly. "Not, apparently, of this physician. Tell us, Polly, how many of your patients survive to this day?"

Polidori flushed. "You are not yet dead, my lord."

Byron flourished the bottle. "Due to my daily prophylactic," he said. "I am pickled. I am preserved. My liver and lights will outlive us both by many years." He poured generously into his glass. Only Mary noticed how his hand trembled.

"Hardly," said Polidori darkly. "If your lordship's drinking does not pickle his brain as well, his other ... endeavors ... will surely bring on worse disease."

Byron's hand froze, his glare locked on Polidori. Claire flushed. "To what do you refer, Doctor?"

Polidori glanced at her, at Mary. He looked away. "I must keep confidence," he said grimly. "But his lordship's mode of living is ... not wise. It could be ... injurious. I cannot recommend it."

Perhaps only Mary caught Claire's low gasp, the half-arrested gesture of protection as her hand darted towards her belly.

"Either row or swim, Polidori, but do not speak again!" Byron growled, his eyes closed.

Polidori's mouth set in a grim line. "Am I never to speak?"

"Oh, come," Shelley said, ever the peacemaker. "No need for this among friends. We need not argue."

"Is conversation open only to those whose opinions march with his lordship's?" Polidori sneered.

"Plague take you!" Byron snapped at Polidori.

"Plague, your lordship says? Indeed, does not the plague take the innocent with the just? Where is your sublime Nature then, my lord? When the infant dies at the breast, where is your sublime Nature?"

Unbidden, the image of her dead daughter flashed into Mary's brain. She turned her face away from the others, felt Shelley's hand on her shoulder.

"Doctor!" Shelley said sharply.

"I ... I beg your pardon," stammered Polidori, glancing white-faced at Mary.

"Row, damn you!" growled Byron.

"I will not," Polidori said defiantly. "The oars roughen my hands, which should remain soft for my examinations. Would you have a calloused surgeon, my lord?"

"Your callouses are elsewhere, whelp," Byron said. "Mostly on your social graces. Fletcher, take the oars."

The boat rocked as the big Englishman exchanged places with the doctor. Mary, her eyes closed, rested a hand on her belly. It was empty now, but she remembered her daughter kicking, the quickening of life, a life that had died so quickly, so quietly, despite all her care. Was it a judgement? Perhaps the doctor was right; Nature had taken her child, so how could it be noble?

"Perhaps it is in the nature of Nature to be neutral," Shelley said. "Man in his original state knew nothing of good or evil. Therefore he had to learn to do evil—"

"Or good," growled Byron.

"And who taught him?" Claire retorted to Shelley. "Who taught him good from evil?"

"Nature alone," he responded. "Only Nature knows how to justly proportion to the fault the punishment it deserves, so Nature teaches justice."

"'Twas Eve," said Byron mischievously, looking over the rim of his glass at Polidori. "Did she not eat of the apple, and thus bring sex into the world? And if that is not the root of all evil, what is?"

"Pride," said Polidori dryly.

"Nay, 'tis custom and tyranny alone at the source of evil," said Shelley with some heat. "Were it not for the custom of the world, that decrees that most men live under the boot heels of others, then were we all equal, in good and evil alike!"

Byron laughed. "But no, we are not so equally disposed, my Shelley. You, perhaps, are all good, and I all evil. Thus are we well balanced, yet neither of us is whole!" He swung the bottle, coming dangerously close to Polidori, who ducked.

"You flatter me," said Shelley, smiling. "I am not the being you describe."

"Are you not?" Byron upended the bottle; finding it empty, he flung it over his shoulder to land with a splash in the water. "Are you not, my Shelley? Yet you would teach all mankind your philosophy. You would have us all live in Nature, and reason together, and eat only vegetables. Come, come, admit it. You would be our newest savior!"

"Our savior, if we need one, will come from just such a background as you describe," Shelley said seriously. "A natural man, one raised far from cities and the corrupting influence of the world."

"A saint! I do declare it, a saint and a savior! What think you of that, my Polly?"

"My lord!" protested Polidori.

"Ah, we have offended his Catholic majesty," sneered Byron. A sudden breeze whipped the waves, and the vessel lurched. Claire and Mary clutched for the gunwales and Byron struggled up to grasp a line.

"Hah!" he cried. "See how the gods reward philosophy! When we drink, when we whore, when we sing, the winds smile upon us. But let us discuss the perfectibility of man, and the storm draws near. Help me tie these sheets, Shiloh!"

Mary watched as the two men, moving almost as one, raised the sails. They expertly caught the wind, and soon Fletcher had shipped the oars while Shelley took the tiller. Pushed by the wind, the boat made good time across the water. The wind was loud enough to suppress further discussion of philosophy, and Mary had to hold her hat onto her head with one hand.

Byron returned to his sulk and his brandy. Claire sat next to him, leaning into his shoulder, her curls whipped by the wind to mingle briefly with his. She curled one hand into his lordship's elbow. Byron said nothing, not protesting, and stared off across the water, drinking.

Over the whistle of the water and the wind, Mary caught a faint melody: Claire was singing softly to Byron. As the boat raced across the lake, Mary sat and wondered what he would say when he learned of Claire's babe.

She feared the worst; Byron was deep in despair and grief over his recent scandal, his separation from his daughter, his self-imposed exile from England.

He will reject her, thought Mary. His own babe, and the woman who bears it. Perhaps Polidori is right: he is a monster.

Chapter XVII - Polly Buys a Watch

> ... the strange system of human society was explained to me.
> I heard of the division of property, of immense wealth and
> squalid poverty; of rank, descent, and noble blood.

> —*Frankenstein*, Volume III, Chapter V

Shelley handed Mary over the gunwale onto the dock, then turned and held out a hand for Claire. "Come, child," he said. But Claire hung back, looking to Byron, obviously hoping he would be her escort. Byron ignored her, climbing out with a clumsy, lurching movement that set the boat rocking. Claire stumbled, righted herself, and finally accepted Shelley's hand up.

"Where shall we start?" inquired Byron, shrugging himself into his blue coat. "The tailor? The wine seller?"

"The chandler's," said Mary firmly. "We are running low on candles."

Shelley grinned down at her. "Because we sit up until dawn every night?"

"But how else?" Byron said. "We are creatures of darkness, it is affirmed on every side, is't not, Polidori?"

The doctor, climbing out of the boat by himself, scowled. "'Tis said of yourself, certes."

Byron snarled and started off up the slope of the cobbled street towards the city gate, his lameness offset by the cane he carried. Claire hurried after him and, catching up, slipped her hand through his arm. His only reaction was a slightly stiffer back. Mary took Shelley's arm and they started up the hill.

"I have been thinking, my love," said Shelley. "Poor Fanny is left alone in England, without our company or our conversation. May we not remember your sister with some small gift?"

"A generous thought," Mary said. "But there is the matter of the candles, and the new sheets for our bed, and William needs a new shirt. I had hoped to visit a fabric seller's—"

"What? You will not even give passing glance to a book store?" cried her lover. He grinned down at her. "I know you need more ink, and I a new pen knife. We must stop at a bookseller's."

Mary smiled, but it was a thin, tight smile. She didn't want to go into a bookstore. It would remind her too much of Skinner Street, and her father's distant smile, and her step-mother's harried contempt. Mrs. Godwin had once fancied herself on the lower rungs of society; now she waited behind a counter on women who had once invited her to tea, and knew herself to be beneath their state. Even Mary, raised on egalitarian principles, had felt her self-loathing and contempt, so that the very air of the bookstore had been bitter and poisonous. She had no desire to remember it in any further detail. Still, it was useless to argue with Shelley.

Polidori puffed up the street behind them. "His lordship said he was looking for a new watch today," he offered. "A shop in the Rue de Rive caught his eye two days ago. It had a handsome astrolabe in the front window, and a fine collection of timepieces."

"I declare I do not know why Albé needs a timepiece," Mary murmured to Shelley. "He gets up after noon, goes where he pleases when he pleases, and dines at his own hour. Indeed, he has no use for anyone else's time but his own, so what schedule need he keep?"

Shelley only chuckled and patted her hand. He looked over her head at Polidori. "An astrolabe, you say?"

It was not far from the jetty where they had tied the boat (with a generous tip to the guard, to see that it was there when they returned), to the lower part of the city proper. They walked up the gentle slope of the cobbled lane, with huge warehouses lining the way. Passing them, their high walls shut out the sun, and a chill passed over Mary. She wondered again where her shawl had disappeared to, and calculated the cost of a new one. She felt sad, knowing that the finest shawl in the world could not match the value of her lost mother's only physical legacy to her. She and Fanny had shared it, and now she had lost it, and Mary wondered if Fanny would ever forgive her.

Shrill cries met their ears as they emerged into a common plaza. Street vendors hawking sausages on a stick, beer and bread converged on the party as they left the narrow street. Shelley laughed to see them, the joy of life that always bubbled just under the surface of him freed by the attentions of the peddlers. Ahead, Mary saw Claire tugging Byron towards a dressmaker's, and flushed. Was Claire really going to dun her lover for clothes, like a common mistress? Was Claire really so ignorant of how Byron would regard this? She pulled at Shelley. "Come, let us catch up to them."

Shelley, tossing a coin to a vendor, bit into an apple absently and nodded his agreement. They pushed their way through a crowd hot with bargaining shoppers, dodged a horse-drawn cart full of cabbages lurching through the square, and emerged onto the paved sidewalk before a row of shops. Claire and Byron stood side by side, not touching, looking in the window. Mary and Shelley stopped beside them.

"Just a small one," Claire was saying. She pointed to a golden locket in the front of the display. "Only large enough to keep a lock of your hair in, B."

Byron shifted from foot to foot, looking uncomfortable. "'Tis an awfully vulgar design, sweet."

Mary felt her face go hot again. Was Claire really begging for trinkets, like some prostitute? "Claire," she hissed, and grabbed her arm. "May I speak to you?"

Claire stepped away with her, and Byron took the opportunity to duck into the shop. Polidori followed him, but Shelley stayed looking in the window, musing. Mary pulled her step-sister into a doorway. "Must you be so common?" she whispered fiercely. "To ask Albé for a locket, it's as if you were a ... a woman of the street."

Claire tossed her head. "Why Mary, how very vulgar of you. Does money not belong to whoever can use it best? Are we to be bound by the artificial rules set out by the very society we despise? I am surprised at you."

"Do not attempt to read my father's work back at me," Mary blazed. "You know his strictures on money apply to those who are benefiting mankind. How would a gold locket benefit mankind? You demand it only to feed your vanity. Indeed, it is in the nature of a trophy, I believe!"

"No more a trophy than Shelley's son is to you!" Claire hissed back at her.

Shocked, Mary blinked. "A trophy? You see William as a ... a prize? You cannot be so cold!"

"Cold? I am cold? When you flaunt your victories at me at every turn! Shelley in your bed, your son in your arms! And what am I left with? Only what I can grab!" Claire's voice rose to a shrill descant.

A shadow fell across them, and a large man in an apron appeared in the doorway. "Qu'est-ce qu'elle a?" he said, frowning at them.

Shelley was at Mary's elbow, reaching for Claire. "Come, let's go into the watch shop. I was thinking of buying a trinket for Fanny."

Claire, still glaring at Mary, ostentatiously grabbed for Shelley's arm. The two of them preceded Mary into the shop.

Inside, the smell of wax and metal and oil mixed with the scent of tobacco from Byron and cabbage soup from the back of the shop. A small, wizened man with a tasseled cap was showing a large gold watch to Polidori. Their conversation, in halting French, occupied them while Byron strolled around the shop, tapping his cane restlessly and glancing up at the wall of clocks. Shelley, fascinated, stopped in front of an orrery. The earth, her continents outlined in red, spun freely on an assembly of gears. Shelley turned a wheel, and a golden ball representing the sun twirled. Around it spun two inner planets like marbles, and a tiny moon circled the Earth.

"A scholar's toy," murmured Byron, looking not at the machine but at his friend. "For this, Bruno was burned at the stake. Surely an object lesson for every free-thinker," he said.

Shelley was not listening, but carefully turned the model, observing how the moon kept pace with the turn of the Earth. "See how you can line up the Earth and moon with the sun," he said.

"But I do not see how an eclipse can be produced. Ah, I see. Let us turn it towards the light, thus, yes. Now see? In London, there is an eclipse of the sun, but in Switzerland, not." He demonstrated, turning the tiny jeweled planets on their rings until he achieved the line-up he desired.

Byron clapped his friend affectionately on the back. "Oh, but here we would not know it if the sun were eclipsed every day," he said. "This accursed weather blocks all sight of it from noon onward." He turned, seeing Polidori pointing at another watch. "Oh, do make haste, Polly," he said irritably. "We do not have all day. I, for one, do not care to be rowing back across the lake in a downpour."

Polidori glanced up. "'Twill not be your lordship rowing, I vow," he murmured. He held up a gold watch the size of his palm to his ear, shook his head. He said something in French to the shopkeeper, who frowned and burst out in furious French.

"What says the man?" said Byron impatiently. "Claire! See if you can make out what his trouble is!"

Behind him, the shop door opened and an older, well dressed couple entered.

Claire, still clinging to Shelley, pouted a bit. "I do not know."

Byron frowned. "Damn your impudence! You know my French is worse than my Italian."

Polidori glanced over his shoulder. "That is very difficult to believe, my lord," he said mockingly. "As your Italian is virtually non-existent. He demands forty guineas for the watch."

Claire and Mary both gasped at this enormous sum. Shelley drifted over to the counter. "Forty guineas? My word! It must surely be the finest watch in Switzerland."

"No doubt it calculates the date of Easter for the next hundred years," Byron said dryly. "But in any case, it is above your touch, Polly."

The young man looked away. Mary caught his look—cold, angry. Why must Byron constantly humiliate the boy by reminding him of his "inferior" station? "A doctor should have a good watch," she said, not quite sure why she was defending this callow young man. Obscurely, she felt a certain maternal instinct towards him. "Does he not regularly take your pulse, my lord? You would surely want him to use a watch suitable for the 'station' of his patient?"

Shelley looked sharply at her, then smiled. Her dig at Byron's vanity amused him. "Assuredly," he said. "Nothing less than a forty guinea watch for the personal physician of the famous Lord Byron."

The older couple's heads swung round at the sound of his name. Mary felt that sinking feeling in her stomach she always got when public censure reared its head. Shelley, oblivious, drifted fingers along a counter filled with lockets, and Byron glared at Polidori. But Mary saw the woman turn to her companion and whisper. The man frowned at Byron.

Byron leaned on his cane. "Damn the both of you. Very well, Polidori, buy the cursed watch. If you wish to pass yourself off as a gentleman, good luck to you."

Polidori set the watch carefully down. "I ... I cannot afford it, my lord," he said.

Mary winced. She knew the embarrassment of low funds; she and Shelley lived with it constantly. Shelley never seemed to care that they were at the parish door every quarter. "Perhaps my lord's consequence extends to a subsidy," she said.

Claire tossed her curls. "Surely Godwinian principles apply here," she said to Mary. "A doctor in need of a watch is surely a benefit to mankind. Give him the money, Byron."

Polidori, momentarily nonplussed, looked from Shelley to Byron. He opened his mouth to reply but nothing came out.

Byron thrust his hand into his pocket, looking harassed. "A watch does not make him a better doctor," he declared.

"But it may make him a better friend," Shelley said, amused.

Out of the corner of her eye, Mary saw the older couple edging closer, curious to see the infamous English poet. Their eager curiosity, so easily dissolving into censure, irritated her. She stepped closer to Shelley to block their view of Byron.

"Friend? Polly?" Byron sounded genuinely surprised.

"No need to strain yourself," Polidori said. His voice was high, strained. His fist opened and closed, opened and closed. "His lordship's good opinion can neither be bought nor sold."

At this, Byron glared at his physician, then drew out his purse and tossed it on the counter contemptuously. "Buy the watch."

"No—" Polidori said.

Shelley put a hand on Polidori's. "Allow his lordship to be useful," he said. Ignoring Byron's black look, he went on. "Be generous. Let Byron contribute something truly good to the world. Even if it be only enough to make up the difference between your purse and the shopkeeper's price."

The shopkeeper, who had been avidly glancing from face to face, apparently understood a sale was imminent. He took up the watch and a cloth, and began polishing it meticulously. He said something in French, and this time Claire tilted her head.

"He says he can let the watch go for thirty five guineas," she said. "Perhaps I can get him to agree to half?"

Byron angrily picked up his purse and poured coins out onto the counter top. They bounced and rang, some of them falling to the floor. "Make you free of it, madame," he said venomously. "And you, doctor. If you come back without the finest watch in Switzerland in your pocket, I shall hold myself insulted." Thrusting the purse back into his waistcoat pocket, he turned and thrust past Shelley. The older couple scampered out of his way, scandalized to be so close to the English devil incarnate. Ignoring them, Byron banged out of the shop. Shelley shot Mary a mute look of appeal.

Mary gathered her skirts and ran out after Byron. The day had turned grey and cold, and the shouts of men and the cries of animals seemed louder. It was all so foreign, so strange. Disoriented, she almost lost sight of the blue coat, the head of chestnut curls.

"Byron!" she called. One or two heads turned at the name, but she pressed on. She caught up with Byron as he hobbled across a gutter between streets and crossed into a quieter lane. "Wait!"

Breathing hard, he stopped, leaning on his cane. When she came up, he looked away. Were those tears on his cheeks? "Leave me alone, I pray you," he said as she came to a stop beside him.

She put a hand on his arm; he tensed as if to throw it off, but let it remain. "Byron ... B. Do not be angry, I pray. Shelley meant no harm to you, you know that. He is your friend."

His shoulders hunched under the broadcloth; under her fingers his arm trembled. "He mocks me. Is that a friend?"

"Mock you? No. You have not sailed with him, dined with him, talked to him all these weeks, and not yet seen how he is with money? How we all are?"

"He is freer with my purse than my wife was!"

"He is as free with his own," Mary said. "You know how he is. Have you not seen him give literally his last penny to a beggar on the street? Money is only a thing to him. It is not important."

"Oh, aye, not important! Because he was born into it, raised with it, will inherit thousands of pounds! Those of us not so fortunate have something of a different attitude! Do you know what it is to be poor, and mocked?" Byron said in a low voice. He glanced up at her, his changeable, beautiful eyes dark with emotion. "Do you know how it is to be 'Lord Byron', and unable to live up to it? To own the home of your dreams, and stable cows in it because you cannot repair the roof? Do you know what it is to have to sell the one place on Earth where you are happy? Because of money. Damned money!"

Mary thought of her feckless father, forever going over the bills, calmly writing letters to complete strangers asking, no demanding, money to pay his debts. "Yes," she said. "I know what it is to be poor. And to be in debt. And for that very reason ..." She turned to face him, forcing him to look at her. "For that very reason, my friend, I refuse to sacrifice friendship on its altar."

His mouth trembled. Mary found herself wanting to put her arms around him, to comfort him as she would William. But here, in this very public place, she could not. "My friend," she said. "Were he down to his last shirt, my Shelley would never ask you for money for himself. I have seen him ask a friend for money, only to turn around and give it away to a ragged urchin in a gutter. He would give you his very heart. For him, money is only a means to an end. He has no ... pride wrapped up in it."

Byron was silent a moment. "Pride." He sighed. "Yes, a besetting sin of the Byrons." He bent his head, looking at his feet, his black boots polished to a high sheen by Fletcher. "Never quote me on that, my dear." He looked up, and a tremulous smile played across that mobile mouth. "I will deny all. We are damned, we Byrons, by money. My father married for money twice, and killed himself when he ran out. My great-uncle spent every groat he could, for sheer spite because he was angry at his heir. They both died and left me nothing but debts and a name of infamy, so yes, pride is my inheritance. Pride and penury."

Mary could think of nothing to say, so she patted his hand that gripped his cane. Lord Byron looked at her kindly. "I am going to the Hotel," he said, giving her its direction. "Tell them to meet me there, and we will have a nuncheon. At my expense, of course," he said, faintly mocking.

"Thank you," she said. His mercurial temperament had swung through black anger to bitter humor again. She wondered how he could live so volatile a life. "We shall be there at one."

Byron leaned over and kissed her cheek, surprising her. His lips were soft on her skin. He murmured. "Tell that bastard Polidori that, having acquired a new watch, he is not allowed to be late. And tell Percy Shelley he is the luckiest man alive."

Before she could reply, he had swung around and stumped off across the lane, ignoring a carriage which was forced to pull up short. As the driver shouted at his indifferent back, Mary watched him go, and thought that possibly Lord Byron was the loneliest man on earth.

Chapter XVIII - The Rake

> I am malicious because I am miserable. Am I not shunned
> and hated by all mankind?
>
> —*Frankenstein*, Volume III, Chapter VIII

Claire and Mary were walking a little ahead of Shelley and Polidori, searching for a chandler's shop. "Must Polly follow us everywhere?" Claire complained. "We cannot have a moment to ourselves."

Since this thought so perfectly mirrored her own opinion of her step-sister, Mary kept her remarks to herself. The sky was beginning to cloud over, and she worried that their trip back might be conducted in the midst of a storm. Yet Claire dawdled along the lanes, looking in all the shops. A music store caught her eye, and with a cry of delight she dashed inside. "Claire, no—" But it was useless. Shelley strolled in after her without a glance at Mary.

Polidori stopped beside her and offered her his arm. "Are you fatigued in this sun?" he asked.

Mary shook her head. "If I follow them into the shop, we will be there all day. If I stay here, Shelley will eventually come out looking for me, and Claire will inevitably follow." Even she could hear the bitter note in her voice.

Polidori nodded towards a bench set under an overhanging sign. "We may at least take our ease, out of the traffic." He led her to the bench and stood beside her as she sat gratefully on the hard bench. He seemed less stiff and formal than he had been that morning, apologizing. Mary felt herself unexpectedly at ease with him. She noted several approving female glances cast his way, and smiled at his utter obliviousness.

He took out his new watch and opened it, then glanced up at a clock on the church tower at the end of the street. "I declare, their clock is a minute slow," he said.

Mary raised an eyebrow. "Perhaps yours is fast."

"Not possible," Polidori said smugly. "The jeweler keeps perfect time on every item in his shop. I am assured that this is most accurate timepiece in Geneva." He closed the case, polished it on his sleeve, and deposited it in the watch pocket of his vest. "By the bye, I saw that Mr. Shelley purchased a lady's watch after you left the shop."

"For Claire?"

"Not at all. He put it in his own pocket. For you, perhaps? Or a sister?"

"I doubt it was for Elizabeth or his other sisters," Mary said. "They have more money than he does."

Polidori looked stricken. "Oh, dear. I beg your pardon. Perhaps I have spoiled a surprise meant for you."

Mary brightened. "Of course. My birthday is next month."

Polidori bowed. "My felicitations, ma'am. I am forewarned, and shall be ready with an offering of my own."

His earnest look reminded Mary of the passage in the gallery the evening before. She smiled tightly and turned her head to look into the shop. But the darkening day had turned the shop window into a mirror, and all she saw was her own face and Polidori's. Where was Shelley? How much longer would he be?

After half an hour, Shelley came out of the shop with Claire on his arm. She was giggling and clutching a few sheets of music. As soon as he caught sight of Mary, Shelley dropped Claire's hand from his elbow and strode over.

"Dearest, I missed you." He caught her hands in his and pulled her to her feet, tucking her hand into his elbow. "Come, we must rendezvous with Albé."

As he guided her, Mary caught sight of Claire and Polidori standing side by side, looking equally bereft as Shelley led her away.

The streets had become slightly less crowded as noon approached and the inhabitants retired indoors for the midday meal. Mary's thin shoes were not much help on the slippery cobbles, and she was glad when they rounded a corner and found themselves approaching the hotel. It was not large, a fairly modest but clean establishment. Mary had feared that Byron would have selected either the most expensive establishment in Switzerland, or a brothel.

The host led Mary and Shelley to a small room off the main room; Byron rose as they entered. His lordship was well into a bottle of wine already, but bowed Mary and Claire to a seat. "I've taken the liberty of ordering," he said as Shelley drew up a chair between the two women. Polidori, looking uncertain, finally settled next to Claire. "They have some exceptional cheeses here; I trust Shelley will eat them?"

"With pleasure," said Shelley.

"Excellent," said Polidori. "Most wholesome. And for Mrs. Shelley, perhaps a boiled egg?"

"And kill the bird unborn? No," said Byron before Shelley could answer. "But I have ordered a milk pudding. Will that suffice for our matron?" He smiled at Mary.

Almost as if his words had ordered it, Mary suddenly felt the tight ballooning feeling in her breasts that signified a let-down. Then a sudden damp feeling, and she felt her cheeks go hot as she realized her breasts were leaking.

"Oh." She looked to Shelley in confusion, but he was pulling a book from his pocket. Claire merely gawked at her, staring at Mary's chest. Mary wanted to kick herself for failing to line her bodice with more absorbent materials before leaving her baby behind. How had she forgotten that William nursed at this hour? She looked around for something to dab at her front.

John Polidori pulled a large napkin from the table and handed it to Mary discreetly. She tucked it into her neckline, concealing the spreading wet patch on her front. She shot the young doctor a look of fervent gratitude; his cheeks flushed.

Byron did not miss this interchange. "Why, Polly, I do believe you are seeking a new subject for experimentation. Shall I be jealous?"

Claire giggled. "I suspect Polly has never seen a breast, save those on a corpse."

Shelley, shocked, said, "Claire!" and Polidori flushed to the roots of his hair, giving his dark complexion an even darker cast.

"Oh, let there be no false modesty here," Byron said. "Are the daughters of William Godwin, the prophet of free love, too shy to discuss openly the pangs of that tender passion?"

Polidori went white. "My lord—"

"What are you doing, Albé?" Mary said sharply. "What has got you in this mood?"

"Mood?" Byron shook vinegar over his boiled potatoes and reached for the salt. "Oh, my mood is nothing. Why, do you not know that you are the object of our dear doctor's passion? Come now, are you not both enamored of our young Italian lover, so ardent and—"

"Stop it!" cried Mary. "This is ungracious of you!"

Polidori, breathing heavily, sat rigid in embarrassment at the opposite end of the table from Byron.

"And unwise," Shelley said drily. "What kind of fool offends his physician?"

Byron laughed. "Of course, you are right, my friend." Byron signaled the waiter to begin dishing out the soup. Polidori continued to glare at his employer, not looking at Mary. "We will cease to tease the young doctor. Ah, Shelley has another book. I see that I am not the only patron of a bookstore today." He half-bowed at Claire. "You may appreciate my find, a collection recently translated from the German. It is called *Fantasmagoriana*, and is full of ghost stories."

Claire giggled. "I shall not sleep for a week!"

"Doubtless, from some cause or other," his lordship said slyly. "Did you purchase a book as well?"

Claire nodded. "I have the newest from Miss Austen," she said. "I believe it came out just last year. This one is *Emma*."

"I cannot conceive why you read that rubbish," Mary said. "Her plots are nothing but schemes for marriage. As if that were all a woman might aspire to."

Claire glared across the table. "Do you not see the subtle critique in each one? The sly joke at—"

"I do not," Mary said firmly. "Moreover, I believe you are

mistaken in your perception. Take, for example, the novels of Mrs. Radcliffe—"

Byron said hastily, "What have you there, my Shiloh?"

Shelley opened the leather bound book. "I saw this at the bookseller's on Montreux Street. It's the first volume of a novel called *Glenarvon*. I perceive that it was published last month, and it is composed of extraordinary, very overwrought prose. Hear, where the heroine first meets her lover:"

The eye of the rattle-snake, it has been said, once fixed upon its victim, overpowers it with terror and alarm: the bird, thus charmed, dares not attempt its escape; it sings its last sweet lay; flutters its little pinions in the air, then falls like a shot before its destroyer, unable to fly from his fascination.

Sipping wine, Byron nodded. "Overwrought, indeed. And who is this reptilian lover?"

Shelley turned back a page. "A Lord Ruthven. Interesting name."

Byron set his glass down with a thunk, his pale face going nearly paper white. "Ruthven?" He extended his hand. "Let me see," he demanded.

Shelley handed over the book and reached for bread. "It appears to be a novel about a woman seduced and abandoned by a lover. I think it—"

"Damn the woman! God damn her!" Byron exploded. He flung the book to the opposite wall, missing Polidori's shocked face by an inch. Byron's face went instantly from white to red and then white again.

Alarmed, Polidori shot to his feet. "My lord! You are unwell!"

Byron waved him away and put his face in his hands. "Damn the woman to hell and back!"

Claire had picked up the book and looked at it. "It does not list the author's name."

Byron's fists clenched, clenched again. "I know who it is," he said, his voice low and guttural. "I know her, damn her. Damn her!"

Claire laid down the book, rose from her chair and came to kneel beside his chair. "Dear Albé," she said. She laid a hand on his upper arm, and he leaned toward her. Claire opened her arms to embrace him, but at the last moment he pulled back.

"The little antelope," Byron muttered. Mary heard tears in his voice, but he kept his head turned away. "It was over, it was finished. I told her and told her. This is her revenge."

Bewildered, Shelley asked, "Who is this 'Ruthven'?"

"He was ... a family connection," came Byron's smothered voice. "She ... I told her ..." He choked to a stop.

"You are saying a woman wrote this?" Shelley asked, bending to pick up the book.

"Who is this 'she'?" asked Claire, confused.

It was Polidori who finally made the connection. "Lady Caroline Lamb," he said quietly. "It must be her work." He took the book from Shelley and glanced into a few pages.

"Lamb?" Shelley said, wrinkling his brow. "Could she be related to Charles and Mary Lamb? I do enjoy their *Tales from Shakespeare.* Mary, dearest, are they not acquaintances of your father?" He looked at her out of innocent blue eyes.

Mary set her mouth in a grim line. "They are. But this Lady Caroline is no relation that I know of." Everyone in London who could read a newspaper during the previous two years knew very well who Lady Caroline Lamb was, and about her passionate, very public affair with Byron. Only Shelley, who rarely read the gossip columns, could have been unaware of it. Mary hesitated, unsure how much to say in front of Byron.

Polidori felt no hesitation. "Lady Caroline is the wife of William Lamb, the Member of Parliament. Her liaison with his lordship two years ago is well known," he said in a low undertone. "Doubtless she still has some feelings for him."

"Oh, doubtless," Byron said with bitterness. "But they are not now what they were, I perceive."

"Then it is as well that you are separate from her," Shelley said judiciously. "If you have no sentiments for one another, or one of you has lost the sentiment, it would be nothing but foolish custom to remain together."

Mary felt a chill come over her. These were almost the very words Shelley had used to justify leaving his wife for her.

Shelley continued. "Love withers under constraint: its very essence is liberty: it is compatible neither with obedience, jealousy, nor fear."

"Or fury, apparently." Byron reached for his wine glass and drank deeply.

"So you conceive that his lordship owes his mistress nothing?" Polidori asked, his voice very quiet. "That he can ruin her reputation, expose her to infamy, destroy her relation with her husband, and walk away scatheless?"

"Ah, there speaks our peasant," Byron said scornfully. "The values of the tradesman, the merchant, for whom reputation has a price. Think you that Caro risked anything at all? She is the daughter of an Earl, married to the heir of a viscountcy, and the cousin by marriage of my own wife. Her friends were shocked by our connection, but she was still everywhere received. And shall continue so."

"I cannot help but note the difference between Lady Caroline's reputation, and our own," Mary said suddenly. Everyone looked at her. "Our friends have fallen away, all but a very few. My own father will not see me, he walks past me on the street, and all because Shelley and I have done exactly as he taught."

"As have I," Claire said staunchly.

Mary looked at her. "Godwin thinks Shelley kidnapped you."

Byron shook his head, then addressed Shelley. "Can this be true? Godwin has renounced you both?"

Mary answered before Shelley could do so, her voice hard. "I have not heard from him directly in two years. We are outcast." She felt a pain in her stomach, almost as if someone had punched her in the middle, but fought to retain her countenance.

Claire blinked, but continued trying to soothe Byron. "Surely the only reason for lovers to remain together is love itself," she said. "The hypocrisy of the world is only the whine of ignorance and prejudice."

"Noble words," sneered Byron. "But I doubt Caro ever read Godwin. I don't know if it was love or madness. She pursued me through ballrooms and public streets. When I think of the scenes, the hysterics, the loud and vociferous dramas enacted in front of all our friends, it is sickening, ugly. But I never insulted her in public, never made her a laughingstock in print—and she calls me a snake!"

Polidori reached for the salt cellar and calmly sprinkled his potatoes. "I would not have credited your lordship with so much sensibility," he said. "I would rather have thought your heart hardened against the wailing of women."

Byron's head shot up, his eyes blazing. "Call me cold-hearted?! Me, insensible! As well might you say that glass is not brittle, which has been cast down a precipice, and lies dashed to pieces at the foot!"

Polidori merely shrugged as he held his employer's gaze. "And yet, despite all this attachment, you deserted Lady Caroline as soon as your liaison became public." He forked his potatoes. "I daresay the lady would characterize your heart in terms more like to marble or brass than brittle glass."

"How dare you!" Byron shot to his feet, fists on the table. "How dare you, sir!"

Claire also rose, and tugged at his arm until he turned to face her. "Dearest, be calm. Don't let him goad you. Come, sit down." She glared at Polidori. "And you! You should be ashamed of yourself."

Mary had said nothing during this scene, only noting a slight tremor in Polidori's hand as he took up a fork. Perhaps only she noted the pale cast to his skin, the tightening of the skin around the young man's mouth. Though he appeared calm, she sensed an inner turmoil. When he caught her looking at him, he locked his gaze to hers; in his expressive dark eyes she read misery and frustration.

I rejected him, and Byron insulted him. Now he takes it out on the man who makes him miserable, she thought. What wayward, hurting creatures we are.

Byron sat glaring at his physician. Shelley cleared his throat, eyes darting between his friend and Polidori. "I regret that I chose a book that offends you," he said quietly. "I had no notion, of course."

"You called it 'extraordinary'," Byron said in a low voice.

Shelley nodded sagely. "And so it is, but not for its portrait of you. Perhaps for its wild expressiveness, its use of—"

"Shelley, I think this is not the time for a literary critique," Mary said abruptly.

Claire took Byron's fist between her hands tenderly; he did not seem aware of it, but his hand opened slowly.

"Of course," Shelley said. He sent a sympathetic look Byron's way.

"A portrait," Byron growled. "It might have been more like if I had given her more sittings." He turned his head away from the others, even as Claire laid a comforting hand on his shoulder. "Women condemn men who 'kiss and tell'," he said. "What of those women who fuck and publish?"

Mary caught Shelley's eye. "Perhaps it would be best if we returned home soon," she said. "I must get back and feed William. He will be fretting."

He reached across and took her hand. "Of course."

"Call Fletcher and tell him to ready the boat," Byron said. Wordlessly, Polidori rose and bowed and exited the room. Claire helped Byron to his feet; the poet looked stooped, older.

As he turned to leave, with Claire still on his arm, Mary stepped in front of him. She laid a hand on his chest and looked up into his eyes. She had noticed before how changeable they were, like her own hazel eyes changing in color with his mood. Now they were brown, his expression hard and yet wounded. "Byron," she said softly. He looked down at her, as if from a great distance.

"Yes?"

She wanted to ask was there a child between him and this Lady Caroline, but what she said was, "Do not be careless with love."

The famous curl of the lip was her only answer. He passed by her without a word, limping out of the room and into the great room of the inn, a storm in his face.

Chapter XIX - God and Man

I now writhed under the miserable pain of a wound, which shattered the flesh and bone. The feelings of kindness and gentleness which I had entertained but a few moments before gave place to hellish rage and gnashing of teeth. Inflamed by pain, I vowed eternal hatred and vengeance to all mankind.

—*Frankenstein*, Volume III, Chapter VIII

Despite the building clouds over Jura, the day was windless. Shelley, Fletcher and Polidori took turns rowing, but Byron sat staring out over the gunwale at the blue water. At one point he shifted, raising his half-empty brandy bottle to his lips. Mary heard him mutter, "I have created a monster," and knew he referred to his mad ex-lover. She felt every sympathy for him, knowing that, even if as a male he was granted more freedom by society, he still suffered the exiled state she and Shelley endured. Aristocrat he might be, and far more conservative than Shelley might believe, but he was still a man beset by doubt and grief.

Beside him, Claire sat in uncharacteristic silence, watching the waves lapping against the boat. Now and then her hand rested on her belly.

Shelley, breathless with exertion, called, "Doctor, I believe it is your turn."

Polidori had followed them silently from the hotel to the dock, and had sat with his back turned during the entire trip. Now he nodded sullenly and stood to exchange places with Shelley. As Shelley passed him the oars, one of them slipped from Polidori's hand and rapped Byron sharply on the knee.

Mary saw him wince, saw him turn away to hide the pain. Polidori took his seat and Shelley settled in next to Mary. He folded her hand into his warm ones; she leaned back into him.

Byron turned back around to address Polidori, who was now pulling steadily at the oars. "Be so kind, Polidori, another time, to take more care, for you hurt me very much."

"I am glad of it," said the young doctor. "I am glad to see that you can suffer pain."

Mary winced at the callousness of this speech, and braced herself for another display of Byron's temper. But the poet remained calm, merely saying, "Let me advise you, Polidori, when you, another time, hurt any one, not to express your satisfaction. People don't like to be told that those who give them pain are glad of it; and they cannot always command their anger. It was with some difficulty that I refrained from throwing you into the water; and, but for Mrs. Shelley's presence, I should probably have done some such rash thing."

Polidori said nothing, but the muscle in his jaw clenched.

"He would antagonize B at such a moment," Shelley murmured.

"He has no common sense at all," Mary agreed.

Shelley dipped a hand into the pocket of his greatcoat and drew out something shining. "I forgot to tell you about this, dearest." He dropped something round and glittering into her hand: a watch.

"Oh." Mary felt her face warm. So this was the lady's watch Polidori had spoken of. "Thank—"

"I was thinking about your letter from your sister, Fanny," Shelley said, leaning close to whisper in her ear. "She seemed so disconsolate. I thought perhaps she would appreciate a trinket."

Mary turned away from him to get a better look at the watch. It was small, feminine, exquisite. Shelley had never given her anything like it. For one tiny moment, Mary had the wild impulse to throw it overboard. But she turned back to Shelley, smiled and handed him the watch. "She will be overjoyed," Mary said. "Do you know, we were so busy in our travels last month I neglected to buy her a birthday present. Thank you, my love."

Shelley kissed her cheek and replaced the watch in his pocket. "We shall bring it back with us when we return. In the meantime, this journey has turned into a row with Charon on the Styx. If we do not jolly Byron out of his mood, we shall be eating stale bread at our own table tonight."

He rose and stepped to the other side of the craft, which wobbled under him. Polidori grunted as he corrected the boat's path.

Sitting by Byron, Shelley stretched out his long legs, until his feet nearly lay in Mary's lap.

Most opinion's the same, with the difference of word,
Some get a good name by the voice of the crowd,
Whilst to poor humble merit small praise is allowed.

Byron stirred. His hunched shoulders relaxed as he looked around at his friend. "What in God's name is that?"

Shelley grinned. "From a poem I wrote to a pretty girl, a long time ago."

"And I am the poor humble to whom small praise is allowed?" Byron grunted. "You are a comfort, indeed, Shiloh."

Shelley leaned back against the gunwale on his elbows; the wind threw his hair into his face and blew it out again, teasingly. "You are surely not concerned with the voice of the crowd," he said. "I am indifferent to it, myself."

"Because it has never roared for you," Mary said. "His lordship is accustomed to being the object of adoration." Her bonnet ribbons, whipped by the wind, threatened to come undone and she retied them.

"Adoration," Byron said. "And excoriation. This—" He waved a hand in Shelley's direction. "This screed of Caro's will damn me forever."

"And your separation from your wife will not?" Shelley was curious.

"Ah, to be divided from a termagant to which one was leg-shackled in a moment of madness? The dream of every man in England, if not the world. They will envy me that, whatever they say publicly," Byron said grimly. "But to have one's dalliances, heretofore winked at, made the common gossip of the world, that is quite another thing."

"She thinks you heartless," Claire said suddenly.

"I did not know you were listening," Byron said.

"I hear everything you say," she said. "I looked at that book. If that is supposed to be you, a portrait of Byron, all I can say is that it is not the man I know."

For a moment, Byron looked blank. Then a curiously innocent look stole across his face. "You ... you move me, my dear."

Claire reached out, and he took her hand and bowed over it from a sitting position.

Polidori pulled on his oars, his eyes on his employer. "Heartless, she says." He pulled again. "I can speak to his lordship's heart. It beats quite regularly, as regularly as my new watch. Unlike the watch, I cannot verify its contents, however."

"No, I have given it away so often, it must be missing altogether," Byron said, still looking into Claire's eyes.

"Missing?" Shelley said in mock surprise. "Why, Doctor, how is it you have not noted its absence?"

"From never having expected to find it at all," Polidori said. "His lordship has been careful to tell the world he is without that organ."

"But I know better," Claire said.

Byron shook his head, dropped her hand, and the mask of the satyr descended again. "I should require you, Polly-Dolly, to locate my heart forthwith. I should not want it stolen."

"Perhaps we should return to the watchmaker," Polidori replied. "Let your lordship commission him to create a replacement."

"Capital!" Shelley clapped his hands together. "A clockwork heart! Always in time, always beating to the same measure."

"The notion appeals to me," Byron said. "A heart that would never speed up with passion, nor slow down with age. What say you, Polidori? Can a clockwork heart be made? How about a clockwork brain or liver? I shall have to have Fletcher wind me every morning, like the grandfather clock in the hallway."

Claire said, "And would you want to be a machine? To feel nothing?"

"Yes!" he said strongly. His fist clenched on his knee, then relaxed. "And no. Of course, no. The great art of life is sensation, to feel that we exist, even in pain."

"Perhaps you could build an animated machine that would feel no pain," Shelley said, musing. "Then Doctor Polidori could smack his knee all day long, with no ill effects."

Mary smiled inwardly. Give Shelley even the hint of a scientific oddity, and he was on it like a hawk on a hare.

"To feel pain, one must be a living thing," she said. "Tell me, Doctor, could you create a living thing? A man? And make him immune to pain?"

Polidori stopped rowing. He took a handkerchief from his sleeve and wiped his forehead with it. "To do so would be to usurp the handiwork of God," he said.

"Or to improve upon it," Mary said. "Shelley is subject to colds. I suffer from the catarrh now and then. How would it be if such a creature were to be free of disease? Or age? Even death might not touch it."

Byron looked down at his foot, now encased in boot leather, but Mary knew he saw its twisted flesh and distorted bone. "Perhaps you could make a man with replaceable parts." He grunted, then leered at Claire. "Some parts wear out more quickly than others, due to rapid and repeated usage."

Claire giggled, gripping his hand tightly. Byron suffered her to hold it, but looked at Shelley. "What part of you would you have replaced? Heart? Brain? Or something more vulgar?"

Shelley cast his head on one side. "Without my heart, I cannot write poetry. Without my brain, I cannot understand philosophy. And without my more vulgar parts, I cannot appreciate women."

Byron smiled slightly. "We must build you carefully, then. A creature with a heart and a brain, one that can live forever, like yourself, on roots and berries. Immortal, perhaps."

"Oh, one hopes not," Polidori said. "Imagine a world full

of immortal beings. They would soon fill the earth with their progeny."

"You have been reading Mr. Malthus," Shelley said.

"To be sure," he said tartly. "Only a fool would argue with his contention: that the population would increase by exponents, while food supply would only double. In a few generations, the population would outstrip the food supply, and all would starve."

Mary looked at him stonily. Shelley laughed. Claire shook her head in disgust.

"A fool, eh?" Byron looked skyward at the gathering clouds. Polidori, do you ever read anything other than medical books?"

Polidori had returned to rowing, and now puffed at every pull on the oars. "To be ... sure, I have.... In fact, I have even read *Childe Harold*."

Shelley laughed. "A touch, Albé."

Byron scowled at Polidori. "But you have never apparently read the debates on population put forth between Mr. Malthus and his foremost critic."

"No, I cannot ... say I have," Polidori replied. "Nor would I wish to."

"A pity," Mary said coolly. She and Claire both stared at him coldly. "Mr. Malthus' foremost critic is my father."

"Oh." Polidori stared, then slowly reddened. "I ... apologize, Mrs. ... Shelley ... I was ... not aware ..."

Shelley leaned over. "The doctor is going to keel over and expire if not relieved. Here, Byron, take the oars."

Instead, his lordship roared, "Fletcher!"

Byron's servant, who had been dozing near the stern, blinked awake. "Sir?"

"Row, damn you," his lordship said. "Else we shall not reach the shore within the decade. The rain is almost upon us."

As Polidori and Fletcher scrambled to change places, Byron put his face in his palms. Claire, her hand released, placed it on her abdomen. "And so you do not believe you have a heart?" she said softly.

"Broken, bruised, patched together perhaps," Byron said.

"Would that Polly-Dolly could make a new one. Even if it defied his God."

"Only God can truly create life," Polidori said stoutly. "In medical school, I attended any number of dissections. I have witnessed the galvanization of corpses, such as Mr. Shelley produced during the storm. I have never seen the vital spark restored to a dead heart." He mopped his brow with his shirt sleeve. "Man is more than a mere machine, to be started and stopped like a clock."

"And in all these researches and dissections, Doctor, did you ever come across the elixir of life? Or some vital principle that could be called into play by the will of Man?"

"I did not."

Shelley winked at Byron. "Then you have surely denied the existence of the soul, have you not? I was under the impression that you are a Catholic, sir."

"I do not mistake the elixir of life with an insubstantial soul," Polidori said defensively.

"So God may grant life without a soul?"

"No, that is not what I meant," Polidori said. "You are confusing me, sir."

Byron reached for the half-empty brandy bottle. "Mr. Shelley is a confusing man," he said. "Come, Shiloh, don't tease our pet Papist. He is not accustomed to atheists."

Polidori ran a finger under his tightly tied cravat. "I will confess Mr. Shelley's works confuse me. I have read your notes on *Queen Mab*. I perceive that you are opposed to religion. But yet you speak of a divine principle. Is it not the same as God?"

"Not at all," Shelley said, eager to defend his principle. "That God you refer to, I vow is an invention of priests and other impostors. But the divine Nature you see about you, that is what really brings life into the world, really creates life. That is my religion."

Polidori shook his head. "Such a 'religion' has no moral center."

Byron laughed. "Then I must convert to it straightaway. Because I have yet to see that avowing a religion, be it Christianity or the Turk, provides men with a moral center." He swigged brandy.

"Perhaps, Polly, you should construct a man with a moral center. Can you do that with clockwork?"

Mary had been staring off across the water at the mountains. She thought about Rousseau, and his man of nature. "Perhaps a constructed man would be stronger," she mused. "Perhaps a clockwork man could be useful. Think of the work he could do, in all weathers, without being made sick or tired."

Byron snorted. "You would create a race of mechanical servants, then? Brava, Mary. A fine opinion from a woman who will not serve sugar because it is grown by slaves."

Claire laid her head on the gunwale. "'The words *slave* and *right* contradict each other, and are mutually exclusive'," she said. "Have you not read Rousseau, B? We can hardly argue for the rights of the natural man, and at the same time partake in that which oppresses him."

"Then it makes even less sense for Mary to want to create a race of slaves," Byron said. He lifted his head to shade his eyes. "And as for the rights of the natural man, I have been called the most unnatural man in Britain." He stared gloomily out across the water again.

"The natural society of man is family," Claire said, her hand still on her abdomen. "Rousseau called it the most ancient of all societies."

Mary glanced up and found Shelley looking at her; in his gaze she read consternation.

Byron tilted up the bottle and drained it. He flung it into the water. "I do not know that I resemble Jean Jacques Rousseau," he said. "I have no ambition to be like so illustrious a madman—but this I know, that I shall live in my own manner, and as much alone as possible."

The rest of the journey was finished in silence.

As soon as the boat nudged the shoreline, Shelley jumped into the knee-deep water. Extending a hand to Claire, he said, "Come, my dear."

Claire stood, steadied herself on Byron's shoulder, and fell overboard into Shelley's arms. He caught her easily and strode off towards the cottage without a backward glance. Polidori scrambled clumsily over the gunwale and waded ashore. Mary stood and began to climb over. Her skirts encumbered her and she tottered, half in and half out of the boat.

"Fletcher, tie us up," Byron ordered. He clasped Mary's arm. "No, allow me." He swung over the side.

"My lord, your boots!" Fletcher cried.

"Damn my boots. I'll order a new pair, made from your skin. Here, Mary, jump down to me."

"No, I cannot."

"Nonsense," Byron said. He glanced at the sky. "In a moment, you will be soaked to the skin. Allow me to help you."

Reluctantly, Mary leaned over the side. Byron caught her in his strong arms and turned towards the shore. "Put your arms about my neck, that way we will be balanced."

This close, Mary smelled him: tobacco, brandy, sweat and under all of that, wet wool. The hair at the back of his neck curled against her hand. His irregular step frightened her a little, but he brought them both to shore securely. Above the waterline, he swung her down and set her on her feet.

"Thank you, B," Mary said. She smoothed her dress.

"Fletcher will bring your parcels," he said. Byron offered his arm. "Allow me."

She took his arm and walked with him up the slight rise. His limp seemed more pronounced; perhaps he had had too much brandy. "Will you stay to tea? I bought some pekoe in Geneva."

"I thank you, no. I am off to the Villa." Having reached the house, Byron swept her a bow and released her hand. He hesitated a moment. "Mary, I pray you will forgive some of what I said. I often say things I do not mean."

"Then perhaps you should say the things you do mean," she said, but smiled to take the sting from her words. Byron smiled slightly, bowed and walked away.

Inside the house, Mary found Shelley coming down the stairs. "I have put her to bed," he said. "She needs to rest. Elise will bring her some tea." He bent down to kiss her cheek.

"You are still wearing your coat, love," she said. "Will you not stay for tea?"

Shelley shook his head and stepped to a case on a sideboard. He opened it, looked to make sure of the pistols within, and then shut it. "I have an appointment to shoot with B," he reminded her. "Would you join us?"

"After I feed our son, perhaps," Mary said. She glanced at the sky. "Will you not wear a hat? It may rain."

Shelley tucked the pistol case under his arm and smiled at her. Then he stepped through the door, admitting a gust of rain-smelling air.

Chapter XX - The Taunt

I learned that there was but one means to overcome the sensation of pain, and that was death—a state which I feared yet did not understand.

—*Frankenstein,* Volume III, Chapter V

It took Mary longer than she had planned to feed William and settle him for his nap. By the time she began walking to the Villa Diodati, the afternoon was darkening again.

As she approached the Villa, Mary heard the crack! crack! of gunfire. This was followed by a brief interval, and she heard men laughing. Rounding the corner of the house, she came upon a familiar scene.

The lawn sloped down from the terrace to the edge of the water, where a low stone wall kept waves at bay during storms. Along the top of this wall stood a row of empty wine bottles, some of which consisted only of a shattered base. On the balcony overlooking the lawn, Shelley and Byron, in shirtsleeves, were re-loading a brace of pistols. A table stood nearby, attended by the stoic Fletcher, on which several firearms lay. Byron stepped forward, raised his pistol, and fired.

Crack!

Mary startled, as she always did, even when expecting the report. She had resigned herself to Shelley's love affair with guns. To her, they were a violent and dangerous diversion, but the son of a landed aristocrat merely saw them as tools for sport, much like a tennis racquet. And Shelley was a very good shot.

"Not quite on target, LB," he said now as Byron stepped back.

Byron caught sight of Mary and immediately pointed his pistol skyward. "My dear, you must give us better warning! Never surprise an armed man!"

John Polidori peered around the baron. "Mrs. Shelley!"

Byron looked over his shoulder at the physician. "Ho, there, Polly-Dolly! You will spoil my aim! Curse this weather!" The last was directed heavenward, whence a light rain had begun to patter the ground.

"It will not affect my aim in the least," said Shelley, busy reloading. "As long as the powder is kept dry, why should rain make a difference?"

"The rain may make a difference to Mrs. Shelley," said Polidori.

Byron cocked an eyebrow at him. "Very well, if you must play the gallant, o'er-leap this balcony and give her your arm through the storm."

Polidori turned a slight red. "If no other man will assist her," he said, looking sharply at Shelley. Shelley, however, was sighting along the barrel of his pistol at a tree limb, paying no attention. "Very well."

Polidori grasped the railing of the balcony. Byron, perceiving too late that the doctor actually intended to jump, called out a warning, but Polidori threw himself over the railing and dropped. He landed solidly ten feet below, on both feet, but the ground was muddy from the rain and he slipped. With a cry, he fell to one side, full length on the grass.

"Oh!" Glancing up to make sure no one was shooting, Mary hurried to his side. "Doctor! Are you hurt?"

Polidori's face was white, and sweat beaded his forehead. "I ... I seem to have sprained my left ankle."

Behind him, the lower terrace doors burst open and Byron limped out, his coat flying behind him. Shelley was right behind him, looking concerned.

Mary helped Polidori to a sitting position. He massaged his ankle, but the heavy boot made it difficult.

"Physician, what ails thee?" cried Byron, but his tone belied his mocking words. He knelt next to the doctor. "Can you stand, man?"

"I ... I shall try." Polidori put out a hand. Byron came to his feet, pulling Polidori. But the doctor winced when he put his weight on his injured ankle. "Oh!" he slipped sideways, but Shelley was there to catch him before he fell. "I beg your pardon, my lord, but I really cannot walk on it."

Byron slid an arm across the man's shoulders. "Shelley, grasp him thus, and let us lock our arms beneath him. We shall carry him into the house. Mary, could you be so good as to get the door?"

Mary held the French doors open as the men carried Polidori across the threshold. As Byron passed her, she saw the strain on his face, and saw the effort that his deformed leg was costing him. But Byron said nothing as they entered and laid Polidori on the sofa in the parlor. They were in the downstairs parlor, which still retained the clutter and scattered apparatus of last night's experiments. The Leyden jar remained in the center of the table.

Fletcher appeared at the doorway, looking anxious. "Cold water, Fletcher," commanded his lordship.

Mary helped settle the doctor on the sofa. "What shall we do for you?" she asked.

"Raise my foot a little," said Polidori. "A few pillows, yes. One more should do it."

"There are no more pillows," said Mary, looking around.

"I will fetch one from upstairs," Byron said. "Shelley, see that he is made comfortable." Byron turned and hobbled up the stairs, leaning heavily on the banister.

"This boot must come off, man," Shelley said. He grasped Polidori's muddied boot; Polidori braced himself. As gently as possible, Shelley worked it off his foot. Polidori said nothing, but his hands clenched the sofa cushions until his knuckles stood out bone-white under the skin. Mary put a hand on one of his, and was rewarded with a look of immense gratitude.

As soon as the boot was removed, Polidori let out his breath in a long sigh. "Thank you, Mr. Shelley."

Fletcher arrived with a bowl of water and some cloths. Mary began wringing them out and placing them on Polidori's ankle and foot.

"Oh, no, ma'am, you must not trouble yourself," he protested.

Mary waved him away. "This could be quite serious, Doctor," she said. "I need hardly tell you that. You should stay off of this ankle awhile."

Byron thumped back down the stairs, carrying two white satin pillows. "From my own bed," he stated, handing them to Mary. As she tucked them under Polidori's foot, he added, "Fear not, they were fresh-laid this morning. I have not yet soiled them with my touch."

Polidori shot him a look of loathing. "Well, I did not believe you had so much feeling," he said.

Mary recoiled. "John! You cannot mean to be so ungrateful for his lordship's generosity!"

Shelley laughed. "Mary, I'm surprised at you, as would be your father. Godwin says that gratitude and other such passions are unconstrained by judgement. They are not to be heeded when determining how we should act. Lord Byron perceives, correctly, that his doctor is essential to his health, so he naturally acts in a manner that benefits Polidori. Why, then, should Albé be owed a pointless expression of empty gratitude?"

"Why, indeed?" retorted Byron. "Best of all, let the good physician abuse me to my face and damn me to my friends; then I shall certainly acquit myself well rewarded. Fletcher, bring the brandy from my study."

Polidori struggled to sit up, despite Mary's caution. "I thank you for your pains, my lord," he said sulkily. "I pray I shall discommode you no further."

Byron stared at him, then shrugged. "As you wish, then. Come, Shelley, our targets await." He stomped out, leaving the doors open behind him. The breeze brought the fresh scent of rain and lake water, and a hint of sunshine.

Shelley stood awkwardly in the middle of the room, until Mary waved him away. "I will deal with this," she said.

When Shelley left, Polidori grasped Mary's hand in his. "Thank you," he said fervently. "Your kindness overwhelms me."

"More gratitude?" Mary said lightly. "My kindness is of no more weight than your gratitude. His lordship needs his physician, and I need my tutor of Italian. I will do what I can to help you, as any person should."

Deflated, Polidori released her hand. "Nevertheless, I am grateful," he said. He lay back on the sofa and closed his eyes. He laid an arm across his face when she placed a cold compress on his ankle.

"Whatever were you doing, jumping over the wall like that?" she asked.

"It matters not," he muttered.

"You did it in response to Albé's taunt," she said strongly. "Why do you allow him to goad you thusly?"

His laugh was short and bitter. "Patronage, my dear ma'am. Patronage. The curse of the educated and unemployed." He removed his arm and looked at her out of unhappy eyes. "Do you know, I am the youngest person ever to receive a medical degree from Edinburgh medical school? I have published poetry. I have written a play. And yet his lordship considers me a secretary." He spat the last word.

"Claire tells me that the publisher Murray has paid you to write about Lord Byron. Have you considered that he may find this objectionable?" She wrung out a cloth in the cold water.

He was silent a moment. "How else am I to live? His lordship promises, but does not pay, like all the aristocracy. And then he taunts me about—"

"About me," she finished for him.

His eyes met hers, full of pain, and then he looked away. "About everything. I am the butt of every joke."

"And you endure it."

"I must. Do you know what the patronage of the author of *Childe Harold* is worth? I hope to get Murray to publish my play, if he likes my notes on Lord Byron."

Mary nodded, understanding very well the difficulties of publishing. "And of course, you are aware that Byron is one of the directors of the Drury Lane Theatre. He can get your play onto the bill."

Polidori shrugged. "I misdoubt it. He has not even read it."

Mary saw sweat on his jaw and wished she had something to ease his pain. "Tonight I will ask him to read it after our meal."

Polidori turned his head, eyes wide. "You would do that? If you ask him, he will surely not refuse!"

She smiled and adjusted his pillow. "You think too highly of my influence on him."

Polidori grasped her hand in his. "Oh, Mrs. Shelley, dear ma'am! This is worth all the pain in my ankle, if you will get him to consider it!"

Mary withdrew her hand but cocked her head. "You say you earned a medical degree only last year, yet you are more anxious to have your play produced. Are you dissatisfied with medicine?"

Polidori shook his head. "Not at all, but my father, he is a translator of Italian works, a literary man. I would have him bear some pride in me, some appreciation of the works of my hand."

Mary's mouth twisted. "I know that feeling right well, Doctor!" She rose to her feet. "Try to rest this afternoon, and I will speak to Shelley."

Polidori granted her an earnest look. "I cannot be more in your debt, ma'am!"

"Gratitude is a useless emotion," she said, but smiled. Seeing Fletcher enter with another bowl of cold water, she nodded to him and went out through the French doors.

Chapter XXI - Targets

*I took every precaution to defend my person in case the fiend
should openly attack me. I carried pistols and a dagger constantly about me, and was ever on the watch....*

—Frankenstein, Volume III, Chapter V

Byron's servant, Berger, had brought the pistols and loading table down from the balcony onto the lawn. There, Mary found
Shelley and Byron preparing to shoot again.

Shelley saw her, turned, smiled, and went back to loading his
pistol. His hand was black with gunpowder. "My Maisie-girl is as
quiet as a little dormouse. I like her that way."

Byron grinned, and Mary had to admit that, in the sunlight
with his tousled hair falling over his wide brow, Byron was an
enormously attractive man. "A quiet woman. What a concept!
Would that I knew one." He raised his arm, holding a loaded pistol, and sighted at the wall at the bottom of the lawn, just above
the water's edge.

Crack!

A wine bottle disappeared in a puff of vaporized glass.

"Oh, well done," Shelley said. "That's five for you, and eight
for me."

"It most certainly is not, my Shiloh. That's seven for me. I am
almost even with you."

Shelley chuckled and stepped forward to take Byron's place
at the head of the lawn, a pistol in each hand. "Come now, be fair,
my lord. You cannot count the one that fell over when you nicked
the wall under it. Nor can you count the one that knocked its
neighbor over. That's not quite the same as shooting it. "

"It's dead, nonetheless," Byron said. He handed his pistol
to Berger to load and picked up a half-full wineglass. "Madame
Mary, how is our good doctor?"

"Well enough. You should not have teased him as you did."

Byron shrugged and knocked back his wine.

Shelley peered over his shoulder. "These are very fine Mantons," he said, admiring the pistols. Looking back to the targets, he squeezed off another shot. One more bottle shattered.

"I protest!" Byron said, laughing. "Come, Shelley! You are destroying my wine bottles faster than I can empty them! Berger, fetch another bottle of the '95 claret."

"Wine will not improve your aim," Shelley said evenly. Sighting down the barrel of the other pistol, he squeezed off a shot. Another wine bottle vanished in a tinkling rain of glass as the the echo of the shot rebounded across the water. "Really, these are too easy. We need a challenge."

Byron placed a chair for Mary, and she lowered herself into it with a sigh. "Are you certain you will take nothing? The day is damnably oppressive. Some ratafia, perhaps? Berger! Damn your eyes, bring us something cold and wet!"

One of Byron's peacocks strutted slowly out of the hedge-copse on their right. Shelley's pistol tracked it unerringly. "What say you, my lord?" he said playfully. "Shall we have peacock for dinner?" The flintlock snicked back and Shelley extended his arm.

"Nonsense," Byron said lazily. "You do not eat meat, so do not try to convince me that you will kill that bird."

> *Never again may blood of bird or beast*
> *Stain with its venomous stream a human feast.*

Shelley laughed, and Byron raised an eyebrow. "You did not think I had read *Queen Mab?* Shelley, Shelley, you underestimate me. But you will not shoot my bird."

"Perhaps it is a monarchist," Mary said. "Shelley, would you shoot a monarchist?"

"Assuredly," he said. "Byron, do stand next to the bird. I can rid the world of two overdressed creatures at once."

"Have you ever fired at a man?" Byron asked.

Berger arrived with a tray, bearing claret, lemonade and gunpowder. Mary accepted a glass of ratafia with a smile. It smelled of cinnamon and peaches.

"I have," Shelley said, lowering the empty pistols and turning back to the group.

"Only when he has been fired upon," Mary said, sipping her drink. The sugary, fiery punch made her eyes water.

Byron raised an eyebrow and his glass. "Well, damn me," he said. "A jealous husband? A jilted lover, perhaps?"

Shelley glanced up, his look cool as he reached for the gunpowder bag. "A government agent."

Byron cocked his head to one side. "A vice and morals committee? Were you arrested for not going to church?"

"I was fired upon in my home," Shelley said calmly. "On a night in February. I heard someone in the house, and went to look."

"Forsaking your pistols?" Byron said archly.

"By no means. I had one with me. I saw someone at the window, and a shot was fired through it. I attempted to return fire, but the powder flashed in the pan. The fiend entered through the window and beat me nearly senseless." Having finished, Shelley fired.

Crack! A twig fell from a high branch.

Byron scowled. "You alerted the authorities? It's a damned thing, when a gentleman is attacked in his own house."

"It was not my house," Shelley said, reaching for a cloth. "I had rented a cottage in Wales."

Byron looked at Mary. "And you, were you not frightened?"

"I was not there," she said calmly. "I had not yet met Shelley."

"Did they catch the fellow?"

"No, although I gave them a drawing of the fiend," Shelley said. "And it was a fiend, I am persuaded. A demon from another region."

Byron stared. "You can jest about this?"

"Shelley thinks it was a demon, but I suspect a more worldly assailant," Mary said. "Shelley was engaged in a political war between landowners and sheep men."

"Well, it's damnable," Byron snorted. "People are mad, I tell you. I am followed day and night, and stared at wherever I go. One grows accustomed, or stays indoors."

Mary shook her head. "Oh, but it is not the same, Albé. You are a notorious rake, someone to condemn with a smile. You threaten aristocrats in their drawing rooms. My Shelley attacks the world at its roots: politics and religion. Men have been guillotined for less."

Berger, who had been loading a pistol, handed it to Byron. He took it absently, pointing it skyward. "So that is why you travel armed, Shelley. I had wondered."

Shelley had finished loading and picked up the pistols. "Never with fewer than three pair," he said. "We have killed all the wine bottles," he said practically. "What shall we culp next?"

"A card? No, we will need all of them later. Perhaps a portrait we do not like? Fletcher, go get that hideous thing over the study fireplace and bring it out here."

Shelley shook his head. "No, too large. How say you to a gold piece? Affix one to yonder tree trunk, and we will see who can come closest to it."

Byron brightened. "Excellent. I used to practice thus at Manton's shooting gallery. But I have not a shilling. Mary? Can you accommodate us?"

Mary felt her cheeks grow warm with embarrassment. Their funds were too low to waste a sixpence, let alone a shilling, on sport. "I fear that I left my reticule at home," she said quietly.

Byron reached into his waistcoat. "See here if I have—yes! My purse. Capital! We shall shoot at this half crown!" He held up the round gold coin.

Mary gulped. A half crown would buy food, clothes, and candles for a week. She felt a trickle of annoyance. She heard her father's voice in her head: Money belongs to those who need it. The principle of utilitarianism was sound, and her lifelong belief in it now rebelled at this waste of good money. She stood suddenly, tugging at her sleeve. "Here. Use this." She held out her handkerchief.

Byron looked at her in surprise. "Your handkerchief? What gentleman would shoot at a lady's pocket square? Really, we are not barbarians!"

She waved it at him impatiently. "Truly, it is of less worth than that half crown, my lord. And the money may be put to better use."

She glanced at Shelley, but he was staring out over the lawn at the lake, thinking. She knew he could not hear them.

A sardonic smile curled in the corner of Byron's mouth. "And what better use can money be put to, than to entertain us? But if you wish it, it will be so. Allow me to purchase your linen, Madame Mary." With a flourish and a bow, Byron handed her the coin and took the handkerchief.

Heat flooded Mary's cheeks. "No, you do not understand. I did not mean, that is, it was not my intent—"

Byron chuckled and waved the white square. "Too late, my dear. Too late. And now for our target ..." He tucked the handkerchief into his sleeve and drew forth a sixpence from his pocket. "Ah, a lesser coin. This will do nicely. Fletcher, set it against that lower limb on the birch yonder." The servant moved off with the coin winking in his hand.

Mary's embarrassed flush now turned to anger. "I meant for you not to waste coin. You mock me, my lord." Her voice shook a little.

Byron burst into laughter. "Waste coin? My good Mary, I have wasted vast oceans of them. Oceans, rivers, deserts of coin. You cannot imagine the line of debtors at my door in Mayfair. I married for money and wasted that, too." His laughter died, he scowled, and suddenly raised the pistol and fired. And missed. "Damn! See what you made me do!"

"Albé, you fired of your own will, in a fit of rage. You cannot blame me if your passions overcome you."

Byron turned to her, mouth open, incredulous, poised for a retort.

"Maisie—" Shelley put a hand on her arm, but stood next to her. "I must agree, Byron. You make yourself disagreeable only out of perversity. Or drink. This canker of aristocracy ill becomes you. Consider, for example, Polidori. The doctor is a man—"

"A man!" Byron swung to the table, caught his bad foot on a

clod of lawn, and stumbled. "Damn the man!" He gripped the edge of the table. "Not even a doctor. See how I still hobble, though I pay him to un-hobble me." Mary stepped forward to offer support, but he waved her away angrily. "As for cankers, what sore upon the ass of society is it who consistently calls for its destruction? You, a country squire, calling for democracy? A country patriot, born to hunt, and vote, and raise the price of corn. Pah!" Reeling now, he stumbled towards the house. "Damn you all!"

Berger stepped past his master to open the door. Byron stumped through it and the servant followed him in. Mary and Shelley were left alone with the smell of gunpowder and the approaching storm. The damp wind ruffled Shelley's hair as he frowned after Byron. "A country squire?" His voice was soft but full of emotion. "Does he think I care?"

Mary patted his arm. "Pay him no mind."

"But I must, my pet. He is the voice of a generation, whether he knows it or not. His poetry is read at every level of government, which means his thoughts are known at every level. And though I admire him for how he says it, I do not always agree with what he says. He presumes an inferiority between us which is wholly artificial, unjustifiable, and unnatural. The true difference between us exists nowhere in reality but in our own talents, which are not our own but Nature's—or in our rank—which is not our own but Fortune's." Shelley stared down at his feet and kicked at the clod where Byron had stumbled. "Sometimes I think he is a slave to the vilest and most vulgar prejudices, and as mad as the winds."

A raindrop plopped on Mary's hand, another on her cheek. Thunder rumbled overhead. "We must go in, my love. A storm is coming."

Shelley looked up, oblivious to the rain pelting his cheeks. "A storm. Yes."

Chapter XXII - Ada and Augusta

I discovered that he, the author at once of my existence and of its unspeakable torments, dared to hope for happiness; that while he accumulated wretchedness and despair upon me he sought his own enjoyment in feelings and passions from the indulgence of which I was forever barred.

—*Frankenstein,* Volume III, Chapter VII

The rain commenced as they entered the Villa; Shelley left the door open so that the smell of rain and lake water wafted through the building. They heard Byron stumping along ahead of them, shouting for Fletcher. On the sofa, Polidori was sifting through some papers.

"His lordship's limp grows worse when he is downcast," he said.

"The outward sign of the inner man," Shelley mused. "How often we judge our fellow creatures by their externalities, by which we are so often misled. Why do we never learn better?"

"You yourself have said it," Mary reminded him. "In *Queen Mab,* do you not recall? 'The beauty of the internal nature cannot be so far concealed by its accidental vesture.' Does that not mean that if Albé's external appearance is beautiful, it is because it reveals the beauty of his internal nature?"

Polidori snorted. "Poets."

Shelley ignored him. "But you must remember the foot," he said. "His infirmity is part of his externalities, so it, too, shows truth. Our Albé is a flawed man, in every definition."

"I fear that we have yet to see his darkest side. That will come soon enough. Claire cannot forebear to give him the news much longer. Polidori has already guessed her condition."

Shelley glanced sharply at the young doctor, who nodded. Shelley shoved a stack of books off a divan and sprawled across it. "Truth will out," he said. "Deception is always abhorrent to me.

You know my mind in this, that when we expose the deformities of human nature, only then can we begin to reform it."

"This is not a deformity likely to be exposed soon," Mary said. "B sees himself as an outcast, a monster because of his foot. Or so Doctor Polidori says." She seated herself on a low stool near the sofa. "How is your ankle?"

"Better. I thank you." Polidori said. "Fletcher brought me some papers to divert me."

Shelley was wandering around the room restlessly. "Tell me, John. As a doctor, you must surely agree that the outward appearance of a man often disguises his inner truth. Do you not agree?"

"Certainly," Polidori said. "A man may appear vital and hale on the outside, while inwardly harboring a cancer."

"Then consider whether Albé's crusty attitude may merely be the hard turtle shell that hides a softer, more easily damaged heart," Mary said. "If he teases you, it is only a form of defense, much like the over-matched force that sallies from a beleaguered castle to engage the enemy by surprise, hoping to overwhelm it."

"Consider, Mrs. Shelley, that a man's outward appearance may also accurately reflect his inner self," Polidori said coolly. "As his actions reflect his character."

Mary stiffened. "And what may we say of a man who hits his employer with an oar?"

Before he could answer, they heard Claire's voice in the foyer.

Shelley and Mary locked eyes, and turned as one when the door opened. Fletcher bowed Claire in. "If you'll be waitin' here, Miss, I'll see if his lordship is at home."

Claire entered, wearing a light green sprigged muslin gown, untying her bonnet. "Oh, Polly, I did not know you were here." She dropped a curtsy, and the doctor replied with a stiff bow from his position on the sofa. "Why Shelley, your face is as black as soot! Whatever have you been doing?"

"Killing Albé's wine bottle collection," Shelley said.

Claire's bright gaze went from him to Mary. "Do you know, dear Mary, Albé is actually working on another canto of *Childe Harold*? Is it not thrilling?"

"Of course," Mary said. Her heart gladdened to see Claire so happy. Perhaps, after all, there could be some rapprochement between her and Byron.

Fletcher re-appeared in the doorway. "Miss, his lordship sends his compliments, and asks if you would join him on the balcony."

"Tell his lordship I shall come directly. It is awfully windy today! And Albé will be dictating, and I shall have to weight down my papers with brandy bottles and ink pots!" Pausing, she looked at Mary. "We have a great deal to do today. Mary, is it possible you could assist us?" She said the 'us' with a proprietary air.

"I shall join you in a few moments," Mary said.

Claire dimpled. "We shall have such a wonderful afternoon!" She dashed through the doorway.

Polidori looked after her for a moment, then shook his head. "You will pardon me, Mr. Shelley, Mrs. Shelley. But I fear that for all her hopes, his lordship regards her only in the light of, er, an amanuensis."

Shelley lifted an eyebrow. "More than that, clearly."

Polidori did not, as Mary expected, rise to the bait. He held out the paper he was holding. "I found this verse among some of his papers this morning."

"More of *Childe Harold?*" Shelley said eagerly.

But before Shelley could take it, Polidori delivered it into Mary's hand.

A single sheet of paper, covered with Byron's scrawl, with blottings and scratchings-out. And, she was shocked to note, blotches that could only have been dried tears. Tears? From Byron?

Shelley leaned close to read over her shoulder, but she turned away, seeking better light.

... Though thy soul with my grief was acquainted,
It shrunk not to share it with me,
And the love which my spirit hath painted
It never hath found but in thee....

Mary scanned down further.

From the wreck of the past, which hath perish'd,
Thus much I at least may recall,
It hath taught me that what I most cherish'd
Deserved to be dearest of all:
In the desert a fountain is springing,
In the wide waste there still is a tree,
And a bird in the solitude singing,
Which speaks to my spirit of thee.

She turned the paper over, looking for an inscription or a title, and found it: *Stanzas to Augusta.*

Tears blurred her vision, and she let her hand fall. Shelley snatched up the paper, reading it quickly. He let out a long sigh and handed it back to Polidori. "Give this back to his lordship," he said quietly. "Don't tell Byron we have seen it."

"Augusta Leigh is his half-sister. He writes to her still," Polidori said quietly. "I ... I mean no offense to Miss Clairmont, but you can see how ... he will never...."

Shelley laid a hand on Mary's shoulder. "Of course, it was rumored all over London."

Mary nodded. "His own sister!"

"Half-sister, actually," Polidori said. "They had the same father, and different mothers. They were raised separately."

She glared up at him. "As if that could matter! Byron stands in the same relation to Augusta Leigh that I stand to Fanny! They have a parent in common! They are almost one flesh, and he—"

"He loves her," Shelley said firmly. "Can you read what we just read, and not know that? Can you not see the strength of that love, that renounces and yet remembers?"

She paced away from him. "And what does that mean for Claire? If he is writing this to his ... sister, he cannot love Claire. He will not love her."

"You think a man cannot love two women at once?" Shelley asked.

Whirling, her hot retort died on her lips as she saw his grin. "Rogue! This not a matter for amusement. She is heading over a cliff, and she cannot see it."

The grin died on his face, and Shelley hunched his shoulders and clasped his hands behind his back. The movement made him look like one of the herons that stalked absurdly up and down the lakeshore.

"Do you know, there were rumors of a child." Polidori spoke in a low voice. "They say that his sister bore him a daughter two years ago. He weeps at night, and I have heard him saying the name 'Medora' in despair."

Shelley shook his head. "I daresay it's as false as everything else we have heard about the man. Look at his politics, his philosophies. Look at his affairs. Why, Albé himself jests about his reputation. What calumny will the world of hypocrites and Custom not hurl at him?"

"You defend him," Mary said. "He has abandoned at least one child in England. I am given to understand that she is only a month older than our own William. Now you tell me there was another child, a child by his own sister? And where is this child? Does he love it? Care for it? Or has he disavowed all of his offspring at once?"

Shelley looked distressed. "I do not know."

"Fletcher!" Byron's voice floated down from the balcony. "Where the devil have you put my—oh, there it is. Come, Claire, I have some verses for you."

Distantly, Claire's giggle wafted down to them from the terrace. Mary leaned on Shelley. "Albé takes her to his bed, while he writes this to another woman. He seeks indulgence and passion from Claire, while all the time his heart is elsewhere. What does this mean for your principle of love?" she asked.

Polidori shuffled papers, his face pale, not looking at either of them.

Shelley shrugged helplessly. "I will speak to him. I will tell him of the child. He will see reason."

Polidori shook his head. "His lordship is not a reasonable man," he said. "It is his disposition to deem what he has, whether it is women or dogs, as worthless. He will not accept this child."

His tone was ominous. "I would not be the one to tell him of it."

Mary shook her head. "No. That is for Claire to do. Oh, why did she do it?" She whirled away from Shelley, her heart wrung.

"Dearest? I do not understand you. You defend her, then decry her. What is amiss with you?" Shelley's voice was gentle. As always, it undid her. She sagged, felt his arms come around her.

"I think of her child, love. I think of him or her, unloved, unwanted by its father. I think of Claire, who loves so passionately and unrestrainedly. I think of their child, growing up despised, ignored. Oh, you do not know what Albé's life was like, as a child. Until I saw that poem, I was not sure he could love at all.

"And even now, I think his capacity for love is as deformed as his leg."

A tap at the door, and Fletcher stood looking around. "Beg pardon, sir" he said stolidly. "There be a lass with your babe at the door." From behind him came a familiar wail.

Shelley grinned. "Ah, the princeling arrives."

The sound woke the milk in her, and she felt the familiar ache in her breasts. "Have them come in," Mary directed. She settled into a comfortable chair as Elise entered. She held William in a brown blanket, his face covered against the light rain.

Polidori was struggling to his feet. "If you will excuse me," he said. "I must go to my room and lie down. All this philosophy is exhausting."

Shelley offered his arm to the young man. "Fletcher, come assist the doctor. We will take you upstairs."

"Very kind of you," Polidori said through gritted teeth. Between them, he limped painfully to the hallway. Pausing at the door, he looked back at Mary. "You see? I limp as badly as his lordship, yet I have not his morals. One cannot judge the inner man from the outer." Before she could respond, he tottered out the door.

Chapter XXIII - Childe Harold

... as we ascended still higher, the valley assumed a more magnificent and astonishing character. Ruined castles hanging on the precipices of piny mountains; the impetuous Arve, and cottages every here and there peeping forth from among the trees, formed a scene of singular beauty.

—*Frankenstein,* Volume III, Chapter I

Elise took young William to the kitchen to make herself some tea. Ascending to the second floor, Mary found Claire and Byron already at work in the drawing room. A large table lay under sheets and stacks of paper, most of them held down with half-empty bottles of wine or assorted bibelots. One stack of paper at the corner of the table lay under a shoe. In one corner stood a hanging birdcage in which a parrot ruffled its feathers and looked out disconsolately on the world.

Claire and Byron sat at the end of the table closest to the windows. Byron's head bent over his paper, his whole body hunched over with the tension of composition. His mastiff lay disconsolately near his feet, massive head on its paws. Claire held a quill pen in one hand and appeared to be writing. Mary knew she was probably copying something of Byron's out into a fair copy, something that could be sent to a publisher. The handwriting of immediate creativity, as Mary knew too well, was often crabbed and skewed, difficult to parse.

Mary laid her wrap across a sofa back. "Shelley has gone out in the boat. How may I help?"

Byron, engrossed in the progress of his pen across paper, ignored this exchange.

"It is hard to think what you might do that I cannot." With a brittle smile, Claire dipped her quill into the ink pot. "Oh, alas, we seem to have run out. Mary, dearest, perhaps you can be of some assistance after all."

Mary drew up a chair near the ink pot. It was nearly empty, so Mary reached for the bottle of fermented oak gall ink and carefully tipped it into the jar. She used a discarded quill to stir the ink until it was well blended, then passed it over to Claire.

Suddenly Byron threw down his pen and leaned far back in his chair, nearly tipping it over. He passed his hand over his eyes and shook his head. "Mary? Good heavens, I did not see you there. I beg your pardon, I am completely engaged with this damned verse."

Mary reached across and took the pages next to Byron. She held them up to the light, reading. Byron's scrawl was not nearly as difficult to read as Shelley's:

Is thy face like thy mother's, my fair child!
Ada! sole daughter of my house and heart?
When last I saw thy young blue eyes, they smiled,
And then we parted,—not as now we part,
But with a hope.

Sole daughter of his house and heart? Mary looked from him to Claire, whose head was bent over a verse she was copying out in her fair handwriting. Byron's eyes were closed, his head back. Mary thought about how Claire would receive this line praising Ada, Byron's legitimate daughter back in England. *And then we parted...*

Determined to spare Claire's feelings, Mary smiled at Byron and reached for a pen. "If you like, I will make a fair copy for you, Albé."

"Thank you," said Byron. "That is most kind of you."

Claire looked daggers at Mary. "I am acting as Albé's copyist," she said. "You should give me that and I will copy it." She held out her hand for the poem.

Byron looked from one woman to another, pleased. "This is amusing," he stated. "Fighting over the honor of correcting my atrocious penmanship? Shall I have Berger bring back the dueling pistols?" He glanced at the window. "It looks to be storming soon.

Pray feel free to use the long drawing room, if you prefer to stay dry."

Ignoring Claire, Mary waved the paper in her hand. "Another canto of Childe Harold?"

"Yes, indeed." Byron looked even more pleased with himself. He gathered up the rest of the pages next to him and handed them to her. "Do feel free to read them."

Mary held them up to the light again.

> *... I HAVE thought*
> *Too long and darkly, till my brain became,*
> *In its own eddy boiling and o'erwrought,*
> *A whirling gulf of phantasy and flame:*
> *And thus, untaught in youth my heart to tame,*
> *My springs of life were poisoned. 'Tis too late!*
> *Yet am I changed; though still enough the same*
> *In strength to bear what time cannot abate,*
> *And feed on bitter fruits ...*

She continued on, line after line of despair and weariness. Her heart sank as his tone grew darker; here was a man succumbing to depression and defeat.

Byron had risen to his feet and now stood with his hands behind him, facing outward. Beyond the window, grey clouds gathered over Mount Jura. "What do you think?" he growled.

"It is ... very different from your previous work," Mary said coolly. *Don't condescend to him. The one thing he wants is honesty.* "This line struck me:"

> *The castled crag of Drachenfels*
> *Frowns o'er the wide and winding Rhine.*

"I fancy we may have passed just such a place on our trip down the Rhine two years ago. Do you not think so, Claire?"

Claire did not look up from the letter she was copying. "It was called Castle Frankenstein, not Drachenfels," she said sullenly.

"Ah, yes," Mary said. "A striking name, to be sure." Her gaze traveled down the page. "And this is striking, too:"

But soon he knew himself the most unfit
Of men to herd with Man; with whom he held
Little in common; untaught to submit
His thoughts to others, though his soul was quelled,
In youth by his own thoughts; still uncompelled,
He would not yield dominion of his mind
To spirits against whom his own rebelled;
Proud though in desolation; which could find
A life within itself, to breathe without mankind.

Mary put the poem down; her hand shook a little. "This is ... very powerful," she said. "The image you raise in the mind, a man wandering alone, cast out, forlorn. Albé, it cannot be you!"

"Can it not?" Byron's voice held an edge; he remained turned away. "We are all of us alone in Nature, Mary. Surely you know that. Shelley does. And he understands what it is to be an outsider."

Mary laid her hand slowly on the table. "Yes. We all do." She drew a stack of blank paper towards her. "If you like, I will copy this out."

Byron turned, his eyes now dark gray as the sky outside. "Thank you," he said quietly. "It is most kind of you."

Claire threw down her pen. "Of course! Give everything over to Mary! Am I not your friend and companion, your confidant? Am I not your partner?"

Byron glared at her, but before he could speak, Mary cut in. "Dearest, perhaps Lord Byron would prefer that you exercise your talents in another direction. Albé, did you not say yesterday that you had bought a book of stories?"

Byron looked from Mary to Claire, a look of understanding dawning on his face. He stepped to the table and took up a small book. "Yes, quite. I would very much like to hear these ghost stories, but they are all in French, which I do not speak. Would you favor us with a reading?" He extended the book to her.

Claire scowled at him, then at Mary. "I cannot read it off so quickly, and besides, there is much to do!"

"All the more reason to start early, then," Byron said firmly. "Come now. Take the book into another room, where our conversation will not disturb you, and practice your translation. Tonight after supper you may read it to us."

"A capital idea!" Mary said. "Do favor us, Sister."

With ill grace, Claire rose and took the book from Byron's hand. "If you wish it," she said, her eyes on his face.

Byron bowed solemnly. "I would be most grateful, my dear."

From the look on Claire's face, it was obvious that she rarely heard this endearment. Flushing slightly, she nodded and went quickly out of the room.

When she was gone, Byron drew in a long breath and let it out. "I feel that I should thank you," he said to Mary. "Claire becomes ... oppressive."

"I perceive a change in you, Albé," Mary said. "Since we returned from Geneva."

Byron ran a hand through his locks. "It's that damned Caro's book. It will ruin her."

"And will it ruin you?"

His smile was bitter. "I doubt it is possible to sully my reputation further than it has been. But she, she has a son and a husband, and they will be affected by society's cruel revenge. You see, she has not only targeted myself, but everyone in our set. Oh, that fiend, she has a gift for grotesquerie. Everyone in Mayfair and Piccadilly will recognize themselves, and cut her dead."

Mary took up a knife to trim a new quill. "And you still care for her that much?"

Byron stared past her at the wall. "I care for them all," he said. "That's the damnation of it."

A smile caught the corner of Mary's mouth. "So you are not, after all, the scoundrel you would have us all believe."

"Believe it, madam. I am all devil on the inside. Do not be misled by what you see."

"I rarely am," she replied. She dipped her pen in the inkwell, drew it across the lip. "All my life, people have judged me by things that are not, well, me."

Byron threw himself into his chair. "Such as?"

"My mother's name. My father's name. Now, Shelley's philosophy."

"Are you not named for your mother, and your father? Are you not even now practicing that philosophy of Shelley's?"

"My name is not me," she said. "As you are not Albé. You are not Childe Harold or your Corsair. You are George Gordon Noel Byron, or maybe you are another name that your mother or sister called you. You are all these names and none of them."

"Perhaps we should dispense with names altogether," Byron drawled. He cocked his head on one side. "That would be a pretty experiment, to write a character who has no name at all. How could that happen, to go through life without a name?"

"A child who dies at birth sometimes is not given a name," Mary said bleakly. "Religious throw away their names when they take the veil. The poor are lucky to have a surname, the rich have half a dozen." She looked up at Byron. "And the fatherless have no name. The nameless are the unluckiest of all. I pray you, Albé, remember that."

Chapter XXIV - Ambush

I perceived in the gloom a figure which stole from behind a clump of trees near me; I stood fixed, gazing intently: I could not be mistaken. A flash of lightning illuminated the object, and discovered its shape plainly to me; its gigantic stature, and the deformity of its aspect, more hideous than belongs to humanity, instantly informed me that it was the wretch, the filthy dæmon, to whom I had given life.

—*Frankenstein*, Volume II, Chapter VI

The night had cleared somewhat, but there was a smell of rain on the breeze. As Mary, Claire and Shelley left the eaves of the Villa Diodati, more clouds scudded across the face of the moon, darkening their path.

They had rounded a path, and the Villa Diodati was out of sight, when Shelley stopped, his whole body rigid. "What's that?"

Mary walked on a step before realizing he had stopped. "What—?"

"Shhh!" Shelley spun on his heel. He peered back along their path, looking past Claire and up towards the meandering path that led back to the Villa. He stepped to one side quickly and stuck both hands into the pockets of his greatcoat. He drew out his pistols; Mary heard him cock them. "Stand back!" he hissed. "There is someone in those trees!"

Mary glanced around. Their path had only just entered a shadow cast by a huge oak. She looked forward into the darkness, backwards up the path, but saw nothing untoward. She strained her ears but heard only the drip of water from the leaves and Claire's soft footfalls behind them.

Shelley took a step forward, his pistols held in front of him. His hands did not shake; his attitude was alert. "Who's there?" he called. Claire gasped, her hand coming up to her mouth. Then she fled towards them, her face white.

"Oh, what is it?" she cried as she reached Mary. Mary flung

an arm around her and shook her head to quiet her. They both watched as Shelley advanced further up the path. Above them the lights of the Maison Chapuis flared and dimmed as fog flowed silently between the house and themselves. Far below, Mary heard the lap-lap of waves against stone. A breeze rustled the leaves overhead.

"Someone's whispering!" Claire said excitedly. "Listen!"

"It's the leaves," Mary said.

"No! I hear them! They're assassins—"

"Shhh!" Shelley glared at them over his shoulder, the shock of hair on his head casting dark shadows on his face. "Be quiet!"

Claire subsided, but Mary could feel her trembling under her arm. Mary wondered if one of them should run back to the Villa Diodati for help. Or down to the Maison. Mary straightened. In any event, any attackers would not find her swooning and afraid. She peered into the shadows.

"Is anyone there?" Shelley called again, pointing his pistols at the empty path. "Show yourself!"

The only answer was a gust of wind that shook more drops from the oak leaves, spattering them. Claire jumped, Mary hugged her more tightly. A thousand years seemed to pass, and Mary felt the cold seeping through her thin dress. Finally, Shelley pointed the pistols skyward. She heard the click-click of the flintlocks as he lowered them. He turned, and his face was pale in the moonlight. "Did you hear them?"

Mary shook her head wordlessly; Claire blurted, "Yes! Whispering! I heard them!"

"No, that was only the—" Mary began.

Shelley motioned them forward. "Quickly. We must get to the house."

Claire shrugged away from Mary and put her hand on Shelley's arm. "It's them, isn't it? The ones who attacked you in Wales?"

Mary remembered Shelley's tale of being awakened one night in his rented cottage, of answering the door and being struck senseless by an assailant. Although the tale had met with skepticism, Mary knew that her lover's revolutionary ideas had made him a target of government spies. She shivered, wondering what brigand with a government's warrant lay in wait for them in the night.

Shelley said nothing, peering into the darkness under the trees. He put one of the pistols back into his pocket and reached out his hand for Mary, ignoring Claire. "Come."

Mary grasped his hand, and he pulled her strongly to him. Holding the other pistol at the ready, he advanced down the path, deeper into the darkness.

A tiny shriek behind them: "Don't leave me!"

Mary glanced back in irritation. "Come along then! Don't dawdle!"

Claire scurried after them, clutching at Shelley's coat.

"Don't hang on my arm," Shelley said tersely, shaking her off with the hand holding the gun. Claire whimpered and scuttled close to Mary.

Huddled together, the three of them walked down the muddy path towards the lighted windows of Maison Chapuis. As they left the shadow of the trees behind, Shelley relaxed a little. "Do you go in, Mary," he said to her quietly. "Lock all the doors and windows. I shall take a tour of the grounds, to make sure we are alone."

Claire clutched at him. "Oh, no! No! You must not go out there alone."

Mary grabbed Claire's hand and enfolded it in her own. Claire's was shaking. "Come now, be calm, sister. There's nothing out there. It was ... an owl, was it not, Shelley?"

He was not looking at her, but rather scanning the vineyard on either side of them, waist high and in full summer leaf. Mary wondered if men were hiding in it. The idea did not alarm her, however; it was as if Claire's fear had sucked all the fear out of her, and she could face whatever danger may lie in wait with calm. Shelley himself showed no fear, only an alert demeanor. His hand holding the pistol did not shake.

They had reached the end of the path and were at the kitchen door at the uphill or rear side of the house. Mary tried the door and found it unlocked, to her chagrin. She held it open for Claire, who darted in and then hovered inside. The smell of ashes and ripe fruit floated out, along with a breath of heated air from the oven. A single rushlight burned in the window. Mary stepped into the doorway, looking back at Shelley.

In the faint moonlight, he was a tall shadow, a footstep, a whisper of movement. A cold gust rattled the leaves of the rhodo-dendron next to the kitchen door. Shelley stalked across the small lawn, his head turning from side to side. Mary remembered his stories of hunting with his father when he grew up. He walked out of sight around a corner. Mary withdrew into the kitchen, closed the door and shot the bolt across it.

Claire stood white-faced in the kitchen, pressed up against the table. Her hands covered her mouth and her eyes were huge in her face. Mary found a candle end and lit it from the rushlight. "Come. We will check through the rest of the house."

"No!" Claire squeaked. "What if there is someone in here? What if someone is hiding?" Her eyes went to the dark doorway leading to the hall.

"Then you stay here and I shall check," said Mary with deter-mination. "No doubt Elise—"

"No! Don't leave me!" Claire's hand shot out and gripped Mary's arm painfully. The candle dipped and bobbed, dancing shadows all over the kitchen.

Mary gently pried her fingers loose. "Walk behind me, then," she said quietly. She led the way into the hallway, and after a mo-ment her stepsister followed, her shoes silent on the hardwood floor.

The pantry was empty, as well as the downstairs drawing room and utility room. Mary led the way upstairs. First she turned to the nursery, where a light shone under the door. She eased the door open; Elise sat drowsing in a rocking chair beside William's cradle. Mary peeped in and saw her son sleeping peacefully on his side, a little milky bubble at the corner of his mouth swelling and fading as he breathed. She backed out of the room, almost step-ping on Claire, and shut the door. A quick examination showed the rest of the bedrooms, and her workroom, to be empty of intruders.

"See?" she said quietly to Claire. "There's nothing to be afr—"

Something banged downstairs, and Claire screamed and leaped up. "Oh my God!"

"Mary?" called Shelley's voice from downstairs. "Are you there?"

Mary leaned over the railing of the staircase. "We are up here, love. All is well."

Shelley's head appeared at the bottom of the stairs, his hair haloed in the light of his lantern. "Nothing stirring without. Perhaps it was a false alarm."

Claire, trembling beside Mary, shook her head vehemently. "No! You scared them away, that's all! Oh, I am so afraid they will be back!"

Shelley chuckled. "Two little mice," he teased. "I shall build a fire, and we shall have light and stories."

Mary forbore to remind him that she had not been the one afraid. Instead, she led Claire back downstairs and hung up their cloaks in the hallway. Shelley was checking each of the windows as she came into the downstairs drawing room. A fire struggled on the stones, and Mary knelt to encourage it. Claire stood in the center of the room, twisting her hands together.

"Do you think it was bandits?" she asked. "Or perhaps someone sent to kill us?"

"No," said Mary sharply. "I think it was wind and shadow."

"Oh, more than that," Shelley said, his smile fading. "I am certain I heard someone behind me."

Claire said nothing, her hands coving her mouth again. Mary poked the fire. "I did not hear anything, love," she said firmly.

"Do you think it was .. a ghost?" Claire whispered. "Or ... or a demon?"

"Not a demon," Shelley said seriously, considering the question. He strode to Claire and took her hands. "Why, you're shivering, my dear! Come, sit by the fire and have some brandy." Tenderly, he led Claire to a chair before the fire and arranged a shawl around her shoulders. "We shall all have some brandy. Mary?"

"A little," she said. "We need more wood."

"I shall fetch it directly," Shelley said, striding out of the room. His boots echoed on the floor, and they heard the door open and shut.

"Claire, I do wish you would contrive to restrain your fears," Mary said quietly. "You set Shelley off when you shriek as you did on the path."

"Not all of us are made of ice," Claire said. "I have too great a sensibility to pretend otherwise. I feel things, you know. Especially those things of the dark world."

Mary poked at a log more forcefully than necessary. "I really have no patience with this nonsense," she said, her mouth firm. "You know there is no dark world. It is only the superstition brought on by the corruption of our intellect by religious cant. Use your reason, Claire."

The front door opened, and a cold breeze gusted into the room. Shelley came through with an armload of wood, banging the door behind him. He dumped the wood on the hearth and stood again, shrugging off his greatcoat. "It is coming up to storm," he said. "A fine, noisy one!" His eyes shone with excitement.

Mary put a log on the fire. The flames leaped up and she settled onto her knees a little way back from it.

"I shall scream, I know it!" Claire said, hugging herself.

"I'm sure of it, also," Mary said dryly.

She caught an amused sideways glance from Shelley, who strode to the sideboard. "Here's a spirit more suited to the night," he said, pouring brandy. He handed Claire a glass of brandy, offered Mary another. She took it and held it in her hands. He flung himself onto the floor in front of the fire, his boots almost in the flames. He flung his wind-tousled hair impatiently out of his eyes. "Here's to spirits dark and light," he said ominously, raising his glass.

"Do you think it was a spirit you saw?" Claire whispered. She inched closer to Shelley.

"I thought you said you did not see anything," Mary said.

"I didn't. I thought I heard something on the path behind us."

"Most likely it was one of Albé's awful hounds," Mary said. The fumes of the brandy, warmed by her hand, rose to her nose. She inhaled. "Or perhaps a fox, hunting the owl. Surely it is ... an exaggeration to make it more than that."

Shelley laughed. "My little Dormouse has nerves of steel. Were I ever to go into battle, my love, I would want you beside me."

"What did it say to you?" Claire asked, ignoring Mary. She sipped more brandy.

"I thought I heard it say my name." Shelley frowned into the fire.

Cold crept over Mary. "Your name?" She sat down next to Shelley, gathering her skirts around her. "Are you certain it was not ... an agent? Like the one in Wales?"

"They follow me everywhere," Shelley said darkly. He stared into the fire, his eyes wide. "I know one was following me all through England last winter. I thought that here, away from London, we could lose them, but they are very hounds of hell."

"Oh, Shelley!" Claire breathed. "Like the one who attacked you in your house? We must call a gendarme!"

Mary looked sharply at her stepsister. "I pray you will not continue in this way," she said. "We are safe now. Let us discuss something else."

But Shelley was not listening. "Perhaps it was a doppelgänger," he said, staring into the fire.

"What is that?" asked Claire.

"A double. Sort of like a twin, only not born to the same mother." Shelley sipped at his glass, one hand idly stroking Mary's hair. "To see it is a harbinger of death."

Mary felt a tiny shiver go through her. It was true that Shelley was hated for his politics, his atheism. Absurd to think that anyone would resent them enough to do him harm and yet ... it was true that he had been attacked in Wales, knocked senseless in Keswick. Whether it was a failed robbery or an act stemming from more sinister political motives, still he had been hurt. Her fingers curled into a fist on his chest, her jaw tightening. The thought that someone would hurt her gentle lover enraged her. She was small, she thought, but even a dormouse can defend its own.

"Let us have something more cheerful," she said. "Shelley, what have you written today?"

He shrugged and looked at Claire. "What has Albé written today?"

Claire held out her hands to the fire. "I recall one passage:

> *Eternal spirit of the chainless mind!*
> *Brightest in dungeons, Liberty! thou art,*
> *For there thy habitation is the heart,*
> *The heart which love of thee alone can bind.*

"Eternal spirit of the chainless mind," Shelley repeated slowly. "A good image. From a heart that loves liberty."

"Yes!" Claire sat up abruptly. "You do understand, don't you, Shelley! Byron loves liberty, just as you do! You know his heart is one with ours!"

Mary sighed. When would Claire abandon her fantasies? "Claire, he does not love you. He may love liberty, and poetry, and the chainless mind, but he does not love you."

"How can you be so heartless!" Claire cried. "Can a heart so pure, a mind so attached to liberty and freedom, be as cold as you imagine? Or is it that you confuse your cold heart with his warm one?"

Mary sat up. "You do yourself no good by this," she said. Her hair had come down. She put up a hand to re-arrange it, but Shelley caught her hand. She left it in his as her hair fell to her shoulders. "Claire, you want him to love you as ... as Shelley and I love one another. But it will never be. Albé is not Shelley—"

"As I am not you! Yes, I understand!" Claire got to her feet, her face red with anger. "Yes, you need not repeat yourself. I know how much you want Shelley for yourself. As if any man could be chained like a dog! Albé does love me! He does, and I will show you!"

Shelley propped himself on his elbows. "Claire, dearest, don't put yourself into a pet like this. Come lie down—"

"No!" Claire caught up a throw from the divan behind her. "I won't stay here with you. Mary wants you for herself. Mary must get what Mary wants!" With that bitter taunt, she swept the throw around her and stamped out of the room. In a moment, they heard the front door slam.

Shelley rolled to his side, getting to his feet. "I had better go after her—"

Mary put a hand on his arm. "No, love. Let her be. She will go to Byron."

"Alone? I must go with her!"

Mary smiled. "I pity the scoundrel who accosts my sister in her present mood. She is likely to kill him."

Shelley caressed her face. "Is it true, what she said? You want me all to yourself? Are you so selfish and backward as all that?" His tone softened the words, but they fell like a blow on her heart. She looked away.

"It is only that you seem so much more involved with Claire and Albé these days. You hardly have time for me."

He tangled his fist in her long golden hair and tugged her downward to his mouth. "I have time for my Maie, always. My life is yours."

His kiss, as usual, sent her thoughts flying. He tasted of brandy, and the warmth of him seeped all through her in ways the fire never could. His arms came up around her, he pressed her to him—

From upstairs, a wail.

Shelley broke the kiss and let his arms fall to his sides. With an ironic chuckle, he said, "We are doomed to constant interruption, beloved."

Mary rolled off of him and stood. Already she heard footsteps on the stairs as Elise brought her charge down. "Be glad he slept as long as he did," she said. "Soon he will be sleeping through the night."

"And we will not," Shelley said.

Mary let a small smile curl on her lips, as she thought of white linen sheets, thunder, and Shelley in the night.

Chapter XXV - Claire's Fury

"Shall each man," cried he, "find a wife for his bosom, and each beast have his mate, and I be alone? I had feelings of affection, and they were requited by detestation and scorn. Man! you may hate; but beware! your hours will pass in dread and misery, and soon the bolt will fall which must ravish from you your happiness for ever. Are you to be happy while I grovel in the intensity of my wretchedness?

—*Frankenstein*, Volume III, Chapter III

A door slammed, someone pounded up the stairs.

"Claire." Mary's voice was grim. Shelley slid quickly out of the bed and pulled on his trousers. Mary found her night rail and struggled into it, silently damning her step-sister's usual awful timing.

"Oh, damn that man. Damn, damn, damn!" Claire was sobbing into Shelley's chest when Mary, puffing, finally caught up with them in Claire's room.

"Here, sit down," Shelley said, guiding Claire to sit on the bed. "Dry your eyes." He searched in his waistcoat for a handkerchief in vain. Giving up on his search, Shelley pulled his shirt out of his waistband and used the tail to dab tenderly at Claire's swollen eyes. "My dear, compose yourself. Tell me what's wrong."

"Oh, God, that man will kill me," she wailed.

Mary winced. "You will wake the neighbors."

"I don't care!" Claire cried. "Let them know what a ... a monster he is! Unfeeling, uncaring monster!"

"Whatever has he said now?" Shelley asked.

"Nothing! He said nothing! He did not need to!" Claire flung up her head dramatically. "He told Fletcher to deny me!"

Shelley frowned. "I don't understand."

"Nor did I, until I pushed past him into the villa," Claire said. She sniffed, and wiped her nose on Shelley's shirt tail.

He sat down beside her on the bed and put his arm around her shoulders. "Tell me everything."

Mary, feeling ignored, sat quietly in a chair.

"He was with that wretched chambermaid!" Claire cried. Her voice rang off the stones of the small terrace. "The cruel, unfeeling monster that he is! I went up to his room. I heard him inside. I wanted to ... to surprise him. He sometimes likes it when I surprise him." She sniffed again. She looked up at Shelley, her eyes full of tears. "He was with the maid! That fat, freckled one who clears up after supper!"

Shelley chuckled and patted her hand where it lay on his knee. "Oh, now, really, Claire! Is that something to get upset about?"

Men would never understand, Mary thought. It just was not in Shelley's nature to lay claim to another, but women, who had the care and feeding of the young, formed stronger attachments. She was sure of it.

"How can you say that! She's ... she's old!" Claire's eyes were alive with anger, her cheeks pink. "She must be thirty if she's a day!"

Mary smiled bitterly. "A veritable ancient," she said quietly. "Why, his lordship himself is a dotard of eight and twenty!"

Claire jumped to her feet. "You are merely jealous!" she cried. "You care nothing for how he rends my heart!"

"But if that is so, why do you pursue him?" Shelley asked, puzzled. "Are you not in agreement with Godwin's teachings? That two persons should not remain together out of stale custom or habit, but only in mutual love?"

"But he does love me, I know it!" Claire said defiantly. "It is only that he cannot bring himself to say it!"

"Which is why, naturally, he takes his servant to bed and denies you the very door," Mary said dryly. "I fear there is a flaw in your argument."

Claire burst into tears. "You wretch. You have everything, I have nothing, and yet you mock me! How can you? Oh, how can you? I want to die!"

"No, you merely want to wake the neighbors with one of your exhibitions," Mary snapped. "Next time, hire a brass band so that they may hear you across the lake!"

"Mary!" said Shelley, shocked. He started to rise, but in that moment, a white-faced Claire snatched a vase of flowers from the bedside table and hurled it at Mary. Only the dim light and Claire's agitation saved Mary, as the pot flew wide and shattered on the wall behind her.

Mary sat without moving, her gaze fixed on the other woman. "Violence is the last resort of fools," she said.

Shelley stepped between them. "No, no, we must not have this. Come, Claire, dry your eyes. I am sure Byron will love you just as much in the morning. You must resist this possessive streak. I tell you, it is only the custom of corrupt society that makes you feel this way."

Mary bit her lips to keep back her retort. Shelley was right in most things, but he had a perennial blind spot where Claire was concerned.

Sobbing, Claire clutched at Shelley's shirt. "Oh, Shelley. Oh Shelley, if only you would ... Oh, Shelley."

Shelley smiled and patted her fondly. "I think it would be best if you went to bed."

Claire looked up at him, awash. "Oh, Shelley, will you not—"

"No, he will not," Mary said strongly. "Claire, you are perfectly capable of coming down from your high state all by yourself. Shelley has better things to do."

Shelley frowned at Mary, but Claire pulled away from him. "Oh, I think you are horrid! Both of you! Neither of you cares if I die!" She turned and flung herself face down on the bed.

Mary stepped out onto the landing, gesturing for Shelley to follow. Shelley thrust his hands under his arms, hugging himself. "I don't understand your attitude. How—"

"Oh, be silent!" The words hissed out of her. "How can you stand her posturings, her temper? How can you be so kind to someone so thoughtless of others?"

In moments of emotional crisis, Shelley became quiet and

very honest. "Because she is like me," he said. "Because I recognize the restless soul in her."

"So you, you love her? You would want a ... three to a bed as well?" Mary's cheeks were hot, her words more so. She hated herself for saying these things, words that gave the lie to what she believed. Or thought she believed. "You would want a ménage, like Polidori says?"

Shelley shrugged. "Why not? You know we should not confine ourselves to one partner, if we so desire. My only objection to Claire is that she is being unfair to Albé. He is acting in accord with his nature. If he were to truly practice fidelity, would he not go back to his wife?"

"That's not what I meant! Oh, why don't you understand me?"

He looked at her, and in the half-light from the candles, his eyes were dark, the dark blue of the lake under a midnight sun. "I do understand you, Mary. Better than you think." He held out a hand. "Come. Let us go back to our room."

He reached into the room to close the door, but Claire rose from the bed and flung herself at Shelley, weeping. "No, no you cannot! You cannot leave me like this?"

Shelley, helpless, had one arm around Mary and the other around Claire. "My dear, what can I do? I cannot make Byron, or any man, love you. I cannot make anyone love anyone else."

Claire, clutching her middle, sank down on her bed, then cast herself upon it. Shelley leaned forward as if to lay a comforting hand on her, but Mary stepped away. He hesitated, then followed her back to their bedroom.

Long after Shelley had fallen asleep with one bare arm across her, Mary heard Claire weeping.

Chapter XXVI - The Somnambulist

> I passed the night wretchedly. Sometimes my pulse beat so
> quickly and hardly, that I felt the palpitation of every artery;
> at others, I nearly sank to the ground through languor and
> extreme weakness. Mingled with this horror, I felt the bitter-
> ness of disappointment: dreams that had been my food and
> pleasant rest for so long a space, were now become a hell to
> me.
>
> —*Frankenstein*, Volume III, Chapter VIV

Mary woke suddenly, with the impression of a fading shriek in
her ears. Had she heard someone screaming? Light flared
fitfully at the window as the storm approached from across the
lake. She rolled to her side, feeling for Shelley, but she was alone
in the bed.

"Shelley?" she whispered.

"I'm here," he said hoarsely. He had pulled on his pantaloons
but had not buttoned the fall; dark hair arrowed downward from
his stomach. He stood silhouetted against the window, his pistols
in his hands. "I hear them. They are outside the door."

They. Mary felt a chill go over her skin, even though she was
cocooned in warm sheets. "It is only the storm. I am sure of—"

A thump against the door. Mary clutched the sheets to her
chin. She heard the ominous click of the pistol cocking. Could it be?
Had footpads, agents of the Tory government entered the house?

Another thump, and a dragging sound. A whimper.

"It's Claire," Mary said with relief.

Shelley pointed his pistols at the ceiling and eased the ham-
mers down. "Go to her." His voice was calm.

Mary dragged her feet out from under the covers. The floor
was cold under her bare soles. Hurriedly slipping her night rail over
her head, she took the duvet off the foot of the bed and wrapped it
around her shoulders. She glanced at Shelley, and at that moment

lightning flared behind him. She saw his face, serene, his torso bare in the moonlight. She smiled inwardly and opened the door.

Facing her, her eyes distant and vacant, stood Claire. She was completely naked, her long dark hair falling over her breast. Mary almost cried out in alarm at the blank and empty look on her features. It was like looking at a ghost. "Claire?"

Her stepsister made no sound, but turned slowly and walked towards the stairs. She heard the cold sound of metal on wood as Shelley tossed his pistols onto the bedside table.

"She will do herself an injury!" Shelley hissed, and strode past her. "Claire! Stop!"

Claire showed no sign of hearing him, but continued slowly to the head of the stairs. In complete silence, she began descending. Shelley was close behind her, hovering. He glanced back at Mary. "Bring a robe for her."

Mary pulled the duvet tighter around herself. "Perhaps if you woke her...?"

"No. It would be futile, perhaps dangerous." Notwithstanding, Shelley laid a hand on Claire's shoulder. She paid no attention, but walked out from under it, still descending.

Mary started down the stairs as well. "She can hear us, can she not? Claire!" she called sharply.

"Don't!"

"But she has never done this before," Mary said.

"It must be the shock of seeing Albé with that other woman," Shelley said. He glanced up at Mary; they were nearly to the bottom of the staircase, with the naked and oblivious Claire leading them. "Could it be her ... her condition?" he asked helplessly.

"Pregnancy has never affected me thus," said Mary. "Perhaps we should consult Polidori."

Shelley grimaced. "I doubt he knows anything of use. Look, she is headed for the door! Some strange power moves her!"

Mary doubted it. Claire seemed to have no trouble negotiating a house in complete darkness that she had only lived in for a couple of weeks. She suspected this was some charade on her step-sister's part, but to what end? Was she really that desperate for attention? For Shelley's attention? And yet, if that was her aim, Mary had to admit it was working. Shelley followed her down the stairs like a shadow.

Undeterred by the conversation around her, Claire walked calmly towards the front door. Passing under the central chandelier, she carefully unbolted the door and opened it. Cold air gusted in; her hair fanned out behind her.

"Shelley, she will catch the grippe!" Mary hurried forward, unwinding the duvet from about her shoulders. "We must keep her inside!"

"It is useless," Shelley said, following her out.

Unhappily, Mary followed both of them into the lower terrace in front of the house. Above, clouds hid the moon, and fog shrouded the shore of the lake below. The cold sound of water sloshing on the shore reached her ears, along with the soft sound of leafy branches tossed by the wind. Rain gusted against her face, then stopped. Shelley's white torso was her only guide; she followed him carefully down the cobbled path. Fog closed in behind her; she hurried so as not to lose sight of him.

"Where is she?"

"Here," came his voice. Shelley had come to a stop. Claire stood before him, teetering on the breakfront wall. Her hair blew in the wind, but she seemed calm, her skin white in the darkness, her form seeming to shimmer and waver as fog drifted past.

"The water is directly below her," Shelley whispered. "Give me the blanket. I will attempt to catch her. I do not want to startle her, lest she fall. She may cry out; be prepared." Mary unwound herself from the duvet and handed it to him. Cold licked her skin. He stepped forward softly.

Mary huddled herself, arms clasped, watching. Claire stood unmoving. Just as Shelley reached her, his foot slipped on a wet stone and made a soft sound. Claire's head jerked, then she caught herself and returned her head swiftly to its former position. The gesture was almost too quick to see, but it was enough to tell Mary that Claire was wide awake, alert to Shelley's movements. This was just another of her attention-seeking hoaxes.

Then Shelley darted forward with the duvet in his hands. Swiftly he caught her up in it, winding it around her. She shrieked and thrashed, then subsided as if fainting. Shelley caught her up easily into his arms and turned back towards the house. Claire's head hung down over his arm, her hair trailing in the wind.

"She wakened, but fainted," Shelley said. "Much as I have done in the past. Let us pray the shock has not been too great for her nerves." He turned and walked back up the path. Mary followed him, her feet numb and slipping on the stones.

Inside the house, Shelley mounted the stairs two at a time. Mary hurried after him, and arrived in time to see him tucking Claire into the center of their bed. "You get in on that side," he was saying. "I will get in on this. We must warm her up."

"We should build a fire," she began.

Shelley shook his head. "No time. The chill may have settled in her bones. It is imperative that the vital force be recalled to her, and she must be warm."

"We should send word to Byron," Mary said.

"I think it would be most unwise to disturb him at this hour."

From the corner of her eye, she saw a brief twitch in Claire's hand where it lay on the cover. Once again, proof that Claire could hear and understand every word. Mary felt irritation at this childish pretense.

"My goodness, her sleep is deep," she said. "Perhaps we should prick her with a needle, to see if she wakes from her faint."

Shelley, who had turned his back to slide out of his pantaloons again, now turned a scowling face to her. "Come, Mary. This is tiresome of you. Your sister needs help, not pinpricks." He climbed into the bed on the other side of Claire, naked against her.

Reluctantly, Mary lifted the covers and slid in. Her sister's flesh was cold as marble. Still, there was a tension in Claire's body that told Mary, veteran of many nights wedged into a narrow bed with her sister, that Claire was awake and shamming.

The bed creaked under Shelley's weight as he climbed in on the other side. He cast an arm across the blankets covering Claire and put her head against his chest. "She will be all right in the morning," he said confidently.

"Why has she done this?" Mary was speaking as much to her conscious sister as to Shelley. "Why now?"

"I spotted laudanum on the table beside her bed as I came past the door," Shelley said. "No doubt she hoped it would help her sleep. This business with Albé, it is distressing to her."

"I would never have called her weak-minded," Mary said. "I have never known her to take laudanum to sleep."

Shelley wrapped both arms around Claire and shifted in the bed, so that the young woman was wedged between himself and Mary. "Many things are changing," he murmured. "Anything is possible."

Soon, Mary felt Claire's breathing change, and felt her body relax in sleep. On the other side of her, Shelley's heavy breathing changed to light snores.

Mary lay awake, unable to sleep, watching the moonlight creep through the shutters before the overcast shrouded it into a dim memory. She remembered her home in London, on Skinner Street near Clerkenwell. She thought of her father's library, with her mother's portrait over the desk. Her thoughts became darker as she remembered coming into the room one afternoon to find her father rigid and unresponsive, in one of his first fits of catalepsy. She thought of Claire's blank expression as she walked down the stairs. Was it possible Claire had somehow developed the same cataleptic disorder as William Godwin? But how could that be, when Claire was not even related to him by blood? From this question, Mary's thoughts drifted to questions about inheritance, and how much children took from their fathers.

Round and round her thought circled, restless, coming back always to one theme: her father. Why, after raising her to believe that marriage was a trap and that freedom of individual choice was paramount, had he cast her out and abandoned her? Had he seen some flaw in her, some imperfection? Mary knew her father had spent his life raising her to be the image of her mother, and she was content with that. To be the mirror of her strong and beautiful mother, to be created and fortified in that image, was much to her liking. But her father had turned his face from her, leaving her cold and alone.

Separated from her lover by her sister, Mary lay alone and wakeful long into the night.

Part Three:

June 16, 1816

Chapter XXVII - The New Man

> He had come forth from the hands of God a perfect crea-
> ture, happy and prosperous, guarded by the especial care of
> his Creator; he was allowed to converse with, and acquire
> knowledge from, beings of a superior nature: but I was
> wretched, helpless, and alone.
>
> —*Frankenstein,* Volume III, Chapter VII

Arriving early at the Villa Diodati the next morning, Mary
found Polidori on the sofa. His pale face, sweaty brow and
disarranged cravat told her he was in some distress; his naked foot
nested in a mound of bandages told her why.

"Let me help," she said, advancing toward him.

He held up a hand. "Pray do not disturb yourself, Mrs. Shelley," he said. "I can manage well enough."

Mary eyed the torn strips of sheeting that lay crumpled on
the floor. "I fear not, doctor. Do allow me to bind up your foot, lest
it begin to swell. You may supervise."

Before he could protest further, she knelt on the floor next to
him and gathered the strips of cloth together.

Polidori let his head fall back; his undone cravat revealed his
strong neck. He closed his eyes. "I am indebted to you, madam, for
your kindness."

"You should supervise me," Mary said. "I would not wish to
bind it wrong. Is there no one to help you? Albé seemed to be
intent on providing you with pillows and every comfort." This last
was said a little ironically; Mary hoped to lighten the young man's
sour mood.

A bitter smile crept across his face, though his eyes remained closed. "His lordship discovered in himself a particular
revulsion for any treatment of a twisted foot," he said. "I can
understand his reluctance, but it still left me fumbling about by
myself, I fear."

Mary carefully wrapped bandages around Polidori's foot and ankle. "Did he not think to call for another physician?"

"I begged him not to," Polidori said. "My reputation is shaky enough in this neighborhood, but to be thought a physician who cannot heal himself would be the very outside of enough." He hissed suddenly and clenched his fist.

"I am so sorry!" Mary drew back in dismay. "I am hurting you."

"Quite the contrary," Polidori said. "Your touch is quite soothing. The fault lies in the joint itself. I fear that the anterior talofibular ligament has suffered a severe strain. If you will be sure to bind the foot in a flatter position—yes. Thank you. That will keep it strong while I heal."

Winding the bandage around his ankle, Mary said, "How long will that require?"

Polidori opened his eyes and smiled slightly. "Alas, I fear that I will not be able to dance at Madame Odier's tomorrow night, as I planned. It would be best to reverse that crossed bandage—yes. Just like that. Do you waltz, Mrs. Shelley?"

Mary kept her eyes on his foot. "No, I do not. But it looks quite ... vigorous."

"I would be glad to teach you, once this ankle is healed. It is quite acceptable nowadays for married women to dance the waltz."

Mary frowned. "You forget, sir. I am neither married, nor likely to be invited to a ball." She glanced up and met Polidori's stricken look.

"I ... I ... forgive me, I pray. I did not mean to be insulting. I only thought you would enjoy it, and sought to allay any fear you might have of ... of ..." Polidori appeared to be lost, and faltered. He lay propped on his elbows, looking miserable.

Mary smiled. "Any fears I might have of impropriety, per-haps? Oh, we are not concerned with impropriety. And in any case, anything Shelley and I might do in the way of dancing would call forth no remarks at all, so long as we are in the company of Lord Byron."

Polidori grinned, showing white teeth. "Very true, ma'am. Very true. Please pull the bandage a trifle more securely, if you will. Yes, that will do nicely."

Mary tied off the bandage and stood. "It is a pity the healing will take so long. If only one could speed it up somehow."

Polidori pushed himself to a sitting position, gingerly lifting his injured foot onto the stack of cushions. "Or replace the foot altogether. I would like a new foot, one that was stronger and more flexible. Imagine how much his lordship would pay to have his club foot replaced with a normal one."

Mary gathered up the unused bandages and began to roll them. "Or soldiers injured in a war could gain a new arm or leg. Perhaps some day science will be able to graft on a new limb, as one grafts on a new peach tree limb."

Polidori fidgeted with his cravat, trying to neaten it. "A novel idea, to be sure! Perhaps we could graft on extra limbs, so that we could have four arms and hands instead of two! Tell me, how would Mr. Shelley embrace such an idea? Would that fit in with his idea of the 'perfectibility of man'?"

"Shelley would probably want to improve on the basic design," Mary said dryly. "Perhaps we could add springs to the new leg, to facilitate jumping off of balconies."

Polidori gazed moodily at his bandaged foot. "I did so at his lordship's urging; otherwise I am not generally given to ... to demonstrations of this sort. Perhaps next time Mr. Shelley will apply a spark to me from his Leyden jar, and I will jump more readily."

Mary closed her eyes, remembering the twitching leg stumps of the chicken galvanized by her lover. "Think of what we might accomplish with such science," she said. "Perhaps we could revive the dead."

Polidori stared at her. "You would so intrude upon the Creator's prerogative?"

Mary smiled slightly. "If the Creator does not intend for us to use science, why did he put it in the world? No, Doctor, I will not allow my mind to be corrupted by the lies of religion, which uses fear to bind men to it. The truly free man will be a man of science."

"Or a man made by science, according to you," he said. He shifted restlessly, seeking a better position for his foot.

"Have you eaten?" Mary said.

"Only a light collation," Polidori said. "I cannot persuade anyone in this house to bring me any meat, even when I offer to pay for it myself."

"Perhaps a strong broth? Or tea?"

"Meat. I offer no offense, Mrs. Shelley, but truly, a man must have meat or he will fall into a decline and ruin his health."

"Perhaps the fluid you need is of a heavenly variety. I can fetch Shelley's Leyden jar directly."

Polidori shuddered. "I beg you, no. The demonstration two nights ago was disturbing. Did you not find it so?"

Mary stared past him. "But to return the dead to life, would that not be wonderful? Would it not mend a thousand thousand broken lives, broken hearts?" She looked not at the window, but into the haunted past, and a pale, still body, so tiny and vulnerable, so cold in her arms. "It is so long before the mind can persuade itself that one whom we saw every day, and whose very existence appeared a part of our own, can have departed for ever—that the brightness of a beloved eye can have been extinguished, and the sound of a voice so familiar, and dear to the ear, can be hushed, never more to be heard. These are the reflections of the first days; but when the lapse of time proves the reality of the evil, then the actual bitterness of grief commences. And for some, it never dies." She looked away from the window, and caught Polidori's startled gaze. "You have heard of my mother, perhaps?"

Polidori half-bowed from his sitting position. "Who has not heard of the famed defender of the rights of women, Mary Woll-stonecraft?"

"Do you know, my father keeps her portrait above his study," she said wistfully. "It is his shrine, his altar. Every day he writes, under her gaze. I have seen him staring at it with tears in his eyes. I think he speaks to it, now and again."

"I perceive that your father has a second wife?" Polidori said cautiously.

Mary nodded. "He married Jane Clairmont, Claire's mother, to provide us with a mother."

"So you are half-sisters?"

"By no means. Claire, who was called Jane then, and Charles, my stepbrother, were from a previous marriage."

Polidori tilted his head to one side, observing. "You were unhappy with the second wife? How old were you?"

"My mother died within eleven days of my birth; my father remarried as soon as possible thereafter, to assure that someone could raise me. It ... it was not a felicitous choice."

"Is this why you abjure marriage so?"

Mary smiled. "No. It is my father's teaching, from his earliest days, that marriage is only enforced prostitution. Oh, I have offended you!"

Polidori struggled to control his features. "No, no," he said hastily—and, Mary knew, untruthfully. "I am sure he has the most, er , high-minded ideals. But is it not hard on you, on your babe, to be in so ... irregular an arrangement?" He pressed her hand. "I will not burden you with unwelcome sentiments, but do consider, dear Mrs. Shelley, what the future will hold. For you, for your son, what will be the outcome? How will he grow up in society?"

Mary removed her hand from his. "Shelley has altered his will to provide for us. And when he comes into his inheritance, we shall live freely and openly as we please."

"So your principles wait on death," Polidori said. "To live on post-obits, is this the utilitarian philosophy your father espouses?"

Mary felt her face grow hot. "You disapprove, of course. You do not understand."

Polidori again struggled to sit up straight. "It is not for me to disapprove or approve," he said. "But it seems to me that this theory of open love, or free love, or what have you, is a very good idea for men, but not for women."

Mary, troubled, looked down at her hands.

Polidori leaned near. "You know that I speak the truth. You

know what they are, these noblemen. They are raised to think only of themselves, to consider only themselves. Mr. Shelley appears to love all mankind—in the abstract. And I have observed his generosity, but it sometimes appears to me that he lives with his head inside a glass bowl, that he does not really understand the causes of the misery around us."

Mary said hotly, "You do not understand! He understands, better than most, the misery of the poor and oppressed! He has suffered for his beliefs! He has been hounded from place to place by vile persons, he has been persecuted. His own father, as corrupt a member of the privileged caste as I can imagine, cut him off for daring to live by his own principles. He was cast out of Oxford for espousing atheism."

"I am aware—"

Mary rose, gathering her skirts. "I have work to do with Albé. Pray excuse me, Doctor." She swept from the room, seething.

But under the anger, she felt fear.

Chapter XXVIII - The Feast of Reason

Oh, that I had forever remained in my native wood, nor known nor felt beyond the sensations of hunger, thirst, and heat! Of what a strange nature is knowledge! It clings to the mind, when it has once seized on it, like a lichen on the rock. I wished sometimes to shake off all thought and feeling; but I learned that there was but one means to overcome the sensation of pain, and that was death— a state which I feared yet did not understand.

—*Frankenstein*, Volume III, Chapter V

As if the previous evening had worn them all out, the households settled into a quiet, unchallenging day. In the forenoon, Mary and Claire copied out more of Byron's verses, or wrote in their journals. Byron and Shelley took the boat out, despite the unseasonably cold day. Polidori remained on the downstairs sofa, reading a book of Italian poetry and scribbling notes. Later in the day, Mary traipsed back down to the Maison Chapuis to feed William and to interview a candidate for the position of cook. This individual was so completely lacking in talent or the ability to speak English that she returned in a glum mood to the Diodati.

The day grew ominously dark as it wore on. Mary considered whether it would not be better for her and Claire to return to the Maison and stay there, but Claire demurred.

"I must be here when Albé returns," she said firmly. "Return if you wish, but I will stay for dinner. You know we have a standing invitation."

Mary did not want to stay, but the fact that they still had no cook of their own made it a moot point.

Shortly after noon, Byron and Shelley returned with the mail; there was nothing from Mary's father. Byron took Claire off to one of the bedrooms, and Shelley engaged Polidori in a game of chess. Mary sat alone in the big drawing room, surrounded by books, letters, and scraps of poetry. She put her chin on her hands and stared out into the gathering storm. She felt restless and ill at ease, but put it down to worry over Claire and her state.

As the sun set, Fletcher and the chambermaid came in with lights, and then called her to an unusually early supper. Once more, bread, soup and potatoes were the order of the day. Though the hour was not much advanced, the chambermaid went around lighting candles as the sky outside grew dark with clouds. Thunder rumbled ominously across the sky as Fletcher served the soup.

Byron and Shelley were arguing over the nature of Man, apparently continuing an argument from their boat trip that morning.

"Man is born free, by nature," Shelley said, munching bread. Crumbs scattered over his plate, where the remains of a Welsh rarebit and a quiche lay mangled.

"But everywhere in chains," Byron said, "Yes, yes, I have read my Rousseau. And you know my opinion of him."

"Then if you know him, you know of his belief that man is naturally good. It is only through the pernicious influence of human society and its institutions that he becomes corrupted."

Polidori signaled to Fletcher to bring him a platter from the sideboard. "And is this not the same Rousseau who abandoned his own children? I read that he lived openly with a mistress—"

Byron laughed. "Remember who sits at this table," he said. "You will find no condemnation of that conduct here."

Polidori flushed a bit. "And his dereliction concerning his own offspring? He forced his mistress to give them to foundling hospitals. Is that the perfectible man?"

Byron set down his fork. "You speak pointedly, physician, of abandoned offspring. Have you some remark to make?" His voice was soft, his tone dangerous.

"He speaks of Jean-Jacques Rousseau," Mary said sharply, heading him off. "There is no need to take such a remark personally, Albé. Rousseau is quite eloquent when it comes to describing the blessings of a state of nature, but nothing could be more unnatural than his 'natural man'."

Shelley looked at her quizzically. "Truly? But surely you agree that Rousseau's description of the unfortunate effects of society on the natural man are substantive?"

"Substantive, but perhaps disingenuous. He seems not even to have understood how criminal his actions were." Mary glanced sharply at Byron, but noticed that Claire was staring down at her plate, her face pale. "His capacity for self-deception, though vast, is only typical of Man."

"How do you mean?" Byron said. "I find this critique, from a woman no less, fascinating."

"As well, perhaps, you should. As a man, you are granted freedoms and liberties we females are denied, and all because of ignorance and superstition. Your idea of 'freedom' is sometimes literally death to us and those we love."

Shelley looked shocked. "Mary!"

She reached over and patted his hand. "Dearest, you know I agree with much of what we both have read of Rousseau. We agree that the nature of Man is basically good, that education is the root of social good. But in his personal life, he fell well short of those ideals for which we often praise him."

"He took them away from her." Claire's voice arrested them all. Fervid, low, fraught with meaning, she raised her eyes from her plate to stare at Byron. Yet it was as if she stared through him, into some other room or place. "His natural instinct, as a father, should have been to protect them. He should have protected their mother. He should have cared for them."

"But she was his mistress, not his wife," said Polidori.

The other four stared at him until he dropped his gaze to his plate.

"Claire is right," Mary said. "Our first duty is to render those to whom we give birth, wise, virtuous and happy, as far as in us lies. Rousseau failed in this. The distortion of intellect that blinded him to the first duties of life made him an example among men for self-inflicted sufferings."

"Would you have had him marry his mistress, then?" Shelley asked, squinting at her over a wineglass.

"Oh, I am content that marriage, as we agree, is but slavery writ small. As a connection between men and women, it is nothing but chains and agony."

Byron lifted his glass. "Hear, hear!" he said, and tossed back the wine.

"But Rousseau's otherwise egalitarian society was more like that of Moloch," Mary continued, stabbing at her potatoes. "Little children were ruthlessly sacrificed to principle, even as the ancients threw their children into a fire for the sake of their false god."

"I perceive the shade of William Godwin haunting us," murmured Polidori.

Mary glared at him, almost hating him for his bad timing, his insensitivity. "Surely the most fundamental characteristic of man is his affections. Yet Rousseau describes his natural man, in his *Confessions*, as satisfying his desires by chance. He leaves his woman on a whim, while she goes through pregnancy and childbirth alone. No matter how civilized or barbarous a society is, surely that man is most noble who loves his woman and offspring with constant and self-sacrificing passion."

"My dear, I have never known you to speak so forcefully against Rousseau," Shelley said.

"Perhaps she is speaking through him to you," Byron said. "I am aware, as are we all, that you left a wife and two children back in England. In that, you have bested me by one, as I have left only a wife and one child. I suppose, Mary dear, that only the good doctor here deserves your respect and praise."

Mary shook her head. "Shelley has not abandoned his children," she said staunchly. "Our son sleeps under this very roof tonight, sheltered and protected by his father's love. He supports and cares for his children by Harriet. You cannot call him indifferent to their welfare."

Byron's hand tightened on his dinner napkin. "Perhaps you see a fault in me, then," he said.

"I see a fault in all men," Mary said. "Less so in yourself, not at all in Shelley, but definitely in Rousseau and the men who made the Revolution after him. Despite his genius and his aspirations after virtue, he failed in the plainest dictates of nature and conscience. It shows us that a father may not be trusted with 'natural' instincts towards his offspring. Only imagine what the children of that man might have become, raised in his shadow, taught by him. Instead, I believe that he was plagued later in life by such guilt, as to color his whole philosophy of the state of natural man."

"So man's natural state is to swive women and abandon their children? This sounds more like a beast than a human being," Polidori said.

"Your mother would not have agreed," said Claire. She looked across the table at Mary, challenging her. "Your mother thought that Man is naturally a creature of reason, that that reason is God-given."

"Yes, Mary Wollstonecraft believed in God," Shelley said. "Therefore she could not agree with Rousseau."

"Her faith is not mine," Mary replied. "Rousseau can attribute only two traits to humans in the natural state: self-preservation and compassion. He says nothing of a divine reason."

"And yet, is this not the state of the true hero," Shelley said. "To preserve his life and reason, and to perfect them? And through compassion, lift up all mankind to the same perfected state?"

"And how shall he lead them to this blessed state?" Byron asked.

"Why, from without. The true hero leads from nature, not from a throne."

"So it is necessary that we all return to a state of nature, to perfect ourselves? I confess, on a raw night like this, I am disinclined to strip bare and run about perfecting myself."

"You would catch an ague," said Polidori. "I cannot recommend it to your lordship."

"But I require an answer," Byron said, his jaw suddenly clenching. "You must tell me, Shiloh. Would it be your contention, or Mary's here," he bowed to her. "That only a man raised outside of civilization, one who grew up with only grim Nature for a teacher, would be a superior being?"

"He would be Prometheus," Shelley said simply. "He would bring true civilization to Man."

"And what of those natural affections of which Mary spoke? Would such a man scatter his seed neglectfully as, as—" Byron stopped, groping for a word.

"As neglectfully as any English lord?" Polidori supplied.

Byron's mouth drew into a tight line. "You live dangerously, sir. But yes, such a creature, driven by self-preservation, would naturally ignore any calls upon his food supply or other needs. And this creature, neglecting his own children, is this the hero you would have as the savior of mankind?"

Shelley leaned forward eagerly to address his answer, but Mary intervened. "You forget, Albé. Rousseau described such a creature as being led by compassion as well as self-preservation. Even the lowliest creature of wood and meadow will give its life to preserve its own young."

There was a long silence, while a footman silently cleared the table of plates and glasses. Shelley toyed with the stem of his glass. Claire folded and refolded his napkin.

Mary looked from Byron to Shelley. Byron's father had abandoned the family shortly after his birth. Shelley's father had cut him off after he married Harriet against his father's wishes. She and Claire were barred from their father's house. Of all the people at the table, only young Polidori enjoyed the full love and support of his parents and family.

Byron said slowly, "I confess, I have had a new experience tonight: I have been entertained by not one but two lady philosophers. A most singular occurrence."

Polidori wiped his mouth with his napkin. "So many poets and philosophers, so much about the perfectibility of Man," he said slowly, "yet not a word about how this is to be accomplished. I take it, Mr. Shelley, that you do not seriously propose that we abandon our cities and towns, go into the woods and try to live? Because I do not think that many of us would long survive so brutal a schooling in perfection. Is there no other way?"

"No way that a poet can conceive, perhaps," Byron said ironically. "Possibly a medical man would know. Did they teach you perfectibility at Edinburgh?"

Polidori met his gaze with composure. "No, they taught me anatomy. Bones and flesh, brain and marrow and tissue. The real composition of man, not the theories of a Swiss revolutionary."

Fletcher set the final course, a dessert array consisting of walnuts, raisins, almonds and oranges, as well as a pear cake, on the table. Shelley immediately held out a plate for a slice of the cake. "Then tell us, Doctor. Among all those anatomies, which is the most capable of perfection? The limbs? Muscles? Where shall we start, to build our perfect man?"

"With the brain," Polidori said immediately. "The seat of reason is surely the point of beginning."

Byron took up an apple and began to pare it. "You would replace the brain of a man with, perhaps, the brain of some other animal? You could make a lion-man, or a dog-man. What wonders would we see! Yet you cannot argue that such a creature would be superior, let alone perfected."

Mary recalled Polidori's notion of the clockwork man. "A machine," she said. "Could a man's brain be replaced by a machine?"

"Such as the Luddites fear?" Byron said, his eyebrows climbing nearly to his hair. "Are we not already replacing men with machines? The frame-breakers and the rioting workers will not welcome your suggestion."

Polidori shrugged. "Machines must be powered. Even if we built a clockwork man, he would be inferior, since he could not move or walk about unless he was wound up."

"We must give him, then, a source of his own power," Shelley said. He picked a raisin up with his fingers. "Give him an electric brain."

The entire company stared at him. Then Byron grinned. "So he would have to be paraded about during thunderstorms? What an imagination you have, Shiloh! I declare, I do not know what you will suggest next."

216

"I suggest a recess," Claire said suddenly. "This talk of mechanical men is making me tired. And the fire has died down. I shall go into the drawing room, where it is warmer. Mary, will you come?"

Without waiting for an answer, Claire rose. A footman stepped forward to move her chair back. Mary was reluctant to end the conversation, but stood. The men got to their feet and bowed.

"We shall join you momentarily," Byron said. "To lose your company for an hour would bereave me."

Mary doubted it, but curtsied back at the men. "We shall leave you to your feast of reason, then."

Chapter XXIX - The Challenge

Some volumes of ghost stories, translated from the German into French, fell into our hands. There was the *History of the Inconstant Lover*, who, when he thought to clasp the bride to whom he had pledged his vows, found himself in the arms of the pale ghost of her whom he had deserted. There was the tale of the sinful founder of his race, whose miserable doom it was to bestow the kiss of death on all the younger sons of his fated house, just when they reached the age of promise.... "We will each write a ghost story," said Lord Byron—and his proposition was acceded to.

—*Frankenstein*, 1831 Edition, Preface

As **Mary stepped** across the threshold of the drawing room, thunder crashed like cannon fire overhead. She flinched, then straightened.

"Gracious!" Claire said. "The draft has blown out half the candles!"

Mary took a taper to the fire, and was relighting the candles as Shelley and Byron came in, laughing together. Byron noted her action and clapped his hands together. "Yes, that's the way of it," he cried. "We must have light! Fletcher! Bring every candle we have in the house! Let us fire a blaze to o'erset the levin itself!"

Claire sank into the arm chair nearest the fire, arranging her curls. Byron cast himself into the opposite chair, stretching his boots to the fire. "Shelley! Mary! How shall we amuse ourselves in this dark hour?"

A shadow filled the doorway; Mary turned, her heart lurching. Then she sighed with relief as Polidori limped painfully into the room. "Come, doctor," she said. "There is a chair here, and a footstool."

"I can manage," Polidori said shortly.

Byron laughed. "No, we cannot have more than one cripple at a time. Shelley, draw up that chair, and the other as well. We may huddle round the fire in better comfort than the yeomen down in their huts in the valley."

Shelley brought two occasional chairs to the fire, and Mary settled Polidori into one, with his foot propped on the footstool. She seated herself next to him. Shelley leaned his elbows on the back of Claire's armchair.

"What is that?" he asked.

Claire lifted the book in her lap. "A book of ghost stories. Albé asked me to read from it tonight."

"Capital!" Shelley cried, his eyes lighting up. "Nothing better for a stormy night!"

Mary looked at Claire's flushed face, her bright eyes, the air of repressed excitement. Claire's eyes kept going to Byron, who was lighting a cigar with a taper. "Indeed," Mary murmured. "We may expect an exciting evening."

Shelley reached past Claire's shoulder and picked up the book. "*Fantasmagoriana.* Yes, you mentioned this one. But this is all in French?"

Claire reached up and took the book back. "I have been practicing all afternoon," she said. "I believe I can translate it for all of us."

Shelley leaned down and kissed the top of her head. "My dear Claire, your talents astonish us all."

"Especially those talents associated with her tongue," said Byron.

Polidori shifted uneasily. "What would you read us, Miss Clairmont?"

She looked to the book. "This one is called the 'Death-Bride'."

"A 'Death-Bride'?" Shelley cried. "It sounds the very thing! Come, Byron, share out some of that brandy, and we shall warm ourselves against a chilling story."

Byron readily complied, filling not only Shelley's glass but Polidori's. He even lifted an eyebrow at Mary, but she shook her head. She fished her sewing out of her reticule, trying to still the nervous, queasy feeling at the bottom of her stomach. Claire was up to something, but she was not sure what.

Quite at ease, Claire opened the book. "I pray you will all forgive me for any clumsy wording," she said. "I have run over the text a few times, but the translation is not of the best."

Shelley raised his glass in a toast to her. "But your French is excellent, my dear!"

Claire smiled. "That may be, but this story has been translated from the German into French. And now I must render it in English, so pray be patient with me."

"Patient? We shall all be dead before we hear it, at this pace," Byron growled. "Proceed, if you please." He leaned on the mantle, staring into the fire and drinking.

Claire flattened her hand against a page, and began to read. "'The summer had been uncommonly fine....'"

It was a fine, though convoluted, story of a dead twin, an inconstant lover, a broken promise and a vengeful ghost. As Claire read in her clear, high voice, Mary grew even more uneasy. Claire had chosen a story of an abandoned, vengeful lover to read to Lord Byron. Was there more to that choice than met the eye?

The story ended with a twist, in which the narrator was revealed to be the ghost. Shelley, who had followed the entire story enraptured, burst into applause. "Oh, well done!" he said merrily. "The scene at the funeral vault fairly made my hair stand on end!"

Byron smiled sardonically. "Whereas the account of the bridal night made me stand on end!"

"Oh, fie, sir," said Claire. "The bridegroom lay dead on the floor!"

"Would that I had died on my wedding-night," he said bitterly.

"Then would we all have lost the felicity of your acquaintance," said Mary calmly. "Fortunately for us, here you are. Claire, dearest, that was really well done. Your translation was seamless."

"Thank you," Claire said. "I was quite surprised when the young woman in the portrait gallery turned out to be the ghost."

Polidori shifted his foot uncomfortably. "I would there was so attractive a ghost in our gallery. It runs next to my bedroom."

Byron snorted. "Our Polly would like a comely phantom to drift into his bedchamber, belike. Only, would it warm your bones to swive a dead woman? Or freeze them? I confess that I myself have heretofore confined myself only to the living." He tossed back the remaining brandy and reached for the bottle. "Perhaps you can open up new realms of research into the dead, my Polly."

Polidori's face flushed. Mary leaned forward. "He is drunk, Doctor," she said. "You know not to pay him any attention."

Shelley was bent over the book of stories with Claire, helping her choose another. Byron seemed frozen in place, staring into the fire, paying no attention to anyone.

"He treats me abominably!" Polidori hissed at her. "Like a child or a mental deficient."

She looked at him levelly. "Why do you remain, then?"

He looked at her with surprise. "Why? But what should I do?"

"Leave," she said. "There is nothing to keep you, other than your own will."

He blinked at her, open-mouthed, but said nothing. After a moment he flushed more deeply and looked away.

She put a hand on his arm. "Tell me you do not stay for me," she said.

He looked back again, and this time his eyes were full of anguish. A beautiful young man, hardly older than herself, and yet so unworldly, so conventional, and so lost. She felt a deep sympathy for him, but nothing more. What would it take for him to grow up?

"I do not stay for you," he said in a low, tight voice. "But I do not leave for you, either." He turned away and stared into the fire.

"Come, we have another candidate," Shelley cried brightly. He held up the book of ghost stories. "Polidori has chosen it, after a fashion."

"I?" Polidori looked astonished.

"Yes," Shelley said, handing the book back to Claire. "You mentioned the portrait gallery. Claire informs me that there is a story in this book called 'Family Portraits', a chilling story."

"Let us hear it, then," Mary said. Any distraction would be welcome now.

She noted the high color in Claire's cheeks, as the girl leaned closer to the fire. This brought her closer to Byron, who did not move. "'Night had insensibly superseded day'," she began.

Outside, thunder muttered ominously, and rain pattered against the windows. The candles had burnt low in their sockets, so that now the fire cast a red light over the faces of the group. A log fell with a thump in the fire grate, sending up a handful of sparks. Byron lit another cigar, and the smell of it filtered through the room, laced with the smell of brandy, Mary's own lavender scent, and the lingering odor of cooked beets.

The story was convoluted: a portrait that fell and killed a young woman, her grieving fiancé's discovery of her near-twin in another city, the doomed romance, the ancestral portrait of grisly visage. Mary was struck by the way the story enfolded other stories inside itself, drawing the listener deeper and deeper into a tangled story of a family destroyed by a nightmare specter. Entering a castle at night, this ancestral ghost kissed his descendants, all of whom but one died before adulthood.

Byron interrupted at this point. "This is a tale I have heard elsewhere, I think."

"You are disingenuous, my lord," Mary said. Shelley's gaze met hers, and he nodded. He put a hand on Claire's shoulder. "Do halt a moment, dearest."

Obediently, she put down her book while Shelley strode to the over-filled bookcase. He scanned the titles, moved a few, and then came up with a small volume. "Ah!" he cried. "I knew it. As do you, Albé:

> *Nor ear can hear nor tongue can tell*
> *The tortures of that inward hell!*
> *But first, on earth as Vampire sent,*
> *Thy corse shall from its tomb be rent:*
> *Then ghastly haunt thy native place,*
> *And suck the blood of all thy race;*

There from thy daughter, sister, wife,
At midnight drain the stream of life;
Yet loathe the banquet which perforce
Must feed thy livid living corse:
Thy victims ere they yet expire
Shall know the demon for their sire,
As cursing thee, thou cursing them,
Thy flowers are withered on the stem.

Shelley snapped the poetry book shut. "I recall that passage all too clearly. Do you not, Claire? It kept you awake half a week, I do believe."

Polidori had leaned forward, fascinated. "I am not familiar with the work, Mr. Shelley. May I see?"

Shelley handed him the book. Mary caught sight of the title: *The Giaour.* "Of course," she said. "One of your Turkish works, Albé. It made quite a sensation when it came out last year. But do you say that this tale of the 'Family Portraits' is the same?"

Byron, who had scowled through Shelley's reading, shook his head, making his dark curls dance. "Not at all. It only tells me that they spring from the same source. This story may be from Germany, but it was written by someone who has traveled in the East."

"Is that where you picked up the story?" Polidori asked, paging through the volume. "About this 'giaour'?"

"I ran across it in Greece," he said shortly. "Where the term they use is 'vampire'."

A silence fell on the room as he said the word, and the shadows seemed to thicken about the room.

"The vampire superstition is still general in the Levant. I recollect a whole family being terrified by the scream of a child, which they imagined must proceed from such a visitation. The Greeks never mention the word without horror."

The book of ghost stories slipped from Claire's grasp; her hands went to her throat. "The ... the creature drinks blood?"

Byron eyed her. "Not just any blood. The blood of its own children and grand-children."

"And the ignorant believe this?" Polidori said incredulously. "I can scarce credit that anyone with reason could believe such a tale."

"Oh, but the ignorant and superstitious will believe any tale," Shelley said. "Cloak it in romance, or religion, or the history of kings, and they will believe the dead can rise and talk."

Byron looked curiously at Shelley. "I thought you believed in ghosts," he said. "Do you not hold with Wordsworth?"

> ... 'tis falsely said
> That there was ever intercourse
> Between the living and the dead.

"Of course I believe in ghosts," said Shelley. "I may even have seen one or two!"

"But you are an avowed atheist," Byron said. "Surely none could believe in ghosts without believing in God."

"There may be no God in the sense that the church decrees," Shelley said thoughtfully. "But there is something beyond this life. It is hard to credit that those vital persons we have known and loved, whose vitality and essence are so forcefully presented to our perception every day, will vanish like this candle." He blew out the candle standing on the table beside Claire, who flinched. "It is unreasonable to think that the soul of man does not endure beyond the grave."

"And do you believe that the dead can return? As other than ghosts?" Polidori said.

"As vampires, you mean?" Byron answered. He shook his head. "You are a man of science. What would convince you that the dead can rise?"

"But the experiments you talked of," Claire said breathlessly. "The electricity, the movement of the limbs—"

"Is that enough to convince you?" Byron said. He looked around the room. "Is that all it would take? A pretty tale, dressed up with some science?"

"You yourself said the people of Greece believed it," Polidori said. "Are they all fools and dolts?"

"They may well be," Byron said. "Though I have ever thought them a brilliant and brave people."

"I find it odd," Mary said. "That a man who could write *The Giaour*, about monsters who destroy their own children, is stymied when it comes to writing about ghosts."

Byron rounded on her, fire in his eye. "Stymied?"

"Surely all it would take," she said coolly. "Is a pretty tale, dressed up with some science."

Shelley applauded softly. "You have it, my love. Surely, Byron, you who have introduced vampires into the educated world can perform a similar service for mere ghosts."

"Or you could write a story about vampires, rather than a poem," Mary suggested.

Byron shook his head. "Cover the same ground twice, like a hunter after a fox who has doubled back? I think not. Besides, I have a personal dislike to 'vampires' and the little acquaintance I have with them would by no means induce me to divulge their secrets." This last was said with a toss of his curls and a sneer on his lips.

Polidori looked down at the volume of poetry in his hands. "Methinks his lordship feels himself inadequate to the task."

Silence fell like a lead weight. All stared at Polidori, unwilling to look at Byron's red face.

Don't do this, Mary thought silently. Do not taunt him.

But Polidori, true to form, could not resist one goad too many. "Perhaps I shall write a play about a ghost, and outshine your vampire."

Shelley chuckled. "Let us hope it contains no 'goitered idiots of the Alps'."

Byron drew himself up to his full height, looking down at Polidori. Then he looked up, meeting Mary's cool gaze. He looked around, at Claire, then at Shelley. "Very well then," he said in a low voice. "We shall each of us write a ghost story. And we shall see which of us is published first."

"Will you include the ladies in this challenge?" Shelley said, arms crossed on his chest.

Byron blinked. "The ladies?" His smile came and went like lightning leaping across the Alps. "Of course. Though we must not, perhaps, expect much."

Claire rose to her feet, carefully gathering her skirts. "You do not expect much from Mary or me? How poor an opinion you have of us." Her voice held a taut undercurrent. Mary could not determine whether it was fear or anger.

Byron looked taken aback. "Well, of course, if Mary ... but to grovel in the charnel house, among tombs and decayed corpses, surely that is unwarranted for two young ladies of taste."

Claire faced him squarely, her head high. "Albé, you mention Mary but not me. Have I nothing to contribute, do you think? Have I nothing to give you?"

"To give me?" Byron frowned. "I do not take your meaning. Do you want to give me a story?"

Shelley's head turned, his eyes met Mary's with an alarmed look. He stepped forward to put a hand on Claire's arm, but Mary waved him back. If this was the moment her step-sister had chosen, let her carry it through, she thought.

"I have more than a story to give you, Albé. I have that which no man can give you, no matter how educated, no matter how polished his prose."

Byron blanched. "I do not take your meaning, Claire."

"I am with child."

Chapter XXX - Byron Refuses

If I have no ties and no affections, hatred and vice must be my portion. The love of another will destroy the cause of my crimes, and I shall become a thing of whose existence every one will be ignorant.

—*Frankenstein,* Volume II, Chapter XXI

There was a long silence, and then Byron said, very deliberately, "So. What is that to me?"

Mary winced.

Claire gasped. "But ... it is yours! We have made a child, together."

"So you say. I do not even know it is mine."

Claire's hand flew to her throat. "Oh, you do not mean that, I know you do not! You know I was a virgin when I came to you. You will not deny it!"

"Mayhap you were, when you came to me," Byron flung at her. "But since? For all I know, it is Shelley's. Half the world believes you are already his mistress, with your sister."

Mary felt it like a blow to her middle; her ears rang. So even Byron suspected...!

"—take care of your responsibilities!" Claire nearly screamed.

"My responsibilities? My dear, I am not agreed that it is mine at all."

"Is this all I am to you?" Claire blazed. "That all our times together, when we have had such bliss—"

"Bliss? Are you actually going to use that word? I have had bliss, as you call it, from my own valet and chambermaid that surpassed any passages we may have—"

"You lie! You are trying to tease me out of my temper!"

"I assure you, Claire, my chambermaid has more experience and better—"

"Byron! Let us speak aside—" Shelley said.

Claire overrode him, blazing at Byron. "Oh, do not take me for a fool! I know your teasing ways. I know you, your passions, your night terrors. I know how you sob in your sleep—"

No, thought Mary. Don't remind him of his vulnerabilities, not now. Beside her, Polidori stared from Byron to Claire, an embarrassed look on his face.

"Only at the thought that you are with me," Byron's voice was hard. "Do not quarrel with me, Claire. I will win. You know it. You know you cannot rage me out of a decision."

Shelley stepped forward, a look of concern on his face. "Albé. Claire. This is not—"

"This is no business of yours, Shiloh!" Byron flung at him.

"What will become of your son?" Claire said, and Mary heard the fight for control in her voice. "Will you abandon this child as you abandoned your daughter?"

Byron drew a deep breath. "You are trying to drive me mad," he snarled. "Between metaphysics, mountains, lakes and love inextinguishable, and the nightmare of my own delinquencies."

"You love me. I know you do. And love is enough, is it not? Oh, you, who have loved in such passion, with such depth, I know that you will see this child as our love's own signature."

"More like its period. It is the end of any love I bore you."

Mary clenched her fists, afraid that interfering would drive Claire to some new foolishness.

Polidori said feebly, "Miss Clairmont—" but no one paid him any attention.

"You cannot mean that," Claire said. Her voice held anger, still, but Mary also heard an undertone of fear. "I cannot believe you mean any of it."

"You exasperate me, madame," Byron said. "You persist, in the face of all evidence, in telling me what I do or do not mean. I assure you, I mean every word."

"Albé, George, please—"

"Never call me that." Byron's voice was cold and contemptuous. "Never, ever, call me by my Christian name. You will never be intimate enough for that."

"I shall call you coward and traitor before I am done!" Claire's voice rang out. "You will listen to me! You must, you will acknowledge me and this child!"

"Madame, make any claim you care to. Think you, after what I have endured in England, from my own wife no less, that any scandal from you shall touch me?"

"Care you nothing for your own child?"

"Should I care more for a by-blow than my own legitimate daughter, got on a legitimate wife?" he snarled in return.

"Not yet," Claire said. "Not while I carry this child."

"It is not mine!" Byron cried, and now Mary heard a note of despair in his voice. "Do you know how many bratlings are laid to my door?

"I love you, yet you do not feel even interest for me. Fate has ordained that the slightest accident that should befall you should be agony to me, but were I to float by your window drowned, all you would say would be 'Ah, voilà!'"

Eyes blazing, Byron shot back, "Shall we try it? Here is the lake, handy enough. Fletcher shall hold you under, and I shall examine my feelings as you drift with the tide."

"Byron!" Shelley put his arm around Claire. "This will solve nothing! Claire, you must calm yourself, and Byron, you must be reasonable!"

Claire burst into tears and fled through the doors to the terrace, slamming them behind her. Polidori struggled to his feet, to go after her. Mary laid a hand on his shoulder and shook her head; he subsided into his seat but whispered, "She will take a chill!"

Mary approached Byron, who was staring into the fire, storms in his face.

"That was not well done, Albé," she said. "She is not lying to you. She would not."

Shelley came up with a glass of brandy in his hand and shoved it at Byron. "I am persuaded you are too good a man to desert her, and your own child," he said quietly. "Would you have it raised, as you were, with no father?"

Byron looked from Shelley to Mary. "Damn you both." He

took the glass and tossed the brandy back as easily as if it were water. "And damn her to hell." He wiped his face with his hand. "I never loved her. I never told her I loved her. I made it plain, my God how could I make it plainer? She was nothing to me. Is nothing to me."

"You felt nothing for her? No sentiment at all?" Shelley sounded astonished.

Byron's laugh rang bitterly in the room. "Oh, Saint Shelley is it? You will debauch both of Godwin's daughters, but shy at lifting a light skirt?"

Polidori gasped.

Shelley took no offense, but shook his head. "There is more than mere sexual connection at risk here, my friend. You are casting off your very own flesh."

"And has it not been rent from me, often enough?" Byron raged suddenly. He flung the empty glass into the fireplace, where it shattered. "One child taken by the judge, another never to be—" He stopped himself, choking a little. He leaned both arms on the fireplace. "Now I am presented with this ... by-blow. This unwanted baggage. You have no qualms about adopting orphans right and left, Shelley. Why don't you take it?" He straightened, turned, and looked Shelley in the eye. "After all, it might be yours."

"No, no," Shelley said mildly. "If Claire says it is yours, it is yours. You may rely on it." He looked at Mary. "Perhaps you should see to Claire, while I talk to Byron."

"It will do you no good," said his lordship. "None at all."

Shaken by the anger of the scene, Byron's sharp temper, his sudden violence, Mary hurried to find Claire. As soon as she flung open the door to the terrace, the rain slapped her in the face, cold as ice.

"Claire!"

"Go away!" Claire leaned against the railing as if she would throw herself off of it. The rain had soaked her to the skin. Her thin muslin dress was completely transparent.

"Dearest, you must come in out of the rain," Mary said. She wiped the rain from her eyes, feeling her hair go sodden and limp.

"No. Leave me." Despite the violence of her words, Claire's voice was leaden, lifeless. "I want to go home."

"Impossible, Claire. Come inside."

Claire trembled, either from the cold or emotion or both. "I do not want to go back in there with him."

"You are past that now," Mary said. "Like it or not, you are bound to him now by the life you carry. This is something not even Shelley can understand, but I do."

Claire looked at her out of miserable eyes. "He does not love me." She said it with wonder, like a child who has discovered her toy is broken, at a loss. "He does not want me."

Mary forbore to say "I told you so", and led Claire back into the room.

It was empty, and the door to Byron's study was closed. Mary led her step-sister to the fire. A light foot-blanket was folded across the lounge; she caught it up and wrapped Claire in it. As the girl sat shivering before the fire, Mary yanked on the bell pull. When Fletcher appeared in all his placid solidity, she ordered him to bring hot tea and more blankets. He said nothing, but turned and went.

From behind the study door, Mary heard Byron's voice raised in shrill anger. She heard the quiet murmur of Shelley's words.

When Fletcher brought the tea, she forced the teacup into Claire's hands, and laid more blankets over her. Gradually, Claire stopped shivering, but she continued to stare dully into the fire, saying nothing.

Mary felt sorry for her step-sister, more sorry than she could remember feeling in a long time. Claire, desperate for attention, for purpose in life, had dug the pit she had fallen into.

"You are in despair, now," Mary said softly. She put her hand on Claire's shoulder. "But you know that Shelley and I, at least, will never desert you." She felt bitterness at the back of her throat; she did not want to be tied to Claire forever, but what could she do?

"He shares our principles," Claire said, her voice thick. "He feels as we do, he thinks as we do. And yet he looks only to his own self-interest. All would be well, if he would look to his heart."

"His heart is forever tied to another," Mary said gently. "He cannot be with her, and no other will substitute. I do not believe Albé has any more love in himself to give."

"Yet he lives as though he does," Claire said. "He flirts and swives and laughs, he makes passionate love to anyone and anything. He is so full of life!"

"He is full of despair," Mary said. "These are all his masks, put on to hide the scars beneath. He shows the world one face, but inside, he feels that he is dead. Have you not read his poem, 'Darkness'?"

Claire put a hand on her belly. "He will destroy me. He will destroy the child we have made." She leaned forward to put her head in her hands. "I want to go home. I want to see Godwin."

Mary suppressed a bitter laugh. "He would not help you. He, like Shelley and Byron, lives in a dream."

Claire sat up slowly, looking at her. "A dream?"

"Yes. They live in the mind, they devise principles and theories, they write great poems and books, but the world does not change for them. So they stubbornly live as if the world was as they want it to be, as if by sheer will they could remake it into the society they want. And look what it has got them!" She clenched and unclenched her fists. "Godwin, destitute. Shelley, cut off. Byron, exiled. And always, it is we, the women, who suffer. My mother, who died birthing me. Your mother, turned into a screaming termagant by constant worry. And Byron—how many hearts broken by that man? I swear to you, sometimes I think men are all monsters."

"But is it not worth the sacrifice?" Claire said. "To perfect humankind, to make the world better, is it not sometimes necessary that some must suffer? Must we not set an example?"

Mary's shoulders sagged.

"Marriage is slavery, Mary. We have seen that, you and I. We have seen two good people, your father and my mother, caught in an endless web of conflict and unhappiness, because they cannot separate."

"At least Godwin knows better than to throw a woman onto

the street. But why has he cast us off?" Mary said.

"Because we are stronger," Claire said simply. "We have an education. We have what we need to live independent lives." She straightened and drew the blankets around her shoulders. "And I must find a way to live an independent life without Byron. With our child."

Before Mary could formulate a reply, the door to the study opened. Shelley came out first, looking tired. Mary immediately stood and went to him, and took his hand. He bent over and laid his forehead on hers.

Byron strode out, his eyes red, bags under his eyes, his curls all disheveled. "I will accept the child," he said in a croaking voice. "There will be conditions. We will talk later about its future."

Claire stood slowly, slipping the blankets from her shoulders. "Thank you," she said quietly. She locked eyes with Byron, and there was a long silence. "It will need the love of both of us."

After a long silent moment, Byron turned away. He leaned on the mantel, grabbed a poker and prodded the fire. "It will not have it," Byron said in a low voice. "I will do the poor best that I can."

"I? Do you not mean 'we'?" Claire stood slowly. "Shelley?"

Shelley cleared his throat; his blue eyes looked sad. "We must talk later, my dear. For now, will you not change, and rest? You must not catch an ague."

Claire paid no attention, continuing to stare at Byron out of huge, dark eyes. Her fingers clutching the blankets around her shoulder trembled; drops of water shook from her sodden hair to spatter on the hearth. "Albé?"

Byron would not look at her. "Go to bed, Claire." His voice was weary. "Fletcher will make you up a room. Fletcher! You rag, put Miss Clairmont in a guest room. Make it the farthest one from mine you can manage."

Claire suddenly sagged, as if she were a marionette whose strings had been cut. "Albé, please."

A noise at the door; Mary turned to see Polidori standing rigid, holding a bottle in one hand. His eyes locked with Mary's and his look was hot, angry. But then Claire turned away from the fireplace and the light showed the devastation in her face. Polidori lunged forward.

"Miss Clairmont! You are drenched!" He took her hands. "Your hands are freezing!"

Claire sagged against him. "Help me get her into bed," Shelley said. He glanced over his shoulder. "Mary?"

She gently pried Polidori away from Claire, and put Claire's arm over her shoulder. Polidori pressed the small bottle into her hand. "Laudanum," he whispered. "To calm her nerves."

Byron stepped towards his study. "Polly! Come here, I need your assistance." Polidori glanced back at Claire, then stumped after his master.

Half-dragging, half-walking the stumbling girl between them, Shelley and Mary followed Fletcher to a small bedroom on the other side of the house. Fletcher strode into the room, flinging dust covers off of a small table, an armchair, a desk. He swept back the hangings from the bed and plumped at it.

Shelley led Claire to the armchair and put her in it. "I'll make up the fire," he said. "Do you have anything for her to wear?" he asked Fletcher.

The servant met his gaze squarely. "She has left ... clothing ... in his lordship's chambers before," he said. "I will ask the maid to bring them." He hesitated, his eyes on Claire, and a look of compassion flitted across his face. "If it will help, I will fetch Miss Clairmont some broth." He bowed and withdrew.

Claire leaned forward and put her face in her hands. Mary stood near her, adjusting the blankets while Shelley made up a fire.

"I thought he loved me. I know he did."

Mary stroked her hair, drawing the long tresses through her fingers. "Maybe he did. Do not tease yourself over it now. It is late and you are tired. For your sake, and the babe's, you should rest."

"How can I ever sleep again?"

Shelley snorted bitterly. "Oh, you will sleep. That's the hell of it, my dear. That you can endure great pain and anguish, yet you will continue to breathe and eat and live." He had got the fire going, and now stood to reach for a poker. "As long as one has ties and affections, one is subject to disappointment and pain. Love denied turns to poison so very easily." He put aside the poker, knelt, and took Claire's hands in his own. Gently, he kissed her forehead. "My dear girl, that is why we must love so often, so freely. We must spread love as far and wide as we can, seed it o'er the universe."

Claire's fingers clutched his. "I only wanted to make him happy."

A knock on the door; Mary answered it to find a pudgy maid holding out a bundle of Claire's clothes. She curtsied, peeking slyly past Mary to catch a glimpse of Claire. Mary moved to block her view, and took the clothes. "That will be all, thank you very much," she said firmly, and closed the door.

Shelley had touched his forehead to Claire's, and the two of them sat holding hands, close before the fire. Mary stood with clothing in her arms and looked at their silhouette. What was to become of Claire? What would Godwin's reaction be, he who had always thought of Claire as a victim of Shelley, not an accomplice? What would become of the child? It was not even born yet, did not show below Claire's bodice yet, but already was a source of trouble and tears. She had no illusions that Byron would share Claire's life, share the child, would take any trouble at all over it. Thinking of her sister Fanny, forever scorned for her illegitimate birth, Mary feared for the future of Claire's baby.

The child was not yet born, she thought to herself. Yet it is already rejected.

Mary laid out the dry clothing on the counterpane: at least the chemise had been laundered, so she could get Claire into that and then into bed.

Shelley rose from the fireplace, releasing Claire's hands. "I will go to him," he said simply.

Mary walked with him to the door; just as she opened it, thunder pealed overhead. She leaned to whisper in Shelley's ear. "The weather is worse indoors than out, I vow."

Shelley nodded quietly. The windows suddenly rattled as the wind threw rain at it like an assault of gravel. "I wish we could take Claire home. But I fear that in this downpour, we would be soaked before we progressed five feet."

Mary agreed. "We must stay here."

"And Albé will be up all night. If we let him go to bed, he may change his mind about Claire," Shelley said. He glanced past Mary to where Claire sat staring at the fire. "Put her to bed, then rejoin us. Let us see if we can keep his lordship's mind occupied tonight, lest he brood."

She nodded, and he left. Mary helped Claire to shed her soaked clothing and then toweled her off. She helped her into her shift, made sure her hair was dry, and led her to the bed.

"I want to go home," Claire murmured at one point.

"It is too stormy," Mary said.

"Not that home. My home. I want my mother."

Mary sighed inwardly. She could not imagine Jane Godwin's reaction to her daughter's out of wedlock pregnancy by the notorious Lord Byron. "My dear," she said, "you really must get into the bed."

A knock on the door again, and this time Claire whirled towards it. "It is he! He has come!"

"Byron? No, Claire, he—"

"Oh, not Albé. I mean him, the demon who walks in his shadow, the dark angel!"

"Claire, what do you mean? You are raving again." Mary pushed her step-sister towards the bed. "Get in, and I will answer the door."

Claire crept in between the covers, and Mary stepped to the door. She laid her hand on the latch, but hesitated. Claire's fear, or the weather, or the scene with Byron, had unnerved her, and she wondered, just for one tiny moment, what stood on the other side of the door.

Mary drew a deep breath and yanked open the door.

John Polidori, looking startled, stood with a tray in his hands, on which rested a covered bowl. "How is she?" he asked.

"I have brought a restorative."

Mary ushered him in. "Thank you, Doctor." She took the tray from him.

Polidori cleared his throat. "I am glad to offer my services in a professional capacity," he said importantly. "I am trained in obstetrics, as well as other faculties."

Claire glared at him over the rim of the bowl. "Did he send you? Does he now care at least for his own flesh and blood?"

"In my capacity as his lordship's physician, I must look after his interests. Including, er, his children."

Mary and Claire both stared at him. Slowly, a pink flush climbed Polidori's cheeks.

He bowed stiffly. "Pray excuse me, ladies." He bowed himself out and shut the door.

Mary looked at Claire, and Claire at Mary. "I could almost laugh," Claire said. "He is so ridiculous."

"Yes," Mary said, handing her the bowl and a spoon. "But of us all, he is the only one who is ... normal."

"Normal?" Claire scowled into her cooling broth.

Mary busied herself spreading the damp clothes before the fire to dry. "Byron's father abandoned him in childhood. Shelley's father has cut him off. Godwin has rejected all intercourse with either of us," she said as calmly as she could. "But John Polidori was raised in a loving family, with a father who supported him. He is neither cast off nor inclined to cast anyone off." She rubbed her face with her hands, then extended them to the warmth of the fire.

"To Polly, we must seem like a collection of outcasts."

Chapter XXXI - Principles

.... when I considered the improvement which every day takes place in science and mechanics, I was encouraged to hope my present attempts would at least lay the foundations of future success. Nor could I consider the magnitude and complexity of my plan as any argument of its impracticability. It was with these feelings that I began the creation of a human being.

—*Frankenstein,* Volume II, Chapter III

Claire finally dropped off into an exhausted sleep. Mary watched her awhile, and then crept out in search of Shelley. She found him standing on the balcony, watching the wild weather. He was soaked to the skin.

"Shelley!" she brought him his greatcoat and he shrugged into it. "You must come inside."

"She was right to come out here," he said. "Claire followed the right instinct, consulting with Nature."

"Her consultation may result in poultices and emetics ere morning," Mary said practically. "I will not have two patients on my hands! If you do not come inside immediately, I shall—I shall call Doctor Polidori!"

That name was enough to break the spell of sky and rain, and Shelley stepped back over the threshold, dripping water on the carpet.

They settled before the fire; Shelley poked at it thoughtfully.

"Byron?" Mary asked.

"Went to bed," Shelley said. He grimaced. "I believe he took the chambermaid with him, or perhaps his valet."

"Or perhaps both," Mary said. She laid a hand on his. "What will he do? About Claire?"

Shelley shook his head, water dripping from his curls onto the hearth. "He will acknowledge the child, and will provide for it, only—"

"Only what?"

Shelley rubbed his eyes. In the firelight, he looked older than his years. "He will only agree, if she gives the child to him."

"What? Monstrous! You cannot allow it!"

Shelley looked at her out of innocent blue eyes. "Allow? It is not mine to say yea or nay, Mary. He refuses to let her raise his child. He will not have it raised by 'atheists'." His tone was bitter.

"She is talking of returning to my father's house," Mary said. "Godwin will not accept her or the child. If Claire attempts to return home, if she tries to have the child at Skinner Street, with my father and her mother there—Oh, Shelley, I cannot imagine what he will say!"

"Claire wants Godwin's good opinion," Shelley said. "Is mine not enough?"

"Dearest ... no." She swallowed. "Despite all he has said about marriage, about love, despite all that you agreed together in your long talks, my father's good opinion of me—or Claire—is not sustained when I actually live as he taught."

"And your own?"

"My own?" Mary frowned.

"Is your own good opinion of Mary not enough to sustain you? Or must you have the support of Custom, and the world, and all those chains we have thrown off?"

"Have we thrown them off? Or have you, my love, freed yourself only?" She could hear her voice growing sharp, but could not prevent herself.

"But we are equals, above that world of shadow and hypocrisy! We are free, my Mary!"

"You, perhaps, are free, as all men are freer than women. Albé is free. Polidori, even, is free. Claire and Mary, however, cannot have the freedom in this world that we were promised."

"But—"

"Promised, Shelley! From the hour I was born, I was told that the world could be reformed, perfected, if only we lived reformed and perfected lives, if only we stayed true to principle."

"Yes," Shelley said eagerly. "And by example—"

"Example? Do you know know what we are examples of? Me, Claire, Fanny—all three of us are rejects. We are examples of decadence to the entire world! As are you and Albé!"

Shelley looked distressed. "Why do you care what those snickering hypocrites think?"

"Shelley, if I am to be an example of a better world, perhaps it would be useful if I were not regarded with loathing."

He paused for a long moment. "Does this mean you no longer hold to those principles—"

"Oh, Shelley, do stop philosophizing for one moment!" Mary cried.

He held out his arms and she stepped into them. He folded his arms close about her; she smelled wet wool and sweat, and took comfort in the scent that said Shelley to her heart.

"When we are together, when we are alone, just you and me and Will-mouse, I care nothing for the opinion of the world. Oh, why can we not just live quietly somewhere, we and our children, and write and dream and live as we will!"

He said nothing, but rocked slightly back and forth, as if comforting a child.

"But there is Claire," she added reluctantly. "She has nothing. You know that she will not have Byron, despite her scheming and wishing. What is she to live on?"

"Of course I will support her. And the child," Shelley said.

"Which everyone will say—all those snickering hypocrites across the lake there—is your child."

"I do not care. You know this."

"You should care, Shelley. Not for your sake, not even for Claire's. You choose to cast off the world, as it casts you off. So does Claire. But the child will grow up despised and rejected by the world, for no fault or cause of its own."

"Who cares if fools despise you?"

Mary wrapped her arms around herself. "I would not, if it were from my own actions, my own choices. But my father made Fanny infamous when she was barely a child."

"You refer to your father's publication of your mother's papers. But that is a sublime book! Your mother's life is a shining example of merit, of courage—"

"It made Fanny the most notorious bastard in England," Mary cried. "Yes, my mother was courageous, and yes, he loved her! But to show his love that way, to publish her private papers, her journals, her failures and doubts, was to strip her naked before the world!"

"You blame him for publishing?" Shelley asked soberly.

"I blame him for not realizing the effect it would have. Had he kept those things private, just for myself, Fanny, Claire, yes, that would have been unarguable. I am persuaded my mother would have kept nothing from me, would have opened her life to me on every level. But to grow up knowing that her very name—my name!—is condemned without justice, without understanding—"

He grabbed her shoulders and spun her to face himself. "He lived by the same principles as she! Would you have had him honor the woman he loved—such a superb woman as she was—by abandoning those principles?"

Mary looked into his eyes. "My mother's first care would have been for her children. Not her principles." She stepped back, and he released her shoulders, staring at her. "My mother would never, never have abandoned me as he has."

"So because he rejects you, you reject his principles? I am distressed."

"We spoke of the principle of life, did we not? We spoke in terms of chemistry and animation, of electricity and subtle fluids. We did not speak of the real principle of life, Shelley. We did not speak of love."

He shot both hands through his hair, causing it to stand up on end, like the halo around an earthly angel. "But we speak of nothing but love, sweetest."

"No, you mean something else when you speak of love. The sympathy for a human being, a child, that is what I mean by the world. Oh, will you men never understand true parenthood, true creation? We are more than mere objects of enquiry! What forms us, what makes us what we truly are, is not atoms and parts and medullary particles, not principle and idea and belief, but connection."

"Of course, but—"

"Not 'of course'! You perceive it, blindly, with open heart and wild verse. But Godwin, Godwin never perceived it at all. To him, I was a philosophical experiment, nothing more."

"No, Mary, no. He loves you, I know it."

"But he has cast me off. I, his creation—he formed my mind as well as my body—he rejects and ignores. I am adrift, like some ice floe on an Arctic ocean."

"What would you then, my Mary?"

"I would be free of him. He will never change. He will never love. Oh, you have shown me what true love is, what true sympathy of mind is, what true equality can be. But he is so inward, so self-regarding, why he makes Byron look generous!"

"But that is exactly how his own *Political Justice* describes the superior man!"

"His superior man is inadequate. He lacks a heart. He was formed without one. He lacks even the imagination to know he lacks it. He raised me with his ideas, never imagining that the world outweighs him, and that what the world will tolerate in a man it will not tolerate in a woman."

"I will never cast you away." Shelley said this in a low, quiet voice, fervent and calm.

Beset by sudden tears, Mary stepped close to him. He wrapped his long arms around her, pulling her into his chest. She smelled rain and sweat and the lavender she had folded into his shirts the day before. "Must I rely on your will alone?" she said, her voice muffled. "Because without you, I am nothing, have nothing in the world. May I not be alone, myself, free and independent?"

"Declare your independence, then, my dearest."

"Shall I write a new *Political Justice?*"

"Or a poem. Or a story. Meet Godwin in his own arena."

"A story—about abandonment?"

"And love." He caressed her hair.

"Or its absence—and principles. And the obsession with them."

"And love." He kissed the top of her head.

"And consequences. The earnest philosopher, blind with ambition, ruins his life and the lives of everyone around him, because he has not the gift of empathy."

"Or love. Come inside, my dearest, and we will go to bed."

Chapter XXXII - Nightmare

... I saw the pale student of unhallowed arts kneeling beside
the thing he had put together. I saw the hideous phantasm
of a man stretched out, and then, on the working of some
powerful engine, show signs of life, and stir with an uneasy,
half-vital motion.

— *Frankenstein,* 1831 Introduction

It started as a familiar dream, the churchyard at Saint Pancras.
Here under the willow stretched the gray stone, the faded grass.
Her dream-self knelt, tracing over the letters of the name that
was hers, that was her mother's, that linked them beyond death:
MARY WOLLSTONECRAFT GODWIN. Over and over her
fingers traced, and behind her she heard her father's voice, telling
her about her mother, teaching her the alphabet from this, her
mother's own grave. Her name. Her mother's name. Letters on a
grave.

The voice behind her changed, and it was no longer Godwin
but Shelley, his cracked soprano whispering words of love, drawing her away from her dead mother and father and the legacy of
early death and lasting notoriety. She turned, seeking him, and saw
that he was far away, standing with her father, fading. The sound
of thunder, faint under their voices, rose and drowned them out,
until the crashing roar shook the very ground. She rose, reaching
out to Shelley, to her father, but they faded and she was left in the
downpour, the sickly yellow light peeping under the edges of the
black cloud above her. A shadow fell across her, and she looked,
and there beside the grave of her mother knelt a man who was
Shelley, who was Godwin, who was neither and both. He looked
down, and from the flattened sod a form rose, pressing upward
through the soil—her mother. And her. The faces were the same.
Lightning blazed, and the eyes of the corpse opened. The creator
and his creature stared at one another, and then both turned their

faces, and looked at Mary—

Mary swam to the surface of the dream, gasping. She sat up in the bed; night enclosed her. Was the nightmare gone? Or was this part of it, still? She didn't have to look, she knew Shelley was gone. No whisper of sleepy breath beside her, only wind moaning outside the shutters, and the creak of the house resisting it. Groping towards the bedside table, her hand fell on cold steel—Shelley's pistol. Her fingers found, and passed over, the cool cylinder of Shelley's microscope, a flutter of papers, the ruffle of a quill pen. Finally, the rough surface of the tinderbox. She clutched it, feeling her heart pound in her chest, almost afraid of what light might reveal.

An abrasive scratch and spark, and the candle caught. The timid flame wavered, danced, tried to die. She pinched away some wax, oblivious to the scorch of the flame. The room looked back at her blankly, emptily. No fright stood above her bed, no corpse looked at her with a question in its dead eyes.

"Nothing," she whispered. "Just a dream." And yet still the echo of terror in her trembling fingers, which made the candle dance and dip.

She looked at the empty bed beside her. Where was Shelley? Here, in the clarity of the deep of night, her mind pictured several answers—writing by a single flame downstairs, or arguing with Byron, or putting a loaded pistol to his head. Or the picture she did not want to imagine, despite all her father's philosophy, despite all her long-held convictions—Shelley in bed with Claire, coupling with her with the same passion, the same energy that broke through her reserve, that revealed to him and to her everything she hid. No, it cannot be. It must not be.

Mary climbed out of the bed, her small feet flinching as they touched the chilled floor. Summer, indeed, she thought to herself. She'd known warmer winters in London. At the foot of the bed lay a blanket; she snatched it around her shoulders, clutching the ends together as she picked up the candle with the other hand. She thrust her feet into slippers, struggling with the recalcitrant heel of one until it finally straightened. She opened the door.

The hallway was not entirely dark; light seeped out from under a door. Polidori? But then the architecture of the house rearranged itself in her head, and she realized it was Byron's door. From behind it came a rhythmic wooden creaking and a masculine grunt. Which proved only that Albé was having sex, but not with whom. Mary glanced down the entry to the gallery, and saw only darkness; Polidori, at least, was asleep.

Noise from downstairs; Mary's hand shook and the flame cast lunatic shadows across the floor. Outside, the wind gusted, then fell ominously silent. It was the dying hour of the world, she thought, when men draw their last breaths and women pray, weeping. The cold seeped through her like water infusing a sponge. The noise downstairs—Shelley at work? She came to the head of the stairs. It was like standing at the brink of an abyss; the circle of damp light emanating from the lamp in her hand died halfway down the stairs. They looked as if they led downward forever. Mary gathered up her nightdress gingerly and stepped carefully down the first few risers. Ahead of her, the circle of light showed her the sharp-limned edges of the staircase, threw ghastly shadows against the walls through the balustrade. Portraits of strangers glared down at her, as if roused unhappily from sleep by her intrusion. Too many ghost stories swirled through her head, a dozen remembered scenes of Bluebeards and monsters and vampire frights.

At the bottom of the stairs, she stood listening. The dining room lay to the left, to the right the drawing room where they had sat up telling stories. A rustling sound came from the dim room, and Mary's heart did a slow roll over in her chest. She took a deep breath, strode resolutely to the doorway, and froze.

Two ghost-green eyes looked back at her from the darkness, shining with cold malevolence. Her hand flew to her mouth. The blanket fell to the ground, and the eyes flickered, following the movement.

"Felix! Oh, for heaven's sake!" The gray kitten pounced forward, tiny claws scrabbling. "How did you get in?"

A cool breeze against her face answered her; the French door stood slightly ajar. Hastily, Mary transferred her naked candle flame to a lamp, lowering the protective glass shield. She turned up the flame, and the room emerged from darkness. A fallen decanter on the sideboard dripped the dregs of its contents onto the carpet. Papers lay in wind-scattered confusion across the carpet. Mary detoured around an overturned chair. Ahead of her, the glass of the French door reflected her lamp again and again. She halted, but the reflections continued to move.

Mary realized she was seeing not the reflection of her lamp, but lights beyond the window, lights moving in the darkness. She thought of ghosts, perhaps the ghost of her mother, of her daughter. Ghosts that walked without heads, ghosts that killed their own children, ghosts that drank blood. She froze, unable to move, seeing the lights move and bob eerily. The French door swung gently open.

Chapter XXXIII - Frankenstein is Born

The idea so possessed my mind that a thrill of fear ran through me, and I wished to exchange the ghastly image of my fancy for the realities around. I see them still; the very room, the dark parquet, the closed shutters, with the moonlight struggling through, and the sense I had that the glassy lake and white high Alps were beyond. I could not so easily get rid of my hideous phantom; still it haunted me.

— *Frankenstein*, 1831 Introduction

From the darkness beyond the glass, a familiar voice: "I arise from dreams of thee / In the first sweet sleep of night, / When the winds are breathing low, / And the stars are shining bright...."

Shelley ...

Dizzy with relief, Mary felt her heart grow light. She ran to the window, heedless of her thin nightdress, the flaring lantern, her unbound hair. The night air flung the smell of rain in her face, and thunder muttered along the edges of the world, but it was not actually raining as she dashed out of the French doors and down the steps.

The voice continued, "I arise from dreams of thee / And a spirit in my feet / Has led me—who knows how?— / To thy chamber-window, sweet!"

Down the slippery cobbles of the walkway, across the wet grass she ran. The lamplight skipped and leaped around her, finding a sudden rosebush, a stone in her path. She danced around all of them, hearing the rich voice in the darkness ahead of her. The waves lapped more loudly along the shore as she approached.

"Shelley!" she called breathlessly.

A figure ahead of her moved, turned, straightened. "Mary!" Two long strides of those heron legs, and he was before her, taking the lamp from her hand and wrapping her close to him with the other. She smelled brandy and candle wax and the green scent of lake water. His shirt was soaked through, but his chest was warm against her cheek. His greatcoat folded around her like great wings.

"I had a dream," she murmured into his chest.

"I also," he said simply. He rocked back and forth a little with her, his heart beating steadily under her ear. "I dreamed of water, and light, and thee." His mouth whispered over her hair.

Now was the time to tell him how much she loved him, how much she needed him for a guide and mentor, how she had gladly left home and father and all behind. What she said was, "Dearest, you are soaked!"

He chuckled. "Indeed, I am fair drowned, my Pecksie girl."

A shiver went over her, and briefly she felt a dim echo of grief and loss. "You know how easily you catch a chill, my love."

He kissed the top of her head and stepped back. The sheltered cove protected them from the force of the wind, yet a stray breeze caught his coat and flared it around him like a cape. For one moment the lamplight caught him as if in a portrait—the curly hair standing out from his head in a chestnut halo, the thin cheeks, aristocratic mouth and ready smile, the lucid blue eyes, the broad shoulders, the soft collar of his white shirt falling wide. He turned, holding the lamp higher. "I am glad you brought the light. I have been making boats, but my candle blew out."

So simple, so child-like. Mary wondered, not for the first time, if her gangling lover would ever become the serious and sober philosopher her father wanted him to be. She devoutly hoped not.

Shelley hummed a moment, smiled down at her, and sang quietly:

The wandering airs they faint
On the dark, the silent stream,
The incense odors fall
Like sweet thoughts in a dream ...

"No, no, 'incense' won't do. Not exotic enough. Hmm."

The swish and hiss of the waves echoed him as he knelt. Advancing and retreating with the surge, like dancers at a cotillion, his little paper boats wobbled on the black water. Shelley handed her the light and pushed a small boat further out into the water. She saw that each one held a short stub of candle, a tiny flame shining through the paper. One by one they floated away beyond the circle of lamplight, becoming water-fireflies. The wind had died now, and the only sounds were the splash of dying waves against an occasional rock. Across the water a night bird called and was answered; in a distant house a baby cried (not hers). Above, the scudding clouds parted just long enough for Mary to see some stars, before the window was shut by black clouds.

"What did you dream?" Shelley asked, folding another piece of paper into a boat-shape.

"Graves. My father and mother. A storm." And you, merging with my father, she did not say.

"Your mother? Ah, a ghost story." His smile flashed briefly in the dim light. He knelt to place the tiny craft on the water with great care. In his greatcoat with his elbows jutting, he looked like a huddle of sticks. "Were you frightened?"

"Yes, and ... no." She pulled the shawl closer around her shoulders, not for warmth, but as armor, perhaps. "I was at my mother's grave. You were there."

He smiled up at her. "A sweet memory, surely? For me, sublime." He stood and took her hands in his. "You changed me, Mary. You changed me forever that day." He kissed her hair. As always, he recast her memories as their memories.

She stepped back, looking up at him. "You are not my father," she said.

His blue eyes opened wider. "Indeed, not. Do you want me to be?"

She opened her mouth to say no, and then stopped. Was that not precisely her wish? She saw the dream-man, standing over her mother's grave—Shelley/Godwin. Two men merging, becoming the same—her creator, with herself the figure of her own mother, the creation of Godwin. For his careful (and careless) tending of her memory had shaped her in Mary's mind as surely as if he had made her with his hands, and she of clay. Mary stared at her lover. "Do you want to be Godwin? Do you want to be my ... my father to me? My creator?"

Shelley smiled. "How can that be, when you created me?"

"But I am no maker!" It curled out of her in a wail, a desperate cry born of too much pressure, too many expectations laid on too young a heart. "I am no poet. I am only me, I am not Godwin or my mother. I am not Byron or Polly. I am not even you!"

"No," he said simply. "You are yourself. To me you are my Maie girl, to William his mother, to Claire a sister. God knows what you are to Albé. You have been all these women and you will be more. But you are, in the end, only yourself." He thrust his hands into his greatcoat. "You are what you want to be, Mary. That is all and everything that your father taught you. Are you not wise enough, old enough to see that? Wherever you go, whatever you do, you are yourself." He drew his hand out of his left pocket, frowning down at a crumpled handful of paper.

She stared at him, seeing past him. Something in her wailed in despair, something in her opened wide. Her mouth felt dry. A roaring sound in her ears had nothing to do with the wind sighing through the summer-leafed trees overhead. "Myself ..."

Shelley looked up from the letter in his hand. Mary recognized her own handwriting—her letter to Godwin, yet unmailed. "I love you, Mary," her lover said simply. "I will love you forever." No matter what happens, he did not say, but she heard it nonetheless.

She knew he meant it. She knew he would mean it even if he climbed into another woman's bed. And it didn't matter to her, because suddenly, with a feeling of lightness around her heart, she felt something give way. She was not Godwin's. She was not Shelley's. She was not William's. She was not even her mother's.

"I am ... myself."

"Yes," he said. He held the letter out to her. "You do not need him."

He had not broken the seal, but he would know what it said, she was sure. Because he was like that. "I don't need him," she said. And she remembered the dream-man turning towards her, and the figure in the illustration from her mother's stories, and the future-man with the electric brain that Polidori had spoken of. She remembered the grave of her mother, and her father's near-worship of the dead, his determination to make her into her mother again, to bring back to life in her the dead woman in the ground. Death—and life again. Will—and passion. Freedom—and responsibility. Wisdom—and utter folly.

We will each write a ghost story ...

"I'm going back to the house," she said.

Shelley looked down at the letter, up at her. He didn't ask, and she did not answer, but he smiled. He knelt and retrieved a candle end lying in the sand. He held it to the lamp, caught the flame, and handed the lamp to her. "Mind the path," he said. "I think it will rain again soon."

As she walked away, he was folding her letter into a paper boat large enough to hold the flickering candle.

Mary shut the French door behind her, making sure not to lock it. Rain had blown in, and the carpet was damp under her slippers. She trod on something soft.

It was her mother's shawl, lying next to a chair, as if it had slipped off the back. Slowly Mary bent to pick it up. As the light fell on it, she saw that it had been changed. Flowers and vines in green and red and blue meandered from one end of it to the other. Mary instantly recognized her step-sister's handiwork, and clenched the shawl in her fist.

"She had no right," Mary said. She sank into the chair and spread the shawl out on her lap. Claire had embroidered the pure white expanse of wool with an unruly riot of flowers, meticulously stitched in her fine hand. The shawl now looked nothing like the one that had lain on her mother's shoulders, on hers. It had been transformed, mutilated. As lovely as the work was, to Mary it was a defacement. Hot, silent tears fell on her hands as she turned the shawl around and around in her hands. Could she unpick the stitches? Yes, but she knew the pinholes would remain, that the wool would forever bear the mark of its wounding. Scars, she thought. Claire has stitched herself into my mother's legacy. She is trying to insinuate her way even there.

Clasping the shawl to her face, she inhaled deeply, but that faint, lingering perfume she associated with her mother, that faint milky smell that was all she had left of the woman who had died to create her, was gone. Now the shawl smelled of Claire's lavender water, deadening the older, dying scents. Mary sobbed into the wool, bereft. Now there was nothing, nothing left of the brave woman who had defied God and man and the Reign of Terror to live her life on her own terms, who had died bringing her into the world.

Nothing left, except herself.

Gradually her sobs subsided and she used the shawl to wipe her eyes. Then she carefully folded the shawl. It was hers no longer. Carefully she laid it on a sideboard and stepped away. *Let Claire have it now. She will need it when the babe arrives.*

Mary gathered up the scattered papers and set them under a Sevres bowl on the sideboard. The little writing table sat next to the chimney, now smoldering with the remains of their earlier fire. Her lamp flared across the mirror, momentarily doubling the light in the room. The clock read four and some minutes. She didn't care.

Byron's scrawl covered half a page of ivory paper; under it several more pages peeped out. She swept them aside and set down the lamp. Byron had left the cap off the inkwell; carefully she added new ink and mixed it well. Her hand fairly itched to get to work, but she took her time. When she discovered that the nib on the quill had bent, she made a little sound of frustration. Rummaging in the desk, she found a penknife and carefully trimmed it to a new point. She kept thinking of the portrait of her mother, her father's inspiration, his lost love, dead within weeks of their marriage, forever lost, forever mourned. Godwin had tried to resurrect his beloved wife in their daughter, and failed.

She sat and drew the chair closer. She took a deep breath and dipped the pen in the inkwell. When she drew it out, a drop of blackness hung on the end, quivering. From this drop, she thought, she would write her own Declaration of Independence. From this beginning, a story of love and abandonment, pride and arrogance, of a warm heart betrayed by a cold allegiance.

A story of an outcast, who from a beginning steeped in corruption emerged pure and innocent, like her daughter, like young William. An innocent blighted by lack of love, by cruelty, by rejection from those who should love it.

She drew the edge across the lip of the inkwell, steadied her paper with her left hand, and began at the top of the page:

> *It was on a dreary night of November that I beheld the accomplishment of my toils.*

The pen skritched, dry already. As she lifted it from the page to refill it, she heard Shelley singing, coming up the walk. She glanced out of the window and saw the last of his boats drifting, fading.

As she watched, the last one, made from her letter to her father, was borne away by the waves, lost in darkness and distance.

Epilogue

The summer of 1816 was followed rapidly by more tragedy in Mary's life than most women must bear in a lifetime. Within weeks, Fanny Imlay, in despair over her bleak future, committed suicide. A month later, the body of Shelley's wife Harriet, heavily pregnant by another man, was pulled from the River Serpentine—another suicide. Mary and Percy Shelley married a few weeks later; from that date, Mary never again used her father's surname, and was known for the rest of her life as Mary Wollstonecraft Shelley.

On January 13 of 1817, Claire gave birth to a daughter, whom she named Alba, a play on her nickname for Byron, Albé. Byron renamed her Allegra. By then Byron was living in Italy, refusing to see or write to Claire. He had agreed to support his daughter, but on condition that Claire surrender custody to him. Reluctantly, she agreed.

On September 2 of that year, Mary bore a second daughter, named Clara after her first daughter.

In January of 1818, *Frankenstein* was published anonymously. It was an instant sensation, but brought very little money to the cash-strapped Shelleys. In the summer of 1818, one-year-old Clara died in Mary's arms. The following June, the beloved Will-mouse, then three years old, died of malaria in Rome. Mary was pregnant at the time, but for a brief time mourned that she was no longer a mother. The birth of her fourth child, Percy Florence, in November was the only thing that could soften her grief.

In April 1819, John Polidori's expansion of Byron's unfinished attempt at a ghost story was published as *The Vampyre*, the first English novel about vampires, launching a craze for the undead at least as enduring as that of *Frankenstein*. But no further success followed, and after struggling with gambling debts and depression, Polidori committed suicide at the age of 25.

Byron placed his daughter in a convent to be raised into a bourgeois young Italian lady. Allegra contracted a fever and died in March of 1822, aged five years. Byron, who had ignored his daughter in life, had her buried with an elaborate inscription. Claire, angry and grief-stricken, spent the rest of her long life (she died in 1879) as a teacher and governess, estranged from Mary and vilifying Byron at every turn.

Shelley's love of boats proved the death of him. In the summer of 1822, returning from a business trip, his boat went down in a storm; Shelley had never taken Byron's advice and learned to swim. His body was not recovered for many days. It was recognized only by the volume of Keats still in his pocket. Byron was present when the body was cremated, by order of the Italian authorities; Shelley's ashes were interred in Rome next to the grave of his son, William. Devastated, Mary returned to England and made her living by writing, as she raised their only surviving child.

Byron now tried to become the Corsair he had written about. Involving himself in various radical political schemes, he undertook an excursion to Greece in an effort to foster revolution. In 1824, in Missolonghi, he died of a fever. Mary saw his funeral cortege pass her small cottage on its way to his interment.

Thus, in less than ten years, the only persons still alive who had been present at the Villa Diodati on that June night of 1816 were Mary and Claire. Mary made her living by writing encyclopedia articles and other work-for-hire, and published more novels. Claire lived most of the rest of her long life alone, in Europe, as a governess and teacher. To the end of their lives, they remained unmarried, on the edges of society, no longer outcasts, but unrepentant advocates of free love, atheism, and republicanism.

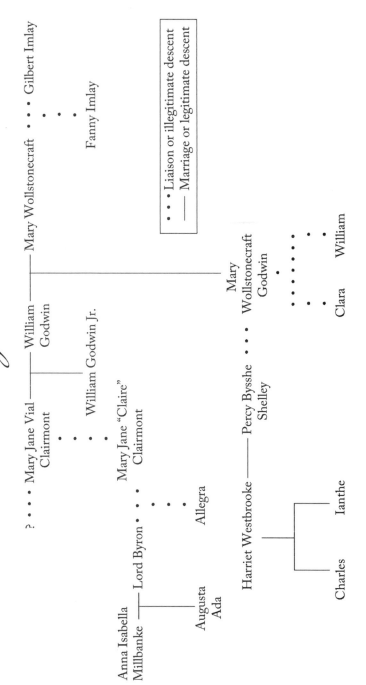

Family Tree

? • • • Mary Jane Vial Clairmont ——— William Godwin ——— Mary Wollstonecraft • • • Gilbert Imlay

William Godwin Jr.

Fanny Imlay

Mary Jane "Claire" Clairmont

Anna Isabella Millbanke ——— Lord Byron • • • Allegra

Augusta Ada

Mary Wollstonecraft Godwin

Harriet Westbrooke ——— Percy Bysshe Shelley • • •

Charles   Ianthe

Clara   William

• • • • Liaison or illegitimate descent
——— Marriage or legitimate descent

ABOVE: George Gordon Byron, 6th Baron Byron, by Richard Westall (d. 1836). National Portrait Gallery, London. BELOW: John William Polidori, by F.G. Gainsford (fl. 1805-1822), given to the National Portrait Gallery, London, in 1895.

ABOVE: Percy Bysshe Shelley, by Alfred Clint (died 1883), after an 1819 original by Amelia Curran. National Portrait Gallery, London. BELOW: Claire Clairmont, 1819, by Amelia Curran (1775-1849). National Portrait Gallery, London.

About the Author

Sarah Stegall writes novels and reviews. Her reviews have been cited in academic television and cultural studies such as *Cult Television, Escape Into the Future, Aliens In America, The Philosophy of The X-Files, Convergence,* and *Reality Squared* (which called these reviews "among the best critical commentary available on the Web"). She is the author of the young adult science fiction novel *Farside*; a series of murder mysteries set in San Francisco: *Deadfall* (Wavelength Books, 2012) and *Deadwater* (Wavelength Books, 2013); and a science fiction novel *Chimera* (Wavelength Books, 2013). With Brian Lowry, Stegall co-authored *The Truth Is Out There - The Official Guide to The X-Files* and *Trust No One, The Official Third Season Guide to The X-Files*. With Andy Meisler, she co-authored *I Want to Believe* (The Official Guide to The X-Files, Vol. 3).

Stegall currently resides in Northern California. For more information, visit her at http://www.munchkyn.com.

Wings Press was founded in 1975 by Joanie Whitebird and Joseph F. Lomax, both deceased, as "an informal association of artists and cultural mythologists dedicated to the preservation of the literature of the nation of Texas." Publisher, editor and designer since 1995, Bryce Milligan is honored to carry on and expand that mission to include the finest in American writing—meaning all of the Americas, without commercial considerations clouding the decision to publish or not to publish.

Wings Press intends to produce multicultural books, chapbooks, ebooks, recordings and broadsides that enlighten the human spirit and enliven the mind. Everyone ever associated with Wings has been or is a writer, and we know well that writing is a transformational art form capable of changing the world, primarily by allowing us to glimpse something of each other's souls. We believe that good writing is innovative, insightful, and interesting. But most of all it is honest. As Bob Dylan put it, "To live outside the law, you must be honest."

Likewise, Wings Press is committed to treating the planet itself as a partner. Thus the press uses as much recycled material as possible, from the paper on which the books are printed to the boxes in which they are shipped.

As Robert Dana wrote in Against the Grain, "Small press publishing is personal publishing. In essence, it's a matter of personal vision, personal taste and courage, and personal friendships." Welcome to our world.

WINGS PRESS

Colophon

This first edition of *Outcast: A Novel of Mary Shelley*, by Sarah Stegall, has been printed on 55 pound Edwards Brothers natural paper containing a percentage of recycled fiber. Titles have been set in Aquiline Two, Bickham Script and Adobe Caslon type; the text in Adobe Caslon type. All Wings Press books are designed and produced by Bryce Milligan.

On-line catalogue and ordering:
www.wingspress.com

Wings Press titles are distributed
to the trade by the
Independent Publishers Group
www.ipgbook.com
and in Europe by
www.gazellebookservices.co.uk

Also available as an ebook.